S

Andy stood stock still as he drank in the sight of the gorgeous girl in front of him. She was stark naked but for a tiny pair of white panties which barely covered the bulging mound of her pussy.

'What are you waiting for?' breathed Gigi tilting her Cupid's bow mouth to his. He pulled her urgently into his arms and their lips locked in a long, impassioned kiss. As she thrust her cunning little tongue into his mouth she pressed his hands to her big round breasts, rubbing his palms across her jutting nipples . . .

Sweet Vibrations

Jeff Charles

HEADLINE
DELTA

First published in 1995
by HEADLINE BOOK PUBLISHING

A HEADLINE DELTA paperback

10 9 8 7 6 5 4 3 2 1

ISBN 0 7472 4634 3

Typeset by
Letterpart Limited, Reigate, Surrey

Printed and bound in Great Britain by
Cox & Wyman Ltd, Reading, Berks.

HEADLINE BOOK PUBLISHING
A division of Hodder Headline PLC
338 Euston Road
London NW1 3BH

This is for Heather and Lennie,
Judy and Cyril,
and above all,
for Vera G.

Variety is the Soul of Pleasure
Aphra Behn [1640–1689]

CHAPTER ONE

A Little Of What You Fancy . . .

'Mr Klein, it is vital that when opportunity knocks, you must be on hand to open the door. This is perhaps the best reason for visiting a reputable astrological consultant such as myself, because regular astral readings will alert you to the approach of Dame Fortune's footsteps.' Mademoiselle Melissa leaned forward from the depths of her plush, upholstered chair to pick up a glass of orange juice from the small occasional table which stood between her and the sharp-eyed, handsome young man sitting in front of her.

'I see,' muttered Adrian Klein. He shifted uneasily in his equally well-padded seat, trying hard to keep his eyes away from the swell of her full, rounded breasts which threatened to overflow over the top of her low-cut pink jumper.

Although the sight of Mademoiselle Melissa's breasts were most agreeable, a scowl of irritation briefly appeared upon Adrian's face. *For heaven's sake, I must be off my rocker to have agreed to come here*, he reflected silently. *I've never heard such a*

3

*load of old flannel, not since that old fortune-teller
read my palm at the Hampstead Heath fun fair last
Easter.*

And it was not as if he needed to be told when to
seize any opportunity that might arise, far from it.
He had been congratulated by his boss only that
very morning for ensuring that all the supporting
stars on the bill with their hot new comedy star
Freddie Amos for the pantomime at the Palladium
were from the Rose and Griffin agency. Although
not even his bitterest rivals had ever accused him of
being a braggart, Adrian was nevertheless proud of
the fact that many people in the business considered
him to be probably the most successful young agent
in London.

There were no problems in his private life – he
had taken delivery of an MGB sports car only six
weeks ago and he had little trouble in meeting the
monthly mortgage payments on his luxurious flat
in St John's Wood. With bonuses and commis-
sions, he had earned more than eleven thousand
pounds last year, which was almost three times
more than his Dad, a hard-working family doctor
with a large practice in a north-west London
suburb.

So it was hardly surprising that Adrian was
unconvinced by Mademoiselle Melissa's patter,
especially since he had been most unwilling to make
an appointment to see her. He had only been invei-
gled into doing so by his sexy new live-in lover, Gigi
Baroja, who was heavily into astrology, flower

power and all the trendy way-out fads and fashions of the Summer of 1968.

'No more blow-jobs until you see Mademoiselle Melissa, Gigi had warned him that morning, tossing her long strands of golden blonde hair away from her face as she swirled her tongue around the gleaming helmet of his throbbing penis. Adrian had chuckled and tried to pull her head down to his pulsing erection but Gigi had wriggled away and swung herself off the bed.

'I mean it, Adrian,' she had exclaimed as she bent over and kissed his forehead. 'You might not think it now, but believe me it's for your own good. You'll thank me afterwards, you see if you don't.'

'Okay, okay, I'll call her this morning,' he had replied with a smile, thinking that if it took a visit to Mademoiselle Melissa to get the gorgeous nineteen-year-old dancer sucking his cock again, this was really a small price to pay.

However, ten hours and a hard day's grind at the agency later, Adrian was feeling far less flexible about the whole business. After all, it was one thing agreeing to a one-off visit but he had no intention of making regular calls to Mademoiselle Melissa's sumptuously furnished South Kensington maisonette.

If I want to read my fortune in the stars, I'll look at Gypsy Lionel's weekly forecasts in the Daily Mirror, he had decided. *I don't need some fucking con-woman, even one as sensually attractive as the curvily voluptuous astrologer sitting opposite, to filch a fiver from my wallet every fortnight for a consultation.*

Despite his well-deserved hot-shot reputation, Adrian Klein was almost always unfailingly polite and soft spoken in all his business dealings. He was about to tell Mademoiselle Melissa that, while he appreciated her interest in his welfare and would carefully consider what she had to say, he had a pressing engagement and would contact her as soon as possible if he wished to take up her offer to make up his personal astrological chart.

He drew a deep breath but before he could speak, Melissa sat up straight and raised her hand. 'No, please don't say anything, I don't have to draw on any clairvoyant powers to know what's been going through your mind,' she said with a rueful smile. 'I've failed to convince you that my star studies can be of any assistance in planning your life.'

'Well, I wouldn't put it quite as bluntly as that,' he began but then he stopped and returned her smile. 'Oh look, I don't want to sound rude but I'm just not into all this hocus-pocus about the stars. Sorry, Mademoiselle Melissa, it's nothing personal, and I know that you genuinely believe in what you do, but it's not for me.'

He picked up his briefcase and stood up to leave but Melissa put out her arm and gently touched his hand. 'Adrian, I may call you Adrian, may I not? And do call me Melissa. I added the prefix of Mademoiselle purely for publicity. Please stay just a few minutes more,' she said softly. 'Gigi told me your birthday was the third of November and I drew up a Hindu chart for you last night.'

'A Hindu chart?' he said blankly, Melissa nodded and explained: 'I really need to know the exact time you were born to make a complete horoscope but if I have the date of birth, I can make up a Hindu chart. It uses the time of sunrise on your birthday to map out the planetary positions and these will give an indication of your personality and future. There is no charge for this initial consultation, so at least let me tell you what the stars foretell for the next week or so.'

Despite his disbelief, Adrian sat down back in his chair. 'Very well, Melissa, if you've gone to all this trouble it would be rude not to listen to your predictions,' he replied, putting his briefcase back on the floor.

'Thank you, Adrian,' said Melissa, flashing her large brown eyes at him. She picked up a sheet of paper from the table and began to read out her report on him: 'Well, I don't think you'll disagree too much with my initial findings. On your birthday twenty-three years ago, Mars to Uranus were in conjunction and this has given you a compelling personality with a strong well-developed mind and body.'

'Say no more, I'm already convinced,' grinned Adrian but Melissa wagged a reproving finger and continued: 'I have to mention that there is one negative aspect in your chart. The constellation Hair of Berenice was in the ascendent and I'm afraid that means you will probably suffer from baldness by the time you reach middle age.'

'I can live with that,' he commented as she continued: 'Over the next few days life will become more adventurous and this will also be a good time to deal with any outstanding business matters. You will be in an ambitious, confident mood and by sheer force or persuasion you will get everyone around you to do exactly what you want.'

'Wow! If only that were true,' said Adrian with a heartfelt sigh, thinking of the meeting he had scheduled for tomorrow morning in his office with the tough impressario, Dickie Segal of Amalgamated Entertainments.

'Oh, but it *will* be true, I promise you,' insisted Melissa, rising from her chair and walking across to stand in front of him. She let her hand fall on his shoulder and then, bending her head down until her face was level with the side of his head, the ravishing dark-haired girl brushed her lips against his ear.

Adrian caught his breath sharply as she whispered: 'Who knows, Adrian Klein, it may begin to happen sooner than you think. For instance, I hardly think I need to be told what you want me to do now.'

He let out a gasp of astonishment as Melissa straightened herself up and then, with one swift movement, crossed her arms and pulled up her jumper over her head. To his delight, Melissa was wearing nothing underneath it. As Adrian stared at her uplifted firm breasts with their large crimson nipples, he felt his prick begin to swell quickly inside the confines of his Y-fronts.

She gave him a cheeky look as she added: 'There, you did want to see my titties, didn't you? Yes, of course you did and unless I am very wrong, you would now like me to take off all my clothes?'

'Is that what the stars told you?' he asked hoarsely but she shook her head and giggled: 'No, you silly boy, I only had to look at that huge bulge in your trousers!'

Melissa unhooked the catch on her long black maxi-skirt and then, with tantalising slowness, pulled down the zipper. She motioned Adrian to reach out and yank the skirt down over her slim hips. With trembling hands he reached out and gripped the skirt but he only needed to give a brief tug before she was able to wriggle it down to her feet. Adrian watched her step out of the skirt and kick off her shoes and then he looked upwards to between her legs where her dark, hairy mound was scarcely covered by a skimpy pair of white bikini panties.

'God Almighty, you have a most beautiful body,' breathed Adrian as he stood up and took hold of her proferred hand. The outline of his cock stood out like a flagpole through his trousers.

'Why thank you, kind sir, I'm sure I'll say the same about yours when I see it,' Melissa quipped as she led him into her bedroom.

'I hope you won't be disappointed,' said Adrian.

He threw his jacket across a chair and tore off his tie. As he sat down on the bed to unlace his shoes, Melissa slid herself down beside him and smoothed her long fingers down his broad back.

'M'm, that's a nice tan. Have you had your summer holidays already?' she asked, sliding her hands round his waist to unclip his belt while he ripped off his socks.

'No, but Gigi and I went to Bournemouth last weekend and the weather was so warm that we lazed around for most of the time on the beach,' he replied. He stood up for a moment to pull down his trousers and when he stepped out of them Melissa took hold of the elastic waistband of his Y-fronts and pulled him towards her.

Slowly she rolled down his pants and she smiled as Adrian's straining truncheon stood up to attention against his flat stomach. 'Well now, here's more proof of astrological science,' murmured Melissa as she slicked her hand up and down his circumcised shaft. 'Each sign of the zodiac rules a part of the body and guess which part is ruled by Scorpio, Adrian Klein, you big-cocked boy?'

Fleetingly, Adrian worried about Gigi finding out that he was playing away from home, but the Archangel Gabriel would have been unable to resist the temptation afforded by Melissa's exquisite nude body. He relaxed and bent his head down to kiss the generous pouting lips of the gorgeous girl. As their tongues mashed together, he slid his body down next to hers on the soft mattress. Melissa took his hand and placed it between her legs, clamping her thighs around it. He ran his forefinger along the length of her moistening crack and then sheathed it up to the knuckle inside her cunny which drove the sensuous girl into an even higher gear of lust.

She clenched and unclenched her buttocks as he whipped first one finger, then two and finally three in and out of her soaking quim. Adrian's heart began to pound and his prick pulsated violently under her provoking caress as he slid his free arm under Melissa's back and clasped her left breast, squeezing the soft flesh and rubbing his fingers against her hardening nipple. She released his cock and grabbed his buttocks as he heaved himself up to move over her. Adrian could feel her sharp fingernails scoring into his bum cheeks, sending stabs of a peculiarly stimulating pain through his flesh as if he were being pricked by ten tiny needles.

When he had mounted her, she pulled his head to hers and their tongues met again, probing the far recesses inside each other's mouths. Then Melissa parted her legs and drew up her knees to allow his shaft the fullest access to her love channel. He eased himself down upon her soft, quivering body and she wriggled her hips to bring her pouting pussy lips into direct contact with the tip of his glistening mushroomed helmet.

'Put your lovely joystick inside me, Adrian,' she commanded. A wide, sensuous smile lit up her face as he eased in the smooth purple crown of his cock between her yielding rubbery love lips, propelling

11

his prick inch by inch inside her warm, wet cunt until their pubic hairs were matted together. Adrian noted now splendidly his own brown curls contrasted with this gorgeous girl's silky black muff.

Melissa pulsed with pleasure as she felt the solid thickness of his hot, throbbing tool sliding inside her cunt. Her loins bucked and her back arched as she writhed in instant orgasmic ecstasy. Then Adrian pulled his prick slowly out of her honeypot until only his knob was left inside her before he drove forward again, burying the length of his rigid rod fully inside her. Again and again she urged him on, meeting each stroke with upward thrusts of her own, crushing her superb breasts under his broad chest.

'More, darling, more,' she cried out, squealing with pleasure as Adrian plunged his throbbing tool in and out of her squelchy slit. Her pussy pulsed around his cock while it slid to and fro inside her welcoming crack and his balls smacked against the back of her thighs.

'You can come inside me, I'm on the pill,' she hissed and she crossed her legs behind his back, locking her ankles together. Her delicious backside was now completely off the bed, giving Adrian free access to fondle her firm young bum as he pistoned his prick deep inside her delicious cunny. From the back of her throat came a deep cry of satisfaction as Melissa arched herself upwards. Her entire body stiffened as, with one great shudder, a tremendous orgasm raged throughout every fibre of her being.

'Aaagh!' he groaned as she slid her hand between

his heaving buttocks and pressed the tip of her finger inside his bum-hole. He came almost immediately, his body jerking as he jetted a fountain of sticky spunk which completely filled her cunny and splashed against the soft folds of her pussy, dribbling down her thighs to mingle with her own love juice onto the crisp white sheet.

Adrian sighed as the throes of pleasure faded away and he withdrew his now deflated cock while they kissed and cuddled in a sticky, sweaty heap. 'M'm, that was really wonderful, I haven't come like that for weeks,' said Melissa as she glanced at her watch. 'I wish we had time for an encore but I have another client to see in twenty minutes.'

'What's the time? Half past five? God, I'm late as well,' said Adrian. 'Could I have a quick shower before I go?'

'Of course you can, the bathroom is straight through the door over there,' she said. As he swung his legs over the bed she added: 'You should make a regular appointment to see me every Thursday afternoon at this time for the next few weeks.'

'OK,' he said, his scepticism dismissed.

'There will be no charge except that I'll expect you to fuck me and don't worry, it will be our little secret, I promise that I won't tell Gigi. Incidentally, there is no need for you to feel guilty about deceiving her, she fucked my boyfriend when Johnny and I visited her in France last Easter. But that's another story, and if you like I'll tell you all about it next week. So, Adrian, do we have a deal?'

He grinned as he heard these words which so often were heard in very different circumstances in the boardroom of the Rose and Griffin theatrical agency.

'It's a deal,' Adrian replied and he gravely shook hands with the lovely naked girl and then padded off towards the bathroom.

He switched on the tap and stepped into the stall. He sighed with the pleasure of release as the hot water cascaded over him, revelling in the release of tension as he relaxed after the delightful, though totally unexpected exercise he had just undertaken.

Adrian gnawed his lower lip as he soaped himself down and he wryly remembered the cautionary words of advice given to him by his late grandfather five years ago when he had moved out of his parents' home and into his own flat. *Ven der putz shtayt, ligyt di seichel oif de fenstehr*, the old man had warned and Adrian heaved a wry sigh as he realised he had just given ample proof of the truth of the old Yiddish proverb. *When the prick swells up, common sense flies out of the window*, it said.

Indeed, Adrian's cock was now almost fully erect again as he soaped the barrel of his thick circumcised truncheon, for part of his mind was still full of images of Melissa, she was a sexy girl and a truly marvellous fuck, but he realised that the agreement he had made with her was fraught with danger. Suppose she reneged on her promise not to tell Gigi of their affair, especially if, as he suspected, after a

14

month Melissa wanted to continue this clandestine arrangement?

Suddenly his thoughts were interrupted by a smooth hand sliding from behind him to grasp his stiffening shaft. Across his back Adrian could feel the deliciously soft peaks of her bare breasts pressing against him as she slid her slippery nipples up and down his spine.

'I thought you had a client coming round soon,' he gasped but the sensuous girl giggled and murmured: 'Yes, but you make me come so quickly we've time for another little fuck.

'Unless you don't want to,' she added unnecessarily, for Adrian's cock was now bucking and rearing in her hand. Despite his concern about being drawn into a situation which might well end in tears, Adrian closed his eyes and let himself be swept up in the whirl of erotic sensation. The insistent rubbing of Melissa's fingers on his cock rooted him to the spot. Then she let go and pulled him round to face her.

'Are you strong, Adrian?' she asked with an impish grin, and when he nodded she moved his legs slightly apart and told him to brace himself.

'Hold my bum for God's sake don't let go!; she ordered as she leaped into his arms, scissoring her legs around his waist as she threw her arms around his neck. His knees buckled for a moment but then he shifted her from side to side until her weight was evenly distributed. His hands cupped her pliant, wet bum as Melissa released one hand from his neck and grasped hold of his cock. She pressed herself even more tightly against him until his helmet was prodding against her sopping snatch.

'Now fuck me!' she whispered fiercely as she slotted her cunny lips around his knob and jerked herself forward until his cock was fully embedded in her pouting pussy.

Adrian had pistoned his pulsating prick in and out of her juicy cunt not more than half a dozen times before Melissa was gasping in ecstatic joy. The sensations were so delicious that in seconds she felt an orgasm building up in her groin, growing bigger as she held onto Adrian's neck for dear life, her body shaking to his savage thrusts. Then she shrieked in triumph as they came together, his spurts of creamy jism lathering the walls of Melissa's love channel. Exquisite throbs of sheer delight hurtled through her quivering body as she shuddered her way through a rapturously exhilarating climax.

Taking care not to slip on the wet floor, Melissa uncoupled her legs from Adrian's waist and her hands from around his neck. They stood panting for breath as the water tumbled down onto their exhausted bodies.

While Adrian was wrapping himself in one of Melissa's large, baby-blue bath towels, the new teenage singing sensation, Sharon Saxon, was just stepping into the shower on the floor above his office at the agency in Albemarle Street. Tony Cavendish, the agent who handled Sharon's affairs at Rose and Griffin, had organised a photo-call in Green Park for the stunning teenager whose latest record, *Why Don't You Stay And Play*? was quickly climbing the charts. The nubile teenage girl had been photographed for almost an hour wearing a tee shirt and a pair of brief athletic knickers by a gaggle of pressmen from all the popular Fleet Street papers. She had welcomed Tony's suggestion that she used the executive wash-room at the agency to change back into her clothes.

Standing directly beneath the shower head, Sharon raised her face to greet the full force of the warm water, screwing up her eyes as it washed the perspiration from her body. It ran in rapid rivulets down her neck, between her high, pointed breasts, across her belly and between her legs where it gathered in the silky blonde curls of her pubic mound before dripping down in a silver swirl at her feet.

What Sharon did not know was that on the other side of the frosted glass of the stall, waiting with bated breath for her to finish her shower, was Carola Watforde, the financial director of Rose and Griffin. Her affairs with female artistes were the subject of shocked gossip among those in theatrical circles who frequented The Ivy, Kate's Club and other noted meeting-places for show business personalities.

Carola, an attractive woman in her late twenties, had overheard Tony Cavendish extend the invitation to use the agency's facilities. Sharon had been wearing only a track suit on top of her tee shirt and knickers and, after the pair had left the agency for the photo-call, Carola had instructed Heather, the new receptionist who was unaware of the financial director's sexual predelection for pretty girls, to inform her the moment that Sharon and Tony returned to the office.

Like all agents, Tony Cavendish was always behind with his admin and so, while he and Sharon were away, it was easy for Carola to arrange for a small sheaf of paperwork to be put on Tony's desk with a crisp memo from herself to say that he had to deal with these matters before he left work that evening. A few moments after Heather called her to say that Tony and Sharon were back, Carola had licked her lips as she sauntered down to Tony's office where he was just giving Sharon the key to the wash-room.

She had met Sharon several times before and she shook hands with the young singer as she said with a warm smile: 'Hello, Sharon, how did you enjoy the photo-call? You poor girl, you look dreadfully hot and bothered.'

'Yes, she is and that's why she's going to take a shower before we go on to the TV Centre for a *Top Of The Pops* recording,' said Tony, pursing his lips as he scanned the memo which Carola had placed in his in-tray. 'Carola, I can't possibly deal with all this stuff now, it'll have to wait till tomorrow morning.'

Now it was her turn to frown. 'I understand that

you're tied up with Sharon but you must check very carefully through the Shackleton contract before Mr Dixon calls New York tonight. There's a great deal of money involved. Look, I'll take Sharon up to the wash-room and bring her down when she's finished while you sit down and give that contract a final once-over. Sharon, you don't mind if I look after you for ten minutes or so, do you?'

'Of course not,' Sharon replied and Tony permitted himself a swift scowl as he muttered: 'See you back here, love, try not to be too long,' as he sat down and gloomily picked up the seventeen-page contract. He had a shrewd suspicion of why Carola had dumped this work on him just at this particular time but he could hardly say anything in front of Sharon. Although Tony had only been with Rose and Griffin for some six months, he knew that Carola had the ear of the agency chairman Teddy Dixon, who would not hear a word said against her.

What Tony Cavendish did not know, however, was that despite Sharon's sweet and innocent young looks, the seventeen-year-old was far more sexually experienced than he realised. She had immediately recognised the gleam in Carola's eye when she spoke to her as being very similar to that of Miss Crispin, a temporary games mistress at Burrell Street Secondary School for Girls, who had insisted on giving Sharon's solar plexus a massage after she had been hurt by a flying hockey stick.

As she followed Carola to the wash-room, Sharon reflected on the incident with the teacher, and how she had laid down on the treatment table wearing only her bra and a pair of regulation blue games knickers. Miss Crispin had smoothed her hands over her tummy, rhythmically stroking her soft white belly. Sharon could sense the desire of the games mistress, who was herself only in her early twenties, to caress the prominent pubic mound which was so invitingly outlined under Sharon's tight knickers.

Sharon loved having her pussy kissed by her boy friend and it had occurred to her that here was a golden opportunity to miss hockey for the next couple of weeks and with a bit of luck for the rest of the term!

'Could you rub a little lower, Miss?' she had enquired sweetly. 'It still feels a little sore down there.'

'Certainly, I'd be delighted to,' Miss Crispin had replied, in a voice crackling with suppressed desire. She let her fingers slide towards the pale wisps of hair from Sharon's pubic muff which peeped out over the top of her knickers.

'Let me take off these silly knickers, you can't massage me properly with these in the way,' Sharon had said mischievously, rolling them down and exposing her gorgeous pussy to Miss Crispin's lascivious gaze.

'Go on, Miss, kiss it better,' she had added encouragingly and as she had anticipated, Miss Crispin lowered her head and placed her trembling lips in Sharon's silky corn-coloured bush. Tentatively at first she had licked gently between the delicate folds before insinuating her tongue inside Sharon's musky cunny.

'Oooooh!' Sharon had panted as Miss Crispin grasped the firm rounds of her bum in her hands and pressed Sharon's slit to her lips. She lapped up the tangy liquid which was beginning to seep out of the teenager's sticky honeypot. In no time at all, she came in spectacular fashion, drenching the teacher's face as Miss Crispin eagerly gulped down her cuntal juices.

Sharon managed to skip games for three weeks after this incident and would have been able to miss even more sports afternoons had not the supply teacher had to leave Burrell Street to fill a temporary post at another school in the area.

So Sharon was not too bothered by the thought that Carola Watforde would like nothing better than to bring her off by kissing and suckin her golden pussy. In fact it occurred to her that keeping on the right side of Carola could be very useful, for it was her department which collected all the money earned from her records and theatrical and TV work. Sharon's parents had insisted that her earnings be ploughed into an investment company controlled by their accountant and she was only allowed a monthly allowance – admittedly generous – on top of her living expenses. But if she played her cards right, Sharon was sure she could persuade Carola to release some cash for a Sunbeam Alpine sports car which she wanted if she passed her driving test next week . . .

She looked around when she stepped out of the shower and though she could not see Carola, she guessed that she might well be peeping through the keyhole. Sharon smiled as with deliberate slowness she reached out for a towel and displayed her lithe adolescent body. As Sharon had suspected, Carola was now almost beside herself with lust as she looked at the singer's tight little bottom and small, high breasts with their adorable pink nipples which appeared to be begging to be sucked.

Beads of perspiration appeared on Carola's brow as Sharon casually towelled herself dry and then, with her feet planted slightly apart, she took a small hand towel and slid it leisurely between her thighs. Then she dropped the towel and pressed her hand on the shiny blonde thatch of pussy hair. She closed her eyes and thought about what might happen that night at the party she was going to with Tony Cavendish after the *Top Of The Pops* recording. It was to be given by the songwriting team of Tim Lempert and Nick Clarke, whose string of hits had made them the hottest property of 1968. Sharon wondered how best to persuade them to pen a number for her next single, especially as Tony Cavendish had told her that he had heard a rumour that the duo had recently been offered a huge sum to write a song for the Wards of Court, whose record *Ring, Telephone Ring* had soared up the charts and won them the accolade of being named the most promising group of 1968 by the *New Musical Express*.

She closed her eyes as she imagined herself naked in bed with both the good-looking young songsmiths. She licked her lips as she pictured the flushed, handsome face of Nick Clarke as she whispered to him to squeeze her breasts and take her titties in his mouth and lick and suck her sensitive erect nipples while Tim Lempert crammed his huge stiffstander inside her tight, juicy cunt . . .

Her fingers moved lower and found the warm, moist crack of her cunny. She splayed open her slit with her thumb and forefinger and then began to stroke herself with an increasing urgency until, overcome with a powerful longing, she inserted two fingers deep inside her moist honeypot.

'Aaaah, aaaah, aaaah!' she breathed as, intoxicated by the scent of her own musky aroma which rose to her nostrils, she almost swooned with pleasure as she finger-fucked herself to an ecstatic frenzy and she let out a little scream of triumph as she reached her own orgasmic climax.

When she had recovered she deliberately turned her back to the door and provocatively wriggled her bum as she pulled on a pair of tiny black panties and a miniskirt in the same colour. Then she slipped on a half cup bra which pushed out her breasts even further and a tight fitting semi-transparent blouse. She completed her outfit by sitting down to step into a pair of Gucci black leather thigh boots.

'Sharon, will you be much longer? You can make

up at the studio,' called out Carola's voice from behind the door and she shouted back that she would be out in just a minute. *Well, Carola, you've enjoyed a free show of the merchandise*, thought Sharon. *But if you want to purchase the goods, you'll have to juggle the books so that I can buy my car.*

Meanwhile, in the penthouse suite at the top of a new three-storey building in Soho occupied by the all-powerful theatre owners Amalgamated Entertainments, were two ravishing dancers, Angela and Charlene. They were attempting to persuade the executive producer, Dickie 'Nipper' Segal, to offer them the last two vacancies in the chorus of *Puss In Boots*. The all-star pantomime would be Amalgamated's big Christmas 1968 London show. But there were six other girls on the short list drawn up by Susan Moser, the group's principal choreographer.

Angela and Charlene had collared Dickie as he alighted from a taxi outside Amalgamated's Poland Street offices. Although they had no appointment with the impressario, he had found it difficult to refuse the two attractive mini-skirted girls when they had begged him for five minutes of his time. He reckoned that the girls knew what they would be expected to offer if – and it was a very big if – they had enough talent for him to instruct Mrs Moser to give them the last coveted places in the chorus line.

'We're both great dancers and we look very sexy on stage,' purred Angela as she lifted up the new

Alan Brooke LP from his desk. 'Mr Segal, let us show you just how good we are. If you'll play the second track, *A Foggy Day In London Town*, Charlene and I will show you our special routine. We wouldn't be able to do this set for the panto but I think you'll like it.'

From the tone of her voice, Dickie realised the girls knew the score and his cock began to swell as he looked approvingly at Angela's long, shapely legs. Happily for Dickie, show business was an activity where he could comfortably mix business and pleasure. Even in his early years after World War Two, when he was putting on shows at only half a dozen tatty provincial theatres, he never gave contracts to girls simply because they were good on the casting couch. On the other hand, if there were two girls with equal talent and one was keen to give him a blow job, then he reckoned this was as good a way as any to make his choice.

Indeed, this was how he acquired his nickname 'Nipper' when, many years ago, an exotic dancer got carried away while fellating him and he had been forced to make an emergency visit to the nearby Middlesex Hospital in Goodge Street.

Dickie Segal shrugged his shoulders and consulted his gold Rolex wrist-watch. 'I can't give you too long, girls as I've an important meeting at the Palladium with Mrs Moser before the first house this evening.'

'That's fine, we won't take up too much of your time,' said the red haired Charlene. She started to unbutton her blouse while Angela pulled off the clip which had held her glossy black hair in a bun. When she shook her head, the long strands of hair fell down her back almost to her waist.

Dickie Segal took the disc from Angela's hand and swivelled his chair round to place it on the stereo record player behind him. As he swung back again and the melodious voice of Alan Brooke filled the room, the two girls swirled gracefully around the office in time to the music as they proceeded to undress each other until both were bare breasted and were clad only in minute lacy white panties.

Then, directly in front of him, the girls wrapped their arms around each other and slid down onto the lush green carpet. Dickie hoisted himself out of his chair and came forward to perch on the edge of his desk and take a closer look at the girls who were now exchanging a mouth-to-mouth kiss. Charlene began to writhe and squirm, thrusting her breasts and her hips forward as Angela ran her hands up and down her smooth tanned body. With roguish smiles the girls traced patterns across each other's elongated cherry nipples with their fingertips and Dickie's eyes were now glued firmly on the glistening bodies of the two semi-naked girls.

'Dickie, why don't you get undressed and join us?' cooed Angela as she suggestively rubbed her palm against the swell of her pubic mound. 'Wouldn't you love me to suck your cock while Charlene licks your balls?'

A wolfish smile flitted briefly across his face as he

picked up the telephone and instructed his secretary to hold all telephone calls until he called her back. Charlene sat up and unlaced his shoes before pulling them off along with his socks while Angela scrambled to her feet and helped him off with his jacket and loosened his tie.

Then Charlene slid her hand up his thigh and smoothed her hand over the bulge which had now formed in Dickie's lap as he held out his arms to allow Angela to take off his shirt.

'What a nice hairy chest you have,' murmured Charlene while continuing to rub her hand sinuously over Dickie's straining shaft. 'I've always found hairy men more virile and from the size of this lovely big cock I'm sure you won't disappoint me.'

'Well, there's only one way to find out,' he grunted, sliding off the desk as he unbuckled his belt and Angela moved round to unzip his flies. The girls pulled down his trousers together and Charlene's hand glided into the slit of his boxer shorts to free his stiff cock.

'Let's move over to the couch,' suggested Angela and they trooped across the room with Charlene still holding Dickie's pulsating shaft firmly in her hand. 'Now you lie down, Dickie Segal, and let us do the work.'

With that, she moved behind Charlene and rolled down her panties which exposed her curly auburn bush to Dickie's entranced gaze. After she had stepped out of the tiny garment, Charlene sat down at the other end of the large leather sofa. Swinging her body round, she lifted her legs to tweak the knob of his pulsating prick with her toes while Angela tugged down his shorts and threw them onto the carpet.

'There, not many dancers can do a shuffle, ball, change step like that,' said Charlene with a wicked chuckle, but she was forced to move her toes down to his tightening scrotum as Angela divested herself of her panties. Her head swooped down to suck Dickie's twitching helmet, lashing his quivering cock with long wet strokes of her tongue.

She shook a fringe of hair from her face as she eased his smooth, wide helmet into her mouth and she sucked slowly, swirling her tongue around the crown of his cock. An ecstatic moan escaped from Dickie's lips as she sucked lustily on his trembling tadger. His hot shaft throbbed as Angela's head bobbed up and down his palpitating length.

His Harley Street specialist, Dr Gottlieb, had recently prescribed a daily dose of valium to counteract the high level of stress in the impressario's life. But as he looked up and saw Angela sucking his cock and Charlene twiddling her toes around his tightening ballsack, Dickie decided that he would cope better with the frenetic pressure of his job if he threw away Dr Gottlieb's pills and spent an hour every afternoon with these uninhibited young beauties.

This pleasing reverie was broken when Angela lifted her head and opened her mouth, releasing his glistening cock from between her lips. Charlene moved gracefully across his body to plant her knees by his shoulders before gently lowering her curly thatch of auburn pussy hair down onto his face.

Dickie's heart began to pound as he caught the arousing aromatic scent of her cunt in his nostrils. He licked and lapped wildly along her sopping slit, nibbling and probing as she ground herself wantonly against his lips.

'Oh yes, keep licking, keep licking,' Charlene gasped as he twirled his tongue remorselessly, lapping up her cuntal moisture. She churned her hips from side to side as he nibbled her clitoris, pressing and licking up under the protective pink hood and then thrust his tongue deep into the depths of her love channel.

Charlene let out a delirious cry of ecstasy as the fierce surge of her climax swelled out from her pussy and cascaded throughout her body. Angela clambered between his legs and clamoured for her to move aside so that Dickie could now fuck her.

Reluctantly, Charlene slid down from the couch and Angela settled herself down between the impressario's muscular thighs. She raised herself and took hold of his rock-hard upright cock and as she slowly lowered herself down, she guided his knob between her yielding pussy lips.

'Wow! I'm so *full*!' she exclaimed as Dickie's prick embedded itself inside her clinging cunny. He stretched out his arms and grasped her soft peachy bum cheeks to pull her towards him. She leaned forward to allow him to kiss her erect, pointed nipples and then they were locked in a pulsating rhythm. As Angela bounced up and down on his sinewy shaft, he felt his penis swell to bursting point. She pistoned herself downwards against the power of his upward thrusts and they met each other's onslaughts with yelps and grunts of erotic pleasure.

As they fucked themselves towards orgasm, the tableau was completed by Charlene who sat on the arm of the settee, frigging herself in time with their lunges and occasionally joining in by slapping Angela's luscious backside as she rode up and down on Dickie's throbbing tool.

'I'm coming! I'm coming!' shrieked Angela as she bucked wildly on his trembling tadger. She shuddered violently when she reached the peak of a superb orgasm which enveloped her in a tidal wave of unadulterated delight. This sent Dickie's spunk racing up his stem and his cock spurted out a fountain of frothy white jism as he emptied himself inside her.

They collapsed down in a sticky heap of limbs as Charlene slid her hands underneath Dickie's scrotum and weighed his hairy ballsack in her palms. 'I'm glad you two enjoyed yourselves, and I hope you've time to fuck me now, Mr Segal,' she chirped up brightly. 'You seem to have plenty of juice left and it would be an awful pity to waste it.'

'By the way, we dance even better than we fuck,' Angela added meaningfully as she sat up. Dickie nodded his acceptance of her remark.

'All right, girls, you've proved your point. Let's all get dressed and I'll dictate a letter to Mrs Moser before my meeting.'

The girls chorused their thanks and Charlene picked up a pen from his desk and scribbled something on a sheet of paper. She handed it to Dickie as she murmured: 'As we haven't the time to finish our fuck, here's my telephone number. Do ring if you want to see me again – and as Angela and I share a flat, if you like we can have another cuddly three-some at our pad.'

'I'll be in touch,' promised Dickie as he drew up his boxer shorts and urged the girls to hurry up and get dressed. 'In the meantime, give me a call if you haven't heard from Mrs Moser by next Wednesday. If I'm not in, leave a message with Miss Leveson, my private secretary.'

Although he was physically tired after this highly charged sex session and the hefty lunch at the Carlton Towers which had preceded it, Dickie Segal felt mentally rejuvenated. While pulling on his shirt, he caught sight of the small phial of Dr Alan Gottlieb's valium tablets next to his telephone. He decided that Angela and Charlene had indeed provided far better therapy than his highly respected physician and, after the girls had kissed him good-bye, he threw the pills into the waste bin under his desk.

As it happened, if Dr Gottlieb had seen his patient dispose of his prescription, he would not have been

31

displeased, but at the time of Dickie's gesture the good doctor was elsewhere.

By coincidence he was at the offices of Rose and Griffin, sipping a refreshing glass of chilled white wine with the agency's managing director, Teddy Dixon, who was voicing his concern about Simon, his eldest son. The pair were shortly to leave town for Stevenage to attend a charity dinner and boxing tournament organised by the Sportsmen's Aid Society on which they both sat on the functions committee.

'I'm really worried about Simon,' confided Teddy Dixon. 'He's twenty-two years old with a first class honours degree in politics, philosophy and economics from Cambridge University. But what's he doing with it? Fuck all, that's what, Alan, even though he can start work at any time here. He knows I would be happy to retire and let him take over the agency once he's learned the ropes, but even that doesn't appeal. With his degree, the world's his oyster.'

'So what's he been up to?' enquired Dr Gottlieb with a resigned sigh. He had heard many similar stories recently from anguished parents about wayward offspring who had rejected the opportunity to take up promising careers and had decided instead to drop out of the rat race before the starting gun had even been fired.

'Nothing, absolutely nothing except that he's left home and he's living with a group of hippies in a squat off the Fulham Road, doing no work and living off the money he came into last year from his grandmother's will. He's not shown the slightest bit of interest in any sort of career, let alone coming into the business and taking some of the load off my shoulders.' The managing director of Rose and Griffin looked obviously unhappy.

'That's a pity, but your eldest boy, Paul, is doing well enough, isn't he?' said Dr Gottlieb. 'When he finishes that two-year research scholarship in computer science at Harvard, perhaps he'll come into the agency and you'll be able to take things a little easier.'

'Not really, Paul's an academic and not commercially minded, but he'll make his way all right. His mother and I aren't too concerned about him or Joannie, our youngest. She's only seventeen and, while she isn't academic, she's having a great time working as a secretary at a PR agency round the corner from here in Berkeley Square.'

Dr Gottlieb spread out his hands. 'Then at least two of the kids seem to have found their feet. Honestly, I wouldn't worry too much about Simon, old boy. It'll all come out in the wash. The middle child is often the one who has to assert his own individuality, because being in the middle can be a no-man's-land position, you know. He has always had to catch up with Paul and I would guess that Joannie might have had more than her fair share of attention, especially as you and Doris were probably over the moon at having a girl after two boys.

'If you want my advice, keep in touch with him to show you're interested in what he is doing with his life but don't try to pressurise him into returning home. Give him some time away from family rules and regulations – once he has shown both you and himself that he can lead his own life without any direction from you, he will have made his point and will settle down into making a career for himself.'

'H'mm, well I hope you're right,' said Teddy doubtfully. There was a knock on the door and Marlene, his nubile long-legged secretary, came into the office.

'Kevin's brought your car from the garage and he's waiting for you on a meter in Dover Street outside Brown's Hotel,' she announced as she passed a large brown envelope to her boss. Here are your tickets for tonight, with directions how to get to the Civic Hall.'

'Thanks, Marlene, we'd better be going,' he replied but she went on: 'Dave Zwaig's secretary called while you were out at lunch and asked if you would call him back before you left the office tonight. She said that Mr Zwaig needed to speak with you very urgently.'

Teddy Dixon grimaced as he growled: 'Damnation, what can David want that can't wait till tomorrow? Alan, would you like to wait for me in the car? I'll be down in a couple of minutes but I must call this chap back. He's one of our American associates and is slap bang in the middle of some delicate negotiations on our behalf. At least these days you can dial New York like a local number. Remember when you had to book a call through the operator? It cost a fortune too.'

After Marlene had escorted Dr Gottlieb to the lift, she came back to Teddy's office where to the impressario's astonishment, she wrestled the telephone out of his hand and put it back on the rest.

'Here, what's the idea? I'm calling New York,' he protested but Marlene shook her head and gave him a saucy smile. 'There's no need to ring Dave Zwaig, there wasn't any message from his office.'

'No message from his office? Well, why the hell did you say there was?' he demanded irritably. 'Traffic can be bad getting out of town and I have to be at the hall at half-past seven to welcome the mayor and assorted local bigwigs.'

'Don't be angry,' she pouted as she snuggled herself against her boss and loosened his tie. 'I just wanted a quickie before you went to your silly old boxing match.'

Teddy breathed hard as Marlene pulled off his tie. 'It isn't just a silly old boxing match tonight. The whole thing's in aid of charity and there's a dinner at which I'm supposed to be the host.' But he made no move to stop her when she started to undress, pulling off her sweater over her head and then unfastening her short skirt to let it drop to the floor.

'Bloody hell, Marlene, I really do have to be at the hall by half past seven to welcome the mayor,' complained Teddy as he saw that she was wearing a black garter belt and stockings but no panties.

Marlene did not answer but simply unhooked her bra and let her large rounded breasts swing free.

She moved purposefully towards him and put her hands on his shoulders as she looked steadily right into his eyes. Instinctively, Teddy slipped his arms round her waist and reached down to clasp her delicious bare bum cheeks and pull her pussy against the mounting swell in his groin.

She let one hand down to squeeze the bulge in his trousers and then, with a giggle, she wriggled free and lay down on Teddy Dixon's infamous casting couch. It had seen even more action than the sumptuous sofa in Dickie Segal's office. She spread her legs wide and stroked her inner thighs, going higher and higher until she was gently brushing her prominent pussy lips with her fingertips.

'Now that's not fair,' said Teddy hoarsely but Marlene still said nothing except look up at him questioningly as she transferred her hands to his belt to unbuckle it before unzipping his flies and pulling out his thick stiff cock from his boxer shorts.

'You only have to fuck me once, Teddy,' she said with a reproachful look. 'Now surely, that's not too much to ask, is it?'

'No, of course it's not, love,' said Teddy, deciding to surrender to her demand as he ripped down his shorts. 'It's the least I can do.'

. *What the heck*, he thought as her warm hand encircled his cock as he heaved himself up over her. *Dr Gottlieb thinks I'm on the phone to New York and if we're ten minutes late getting to Stevenage, tough luck. All the tickets for the event have been sold so the charity won't lose out.*

Marlene raised her knees and opened her legs wide to give Teddy an even more stimulating view of the red chink which lay between her love lips in the midst of her curly dark thatch of pussy hair. Her eyes wide and sparkling, she welcomed his pulsing prick into her, thrilling to the sensation as he pressed home the crown of his rock-hard stiff-stander until his entire throbbing tool was buried in her clinging moist honeypot.

She sighed with delight as Teddy began to pump away, pressing up to meet his thrusts and he drove home with increasing speed as his sexy secretary urged him on, closing her feet together at the small of his back to force every last inch of his straining shaft inside her tingling cunny.

Now Teddy leaned forward and sucked on her raised-up nipples as he pistoned his prick in and out of her soaking cunt, reaming the far walls of her love channel and she moaned in ecstasy as she began to come. Her juices soaked her cunt as, with a tremendous shudder, Marlene reached her climax. Shortly after Teddy followed her to the sexual Nirvana as with a wild cry he spunked deep inside her sopping snatch, a fierce fountain of frothy jism spurting out of his cock. He closed his eyes and savoured the sweet warmth of his orgasm while he emptied his balls inside her.

Reluctantly, Teddy pulled his rapidly shrinking cock out of her squelchy slit and manoeuvred himself off the couch and back on his feet beside her. 'I'd love to continue,' he said sincerely as he pulled up his trousers, 'but I really must go now. But I'm free for lunch tomorrow and we could take a taxi up to the flat for a nice sexy lunch.'

'Okay, and I'll order something nice from the sandwich bar to take with us,' said Marlene happily. She always enjoyed their occasional daytime romps at Teddy Dixon's small apartment in St John's Wood, a little secret hideaway of which his wife and most members of the staff of Rose and Griffin were unaware.

'Hope you enjoy yourself tonight,' she called out as Teddy finished dressing in record time. 'See you in the morning.'

'Bye, Marlene,' he replied, pulling up the knot in his tie until it fitted snugly against his neck. 'Oh, I almost forgot to tell you. I'm having my annual dental check-up tomorrow, so I won't be in till about ten-fifteen. So first thing in the morning, please telephone old Ronnie Dunn and tell him to come round at eleven instead of half past ten. I'm sure he won't mind too much as he knows I've got a cheque from Australia waiting for him.'

He blew her a kiss as he hurried out of the office. While he waited for the lift to come back up from the ground floor, he mentally kicked himself for making a lunch date with Marlene the next day instead of later in the week. The reason for his late arrival in the office tomorrow was not a dental appointment at all. Instead he had arranged a *rendezvous* with Sally Markham, a gorgeous dusky beauty fresh out of stage school who had written to him personally asking if Rose and Griffin would represent her. Normally, Teddy refused to take on beginners who at best would bring only a tiny amount into the coffers of the agency, but the girl had written a personal letter to him and enclosed a colour photograph of herself in a white bikini which accentuated her lavish curves as well as her smooth brown skin.

The lift doors opened and he stepped into the elevator and pressed the ground floor button. Teddy grinned as he recalled how, in her letter, the girl had underlined that she was a close friend of Caroline Sharples, who had been in the year above her at their stage school. She was sure that Teddy would find her as good a performer if he gave her a similar audition as he had given to her chum. Then, remembering the passionate hour of fucking he had enjoyed with the voluptuous Caroline, Teddy decided he needed more time to prepare himself and telephoned the luscious-looking Sally. She agreed to meet him at his private flat next Monday at nine o'clock in the morning.

It was just as well, thought Teddy, that his wife would be away for a few days visiting her sister down in Gloucester. The lift came to a halt and he walked briskly out into the street. As it was, if Sally was anything like as sensuous as her friend, he would be pretty shagged out long before he and Marlene were rolling around on his bed at lunchtime. And Monday was also one of the three mornings when Mrs Webster, the porter's wife, came in at noon to change the bed linen and clean up the flat.

'You look pleased with yourself,' said Dr Gottlieb to Teddy when Kevin, the Rose and Griffin chauffeur, jumped out of the Rolls Royce which had been waiting for the agency's managing director. 'Even though you must have been on the phone for more than ten minutes, I presume your Transatlantic call was worthwhile.'

'Oh yes, very worthwhile, Alan, though even with this new automatic dialling to America, it must have set us back a few bob,' agreed Teddy, trying hard not to smirk as he slid into the back seat to join his fellow passenger.

As Kevin swung the Rolls into Berkeley Square, Dr Gottlieb shut the glass partition between the driver and passengers. With a twinkle in his eye he turned to Teddy and said: 'Splendid! I'm really pleased for you, Teddy, because it must have been a very heated conversation. After all, I can see that you ripped off your tie because you've obviously reknotted it and rather badly at that, if you don't mind my saying so.

'Also, the zip of your flies is at half-mast and the button of the cuff on your right sleeve is undone. So you must have been having one hell of a shouting match with your American associate – or dare I suggest that you were perhaps otherwise engaged with the lovely Marlene?'

The doctor gave a fruity chuckle. Although at first Teddy Dixon was discomforted by his old friend's observations, he laughed as he hastily adjusted his clothing.

'Woe is me, I am undone,' he confessed with a broad grin. He held up his hands in mock surrender. 'But honestly, Alan, it was Marlene's idea to keep me back for a quickie. I knew nothing about it. I really thought that there had been a call for me from New York.'

Teddy opened the cocktail cabinet and poured out generous measures from the bottle of Johnnie Walker Black Label into two crystal goblets and passed one over to his guest. 'Cheers, let's drink to Marlene, a wonderful secretary who can take short-hand and type almost as well as she fucks. But I'd already given her the job before I began enjoying some after-hours privileges. It all began last year when young Adrian Klein threw a small party at the office for the Allendale Sisters when *Emerald Man* topped the charts. It wasn't a big do, we bought some snacks from Marks and Spencer and our own girls served the drinks.

'Anyhow, Adrian left with the Allendales and I heard Marlene tell the other two girls who had been helping her with the drinks that she didn't need their help to put all the glasses back in the kitchen. "That's kind of you, but I'll give you a hand," I said to her – I was planning to stay on myself because Doris was playing bridge with her cronies and I needed to spend a quiet hour or so checking through Freddie Amos's new contract. You must see his new show on the box, by the way, it's really good, there's been a dearth of good comedians since variety theatre died out.

'So I helped Marlene clean up. It seemed a shame to throw away a bottle of champagne which was three quarters full so I suggested we finish it together and I put a record on the gramophone. By the time we finished the champagne, Marlene was settled on my leather sofa like a sleek cat who had found its home in a well padded basket.

'Well, what with the soft lights and sweet music, one thing led to another and soon she was sitting on my lap. We cuddled and kissed and soon my hand was busy unbuttoning her blouse. When I cupped her breast with my hand she sighed and I wasn't too sure whether she wanted me to continue. But when I reached round her back to unhook her brassiere, she leaned forward to assist me and so I knew that she wanted me to carry on.

'I tell you, Alan, it was Marlene who made all the running! "Suck on my nipples," she whispered as I slid the bra straps from her shoulders and caressed her bare breasts. She began to squirm as I sucked one of her large red titties into my mouth while I ran my hand down to her knee and began to slide it up underneath her short skirt. When I reached her mound and pressed my palm against her pussy she sighed and rubbed her hand against my cock. She took off her shirt herself and raised her bottom as I rolled down her tights and panties. Then she helped me undress and when we were both naked we lay locked together, french-kissing like crazy while she ground herself against me, rubbing her pussy against the underside of my hard-on.

' "Do you mind if I go on top?" she asked and when I said: "Sure, why not?" she climbed on top of me and straddled across my thighs. Then she lowered herself gently onto my prick, taking in every inch of my shaft inside her cunt as she wriggled into the most comfortable position for her. As she settled, her buttocks pressed hard on the tops of my thighs. She twitched her shoulders and I watched her lovely firm breasts swing free above me. I squeezed those gorgeous soft beauties as Marlene treated me to a long, hard ride, fucking my cock slowly as she moved up and down and then from side to side and back and forth with her silky wet bush pressed tight against my own short and curlies.

'Suddenly she moved around a little too far and my cock almost dropped out, although my knob just remained inside her slippery cunny lips. I pulled her on top of me again and took control, clutching hold of the fleshy cheeks of her bum and sliding her up and down my cock at a nice easy pace. Then I had a sudden fancy to finish her off in a different way.

' "How about doing it doggy-style?" I panted and she replied: "Oh yes, yes, what a good idea, I love being fucked from behind!"

'She turned herself over onto her elbows and knees, raising her luscious bottom high in the air as I hauled myself up and placed my hands on the warm, smooth cheeks of her gorgeous backside. I passed my fingers inside the cleft between Marlene's bum cheeks and spread open the sticky wet love lips before pulling her buttocks apart and guiding my cock directly towards her dripping quim. I rammed my prick deep inside her juicy honeypot and she squealed with pleasure as I started to fuck her in a slow, steady rhythm. She quivered with every pounding stroke as I drove home again and again into her tight young cunt until we both came. As she exploded I spunked inside her sopping snatch and we collapsed down into a sweaty, spunky heap.'

Teddy grunted with satisfaction at the memory of this superb fuck as he drained his glass. He looked out of the window as the Rolls sped smoothly along Wellington Road along the side of Lord's cricket ground.

'The Third Test Match starts here on Thursday and I've been given a couple of tickets,' said Dr Gottlieb with a wry smile. 'Would you like to come with me, Teddy? Mind, I dare say you'd rather spend any spare time with the nubile young Marlene.'

'Thanks for the offer, Alan, but I couldn't take any time off this week, not even to screw Marlene,' replied Teddy, as he refilled their glasses. 'And in any case, I'm not that keen on cricket. It's nice to go out to the country on a Sunday afternoon and have a picnic while watching one of my boys play – Simon used to be a bloody fine batsman till he got involved with all this hippie nonsense – but to spend a whole day watching a professional game isn't for me. Cricket's getting like football, you know, there's so much money at stake these days that I'm sure the players go out to play thinking that whatever happens, they mustn't lose, so you get more and more draws because no-one's willing to take any chances.'

'Oh, I don't know, what about the way Manchester United beat Benfica a few weeks ago? That was a great game.'

Teddy nodded his head. 'Yes, but it was an exception to the rule. Most teams play to win the European Cup by sneaking a goal and then pulling everyone back in defence. And how many George Bests and Denis Laws are there coming up through the ranks? Precious few, I'll be bound, because the coaches aren't interested in individual geniuses any more. Everything is geared to the hard-running bonehead and the game's going to get more and defensive.

'Mark my words, we'll never see another Jimmy Greaves again,' he concluded gloomily as Kevin jumped through an amber light at Swiss Cottage and gunned the Rolls down the dual carriageway towards Finchley Road Station.

Teddy leaned forward and pulled open the glass divider. 'Steady on, Kevin,' he warned the errant driver. 'You're already up for speeding in Regent's Park. All you need is another ticket and they might disqualify you.'

'Okay, Mr Dixon, but we'll have to push it a bit if you want to be there on time,' called back the chauffeur over his shoulder. 'And anyway, I didn't cross on the red.'

'No, but you go and prove it,' said Dr Gottlieb drily. 'When it's your word against the police, you don't really have a leg to stand on. Mind, a former patient of mine who now lives in America told me an interesting story the other day. I can't mention her stage name, of course, but Patsy was a small-time actress – not on your books, Teddy, and I doubt if you've ever met her – and last year she was playing in some repertory company up in Manchester when she met an American airline pilot. After only six weeks she married him and went to live in a small Californian town about thirty miles south of Los Angeles.

'It's as well that she gave up the theatre because before all this she had come to me with a nasty skin complaint and it took some time before I found out that she was allergic to stage make-up. She was very grateful and when she went back to Manchester we kept in touch though and since she emigrated we still write the occasional letter.'

'She's like a pen-pal, is she?' enquired Teddy and the doctor nodded his agreement and gave a short laugh as he replied: 'Yes, though I promise that our relationship is strictly professional and nothing like what you have going with Marlene! In fact, all being well, Marie and I are going out there to see Patsy and her husband in early October.'

'Good for you, but what's this got to do with being stopped by the police?' Teddy demanded as Dr

Gottlieb pulled out a tiny cassette from his pocket and passed it over to him. 'Patsy slipped while playing tennis and hurt her wrist and won't be able to write for six weeks. So she sent me this recorded message. You've got a tape deck in the car, haven't you? Well, listen to this and you'll see the connection.'

Teddy opened the drawer in which he kept his dictaphone, placed the cassette inside the machine and listened to what Patsy had to say. While she began by sending greetings to Alan Gottlieb and his wife, Teddy listened somewhat half-heartedly. He idly noticed that after living two years in California, Patsy had picked up a slight American twang but her soft voice was still essentially English. Then when she started to describe what she was wearing as she was dictating this letter into the microphone he pricked up his ears.

It can't be less than ninety degrees in the shade and I'm sitting at the side of the pool under an umbrella drinking an ice-cold frozen daquari and thinking about how foolishly I behaved when I was stopped by a traffic cop for speeding yesterday afternoon.

Come to think of it, even though you're no longer my doctor, Alan, as a friend, I'd welcome your advice on what I should do. The point is, Michael and I had a terrible row only the previous evening – before he left for a five day stint flying to Europe – about some lipstick I had found on his uniform. I accused him of having an affair with one of those pretty stewardesses which he denied but I wonder how many people he would have been able to convince after I showed them the smudge of lipstick at the top of his flies!

The next day I decided to go out and see my friend Jill who lives ten miles down the road. We're in the middle of a heatwave right now so I was only wearing a thin pink shirt and a pair of skimpy white tennis shorts. I was feeling so angry with Michael that I zoomed out of our drive in our convertible and I suppose I must have been doing about sixty when all of a sudden I heard the blare of a siren behind me and when I looked in the mirror, I saw there was a motorcycle cop following me. Cursing, I slowed down and pulled over into a lay-by and he parked his bike behind my car and walked over to me.

I remembered what my brother had told me years ago back in England – if you're stopped by a traffic cop, always get out of your car so they're not towering over you and you don't have to look up at them. I opened the door of my car and, first sliding out my tanned left leg, I hauled myself up and leaned against the convertible as the cop approached me. He was a broad, handsome young guy who looked pretty hunky in his blue uniform. I could not see his eyes behind his dark glasses, but I was pretty certain that he was looking appreciatively at my long bare legs as he said sternly: 'Ma'am, have you any notion at what speed you were driving?'

'Not really,' I confessed, putting on a little smile and my best British accent as I added: 'but I suppose you're going to tell me that it was too fast.'

'Yeah, and how! You were clocking up fifty in a thirty-mile-an-hour zone,' he replied as he whipped out a note-pad which meant I would get a ticket. As the fine shoots up if you were going way over the limit, I knew I would be facing a hundred dollar fine.

'May I see your licence please?' he asked me, and I shook my head. 'I'm afraid I've left it in another handbag. But that's only about a mile back so it wouldn't take me long to drive back for it.'

'Don't you know you're always supposed to carry your driver's licence?' he said. I replied that I hadn't lived in California all that long and apologised for my mistake.

'All right,' he said, putting his pad back in his pocket. 'But we'll both go back and remember I'm behind you so don't drive at even a fraction more than thirty miles an hour.'

'I won't,' I said humbly as I slipped back inside my car. Well, I made sure I never went over twenty-eight on the ride home and after he had parked his bike in our driveway, I got out and asked him to come inside the house. He followed me through the front door and into the lounge where I'd drawn the blinds to keep out the blinding rays of the afternoon sun. I pulled them half-open to let more light stream in as I looked for my bag in which I'd put my driver's licence.

By great good fortune, I'd left the bag on top of a shelf which meant I had to stretch up to reach it and although I could not see him, I sensed that the young cop's eyes were looking at the contours of my bottom through the tight stretchy white fabric of my cut-away shorts. This feeling was confirmed when I turned round and saw that he had taken off his sunglasses to reveal his handsome bronzed face.

'Why not take off your cap and sit down for a couple of minutes rest while I fix us a cold drink,' I suggested. It was quite funny really to see him struggle to remember that he was supposed to be writing me out a speeding ticket, rather than yielding to the advances of this curvy blonde lady who was tempting him away from his duty!

'Well, I don't know,' he said doubtfully but I took no notice and sauntered out to the kitchen. With my short golden blonde hair and summer freckles, I felt like one of those sexy French girls in the Feydeau farces. I began to act the part by wiggling my bottom as I sashayed by him. Before I brought in two glasses of ice cold orange juices, I slipped off my bra and rubbed my titties so that my nipples stuck out under my top. This strategy certainly worked because I could see his eyes widen as I brushed my breasts along his arm when I gave him his drink.

We introduced ourselves and he told me that his name was Louis Baum and he had only joined the force last year on his twenty-first birthday after leaving the Army. 'I'm sure you're going to be a very good cop, Louis, especially if you learn the value of discretion,' I said as I pulled up my top over my head and then took hold of his hands and pressed them to my bare breasts. In no time at all we were kissing *furiously and he was tearing off his jacket and shirt while I slicked my tongue all round the inside of his mouth. I wiggled my erect nipples against his hairy chest while I fumbled to unbuckle his gun-belt and murmured in his ear: 'Let's go upstairs, big boy.'*

We staggered out of the room and then Louis lifted me up and carried me up the stairs and into my bedroom. He gently deposited me on the mattress while he sat down on the side of the bed and quickly took off his boots and socks. Then he stood up and tugged down his trousers and shorts to reveal his tight, dimpled little bum. When he turned round, I gasped with excitement as I saw his thick stiff shaft which was standing up proudly against his flat stomach. Louis might not have had the biggest cock I'd ever seen but was none the less beautifully proportioned with a wide reddish dome and a warm shaft as smooth as velvet.

He threw himself down on top of me and plunged his hand inside my shorts as our mouths fastened together. I heard Louis gasp as I pulled down the zip and he yanked them off me together with my frilly little panties in one fell swoop. He could tell from my moistening pussy that I was getting ready for him and then it was my turn to begin panting with pleasure as I felt his fingers pinching my clitty and I quickly squeezed my legs together, trapping his hand between my thighs.

'Yes, yes, yes!' I gasped as his lips travelled down to massage my breasts and nipples. I closed my eyes and breathed deeply as his tongue traced a wet path

across my tummy, down into my golden grotto. He nibbled all around my pouting pink pussy lips and when I felt him working his way towards the tingling bud of my erect clitty, my pussy juice began to drip out of my cunny and down onto my thighs.

Now Louis moved his body around so that I could fondle his lovely balls. They hung hot and heavy in my hands and their hairy sack tasted dry and salty when I licked it. When he kissed my pussy again I copied his actions and within a few seconds we were each mirroring each other's motions. When Louis slurped his lips all along my crack from end to end I lashed my tongue around the long length of his shaft. I shuddered into a series of lightning orgasms when he inserted his tongue inside my cunt and licked out my honeypot.

As soon as he felt my cunny vibrating, Louis's cock began throbbing like crazy and so I got my mouth nice and wet and slipped his veiny pole down into my throat. I guessed that he was on the verge of spunking and with a few thrusts of my lips and sucks with my cheeks, I had him pumping into my mouth like a well-oiled piston. Then, as the cum started to spurt out of his prick, I milked his cock by gulping down all his tasty jism until his balls were emptied.

Louis pulled out his prick from my mouth but continued to frig with his fingers. I rubbed his glistening wet shaft which soon stood up as hard and stiff as before. I placed a pillow under my bottom to give me some extra elevation while he rolled on top of me and I guided his throbbing tool towards my yearning pussy.

'A-h-r-e!' he groaned with pleasure as his prick slid in one smooth movement into my soaking cunt. We were now both at fever pitch and in such haste to enjoy each other's bodies that there was little time for any finesse. Louis started to screw me with short jabs of his thick truncheon but soon we were fucking away wildly and my fingernails raked across his back as he humped into me, holding me tightly by my buttocks as he diddled my bum-hole with his little finger.

'That's it, Louis, fuck me!' I shrieked out loud and bucked my hips back and forth. I revelled in the sensation of having his cock and finger filling me simultaneously and then Louis dipped his head to my titties and licked and sucked deliriously while I shivered my way to a wonderful climax. Then he came too and shot his spunk deep into the palpitating channel of my cunt . . .

We lay in a tangle of limbs, panting with exhaustion at first unable to speak but finally I turned to my new young lover and said: 'Well, you can hardly give me a ticket now, honey, or I'll be forced to tell the press about our local police department's secret weapon.'

He grinned and kissed me lightly on the lips. 'Let's call it quits, shall we? But please, Patsy, don't drive so quickly in a residential area. Never mind the ticket, suppose you ran down a kiddie because you couldn't pull up in time?'

'*You're right and I promise to be more careful in future*,' I said as he turned me over onto my tummy and began caressing my soft bum cheeks. *Could my gallant young cop be up to a third session of love-making?*'

At this point the tape stopped and Teddy Dixon snorted with disappointment as Dr Gottlieb snapped open the lid of the dictaphone and extracted the cassette which he put back in his pocket. 'I was really enjoying listening to that,' complained Teddy. 'What a place for the tape to run out! This girl sounds like a bit of all right to me, Alan. Are you sure you didn't have anything going with her?'

'Of course not, although I can't say I wasn't occasionally tempted to break my Hippocratic Oath!' replied the doctor with a grin. 'But actually, I haven't come quite clean with you. As I said, Patsy was an actress back here but she can't get her American Equity card until she's lived in the States for three years. So to keep herself occupied she recorded a few adult tapes for a chap she met at a party. These sold so well that she began to write her own stories and this was one of her most successful. She said she'd send a sample tape and asked me if I thought there might be a market for them in Britain. What do you think, Teddy?'

Teddy Dixon exhaled a deep breath before he replied: 'Blimey, I'm not sure about that. I'm sure there'd be a big market but I can't see how they could be sold. I mean, you could hardly expect any of the chains to stock such hot stuff, though I suppose you might be able to get away with knocking them out through mail-order. You'd need to advertise them through *Titbits* or *Reveille* but I wonder if the advertising managers would take the ads if they heard the tapes.'

'Yes, but if the ads specified sales to adults only, this might be a way for the ads to be accepted,' suggested Dr Gottlieb. With the clear open A1 road ahead of him, Kevin now put his foot down and took the luxurious car up to a hundred miles an hour.

'Well, if she wants someone to see if anything can be done, I could have a word with Alf Fairclough. He sells a lot of stuff through his Mini-Market ads in the papers and he's just joined my lodge. Come to think of it, if he is interested, perhaps he'd ask Simon to help run the operation!'

'Fine, I'll write to Patsy and tell her what you say. This could work out very well for all concerned,' said his old chum with evident satisfaction.

CHAPTER TWO

. . . Does You Good!

Sharon Saxon was enjoying herself at the party thrown by the songsmith Nick Clarke at his luxurious Kensington penthouse after the *Top Of The Pops* recording. Neither Mick Jagger nor John Lennon had turned up but she had been interviewed by journalists from *Melody Maker* and *New Musical Express* and she had danced with the lead guitarist of one of her favourite groups. As she sat on the stairs munching a sandwich, a shapely coffee-coloured girl of about her own age with a glass of champagne in her hand came up and sat down beside her.

'Hi there, aren't you Sharon Saxon? I loved *Why Don't You Stay And Play*, I do hope it gets to number one in the charts.'

'Thank you,' said Sharon, who did not recognise the girl but unlike many other performers, she was always pleased to chat with her fans. 'But it would take The Beatles or Cliff Richard to knock the new Stones single off the top spot. I'm not too upset about it, though, because as that Avis advert says, when you're number two you have to try harder!'

The pretty dark-skinned girl smiled and said: 'It's nice to hear a singer taking a sensible view of a situation. I hear so many bleating that the record producer didn't know what he was doing or the publicity agent was hopeless, or of course that their material wasn't strong enough – and that last excuse really makes me annoyed because I know how much hard work goes into writing a good song.'

She held out her hand and said: 'I'm Donna Butler, by the way, Nick Clarke's secretary – it's really nice to meet you.'

'Are you?' Sharon exclaimed as she shook hands with her. 'It's nice to meet you too, Donna, and I'd love to be introduced to Nick. I haven't had a chance to meet him yet although I think that's my agent Tony Cavendish with him and Tim Lempert in the corner.'

'Oh, Tony's your agent, is he? I've heard some good things about him,' remarked Donna. 'Mind, if he's trying to persuade the boys to write a song for you, I doubt if he'll have much joy for they're so busy that I can't see how they could take on any more work just now.'

Donna looked across at Sharon's crestfallen face and added quickly: 'It's nothing personal, honest it's not. But look, if you really want Nick to write your next single, when it gets a bit quieter, I'll arrange a little get-together for just the two of you in his study. Tony Cavendish won't be there, so Nick won't feel he's being pressurised.'

'Oh my, will I be safe?' said Sharon in mock fright, placing her hand across her chest.

'As safe as you want,' replied Donna with a large wink as she grabbed two fresh glasses of champagne from a passing waiter and gave one to Sharon. 'Nick's a very attractive guy and, thank God, he likes girls, not like so many of the poofters in this crazy business.'

And then lowering her voice, she added: 'And between you and me, if Nick thinks there's a chance of any pussy coming his way, any girl can run him round her little finger!'

'M'mm, that's good to know,' mused Sharon and Donna downed her champagne and whispered in her ear: 'Nick's also a very good fuck, and coming from me that's a terrific recommendation because lately I've tended to prefer girls to boys. In fact, I was really overdoing the lezzie bit and I have to thank Nick for reminding me of the pleasure of a thick hard cock in my cunt!'

The waiter came by them again and Donna seized a fresh glass of champagne from him. 'Excuse me, I'm a bit tiddley, but what I said was true enough,' she sighed. 'I'd love to be fucked by Nick again but would you believe, we have both been so busy that there just hasn't been time, not even for a quick knee-trembler!'

'Do tell me more,' Sharon said eagerly as Donna gulped down another drink. 'I'd really love to know what turns Nick on.'

Donna shrugged her shoulders and said: 'Well, we

first put it together only last month so I don't know too much about his tastes, but seeing Sara and I in a sixty-nine certainly drove him wild. Sara's a part-time secretary who comes in to help when we have an overload,' she went on, pointing a finger at a willowy strawberry blonde who was talking to Tony Cavendish in the far corner of the room. 'She also likes to mix n' match, if you get my drift, and once we found out that we had this interest in common, I discovered that she must be the best pussy eater in the whole country!

'And I do mean *country*,' Donna added with a saucy laugh. 'As I said, it all started one afternoon in the office. Nick was out of the office till tea-time and Sara and I had been to a super drinks party at Decca to launch Shane Hammond's new record, so when we got back we were both a bit sloshed. Well, while Sara was in the loo, I happened to see a copy of this very rude magazine called *Pink Lips* on her desk. There were lots of photos in it showing beautiful horny girls reaming each other out and sticking dildoes into each other's pussies.

'I was so engrossed in looking through it that I didn't hear Sara come back until she slipped her arm round my waist and cooed: "Does my magazine turn you on, darling? Look at that lovely girl, wouldn't you just love to didle your fingers inside her juicy pussy? And can you imagine how just one lick from your tongue would make her thrash around and send her love juice spurting inside your mouth?"

'She didn't have to say much more, but she pulled me into Nick's office and in no time at all we were stark naked and into a sixty-nine on the carpet. We were really into each other and neither of us were aware that Nick had come back early and was lounging against the wall watching his secretaries licking out each other's cunnies!

'He didn't say anything and we didn't notice he was there till we had brought ourselves off. When I looked up and saw Nick I almost died of embarrassment. I thought he would be angry and fire us and I was so flustered that I tried covering my breasts with one arm and my pussy with the other, but then he smiled and said: "Don't do that, Donna, you carry on – I just hope you'll let me join in the game."

' "Okay with me, boss,' I said and Sara showed she was also keen to continue by reaching up and unzipping Nick's flies. He sat down on his chair and pulled down his trousers. His cock shot up as stiff as a poker and he stroked his veiny shaft as he asked how we were going to relieve him now that we had got him so aroused!

' "Would like you to fuck me?" asked Sara, but he replied: "Yes please, Sara, but first I'd like Donna to suck my cock."

'Now I was happy to oblige, but I hadn't had a prick in my mouth for some time, so I was feeling a little nervous as I dropped to my knees in front of Nick. I grasped hold of his thick stiffie as I crawled between his thighs and began to suck his knob, twirling the tip of my tongue around his helmet.

'Oh, it was absolutely heavenly to have his cock in my mouth! I lashed my tongue around his pulsating prick and then bobbed my head up and down on his thick tool and three short, licking strokes followed by one long, fierce suck was all it needed to send him off.

' "I'm coming, I'm coming," he gasped, wanting to warn me if I didn't want to swallow his spunk, but I didn't try to pull away and I squeezed his balls and gulped down all his tasty jism.'

Sharon wriggled slightly as she felt her pussy moisten while she listened to Donna's confession and she remarked: 'So a good time was had by all.'

'Oh, we didn't stop there – I'd heard a rumour about Nick having amazing stamina and sure enough his shaft was still hard when he slid it out of my mouth. He lay down and told me to straddle him, but before I could move, Sara said: "Hey, what about me, don't I get a slice of the action?"

' "Sorry, Sara, of course you can," apologised Nick cheerfully and he spun me round so that my bum was facing him as I lowered my cunt onto his cock. It was wonderful to watch his truncheon slide all the way up my cunny. While I bounced up and down on it, Sara knelt down in front of me and began licking and lapping at my titties which helped bring me off again before Nick could squirt some more spunk in my pussy.

'We then swapped round and Sara got down on all fours and asked Nick to fuck her doggy-style. He pulled her bum cheeks open and mounted her, sliding his glistening cock in her hot, juicy cunt while she gyrated her hips and rocked around, moaning and groaning softly as he pounded hard into her, grabbing her hips as she reached a huge orgasm. Nick slid his prick out of the crevice between her bum cheeks and I couldn't believe that it was still rock hard! He could see that my pussy was aching for cock so he told me to lie on my back and then he climbed over me and I gasped with pleasure as he slipped his beefy lovestick inside my sopping quim in one long thrust.

' "Fuck me, Nick," I panted and soon he was riding me like a bull. I felt his body stiffen and then his cock throbbed and he shot his sticky jets of cum deep into my cunt. I was overcome by my own climax and I clung on to his shoulders and pushed myself against him as hard as I could while wonderful waves of pleasure swept through me.'

The beautiful dusky girl closed her eyes and a seraphic smile lit up her face as she recalled the marvellous electricity which had surged through her shapely limbs. She leaned forward and whispered in Sharon's ear: 'If you're interested in getting him to write a song for you, Nick loves pretty long-legged blondes and he'll be putty in your hands.'

'Pretty stiff putty, I would imagine from what you've told me,' said Sharon drily and Donna winked at her and said: 'Well, would you like to find out for yourself? If you're shy I'll join in, there's nothing that turns a man on than coffee and cream.'

'Coffee and cream?' repeated Sharon in bewilderment and then the penny dropped and she chuckled: 'Oh, you mean a fair-skinned blonde like me and a black-haired dark-skinned girl like you! H'm, I suppose it could be fun.'

Donna slid a hand around her waist and planted a kiss on her cheek as she murmured: 'What about making a double date tonight? I'd like to see what your guy, Tony Cavendish, has between his legs, though he seems to have disappeared. Mind, as he's looking after you tonight he can't be far away. On the other hand, perhaps you'd rather I didn't try to see if I could interest him.'

'I'm sure you'll have no difficulty in pulling Tony – so long as you can find him,' Sharon replied as she looked around to see where her agent had gone. 'He can't be far away as he wouldn't leave the party without me. If you want to screw him it's okay with me, but I don't think I want to be involved in any foursome, it might spoil our business relationship.'

'Okay, I understand, though most girls in this business are getting shafted one way or the other,' shrugged Donna as she hauled herself to her feet. 'It might sound cynical but, in my opinion, it's better to be screwed in bed than find you're being screwed on your earnings! Rose and Griffin is one of the best agencies but it must be good to have someone on the inside really batting for you.

'Anyhow, while I go and arrange things with Nick, would you like to find Tony and suss out if he would like to stay on with you, me and Nick after everyone else has gone home,' she added as Sharon also stood up and brushed off some crumbs from her skirt.

'Sure, Tony must be around somewhere. I'll come back here once I've found him,' said Sharon. She glided off to look for her agent, but he was nowhere to be found. Then, in the hallway, she saw a small flight of stairs and she realised that Nick Clarke's apartment was in fact a two-floor maisonette. *He must have gone upstairs for a pee*, she muttered to herself as she waited in the hall for him to come down. However, when there was no sign of him after almost five minutes, Sharon clicked her tongue in annoyance and decided to investigate the mystery of her vanished colleague for herself.

She climbed the stairs and on the small landing she paused as above the hubbub of music and raised voices from downstairs, Sharon thought she heard sounds coming from behind one of the three closed doors of what she supposed were bedrooms facing her. She tapped on the door and called out: 'Tony? Tony Cavendish? It's Sharon, are you in there?'

Although there was no reply, Sharon could still hear sounds of puffing and panting coming from the room and so she gingerly turned the handle and slowly opened the door. The room was in darkness except for a lamp by the side of the bed and Sharon grinned as she saw that she had found her missing agent. Tony was lying naked on the bed with a ravishing young girl with big breasts. She was also nude and lying on her back, her legs splayed out with Tony's face buried between her thighs, noisily nuzzling on her pussy with his lips and tongue. At first Sharon watched in silence, admiring Tony's taut dimpled bum cheeks as he scrambled up. The girl grabbed hold of his cock and guided it between her cunny lips.

'Wow! Not too tight, Marilyn!' he protested as she squeezed her thighs together, making Tony open his own legs and lie astride her with his shaft well and truly trapped in her cunt.

Sharon now felt a familiar moist tingling between her legs. She looked on as Marilyn eased the pressure and Tony began to fuck her like a man possessed, pumping his prick in and out of her juicy quim, driving hard and fast and bringing her off time and time again. He slid his hand under her backside and Sharon presumed he must have jabbed his finger up the girl's bum-hole because she now threw herself around in a wild frenzy, bringing her legs up against the top of his back and humping her hips upwards to meet the fierce, thudding strokes of his rigid rod.

'Here we go!' he shouted and crashed down on her, but Sharon noticed that he had pulled out his prick from Marilyn's cunt and was rubbing the red, gleaming shaft along her soft belly.

'Aaagh! Aaagh!' he gasped as he bucked forwards. As he sent a stream of sticky creamy spunk cascading into the cleft between Marilyn's generous breasts, she grasped his quivering cock and milked every last drop out of his spurting length.

Sharon cleared her throat loudly. Tony's jaw visibly dropped when he twisted round to see his young star standing behind him. 'Ah, er, Sharon, this is Marilyn from Consolidated Rediffusion, the ITV television company for the Midlands. Marilyn, meet Sharon Saxon, our new number one singing sensation.'

'Hi Sharon! Tony was telling me all about you before he asked for the millionth time if he could fuck me. I was getting so bored with saying no that in the end I let him have his wicked way,' said Marilyn coolly as she sat up, apparently quite unconcerned not only about being stark naked while meeting a stranger but also at having rivulets of spunk trickling down her tummy. 'You're very pretty,' she went on. 'I'll bet he's been trying his best to get into your knickers.'

'Not really,' said Sharon, shaking her blonde mane. 'He knows I have one arsehole in them already.' To Tony's discomforture, the two girls burst out laughing.

'Well, I've heard it said that lots of laughter and lots of sex are essential in any relationship,' said the affronted agent while he pulled on his pants. 'Don't get me wrong, I couldn't agree more – but not at the same time, girls, if you don't mind.'

Marilyn blew him a kiss and said: 'Ah, don't be a bad sport, Tony. After all, you've had your wicked way with me which you've wanted since we met at that Salute To Israel Concert after the Six Day War last summer.'

'I'm not really cross, though I've never fucked in front of an audience before – at least I don't think so, although someone told me that old Eric what's-his-name from Silverside Records had a two way mirror installed in his guest bedroom down at his place on the South Coast.' Tony chuckled as he continued dressing and as he reached down to the floor to pick up his tie he added: 'Marilyn, you were terrific, bless you. I'm sorry I have to rush away but I promised to take Sharon home.'

After he had slipped on his jacket, he escorted Sharon to the door and Marilyn called out: 'Tony, if you have to leave, be a dear and ask Pascal, that nice French guy from *Paris Match*, if he'd like to come up here and keep me company for a while.'

As Tony closed the door behind them, Sharon asked him to wait a moment and recounted what Donna had told her. He gave a wide grin when she told him that Donna had asked if he would like to make up a foursome when the party ended. 'But not a whoresome foursome, Tony,' she added firmly. 'I'm not getting involved with you in any way outside the office.'

'Fair enough, it's probably for the best,' agreed Tony reluctantly. 'On the other hand, I'd love to get to know Donna better. She's an absolute corker, though I was under the impression that she prefers girls to boys.'

'She swings both ways,' explained Sharon as they walked down the stairs to rejoin the party.

When she saw Donna looking enquiringly at her

across the room, Sharon gave the ravishing girl a thumbs-up signal, but it took the best part of an hour to shoo the last guests out of the front door.

Donna and Tony were cuddling up together on a sofa and Sharon was sitting in a deep armchair when the noise of the front door closing echoed round the now-quiet room. Nick Clarke came back to announce that the caterers had now also left and that they were alone.

'Well, Sharon, at last we have a chance to talk,' said Nick, settling himself on the arm of her armchair. 'Tony and Donna have been bending my ear all night about how you want Tim Lempert and me to write a song for you. I'm flattered, but I hardly think you need us right now. After all, *Why Don't You Stay And Play*? has done very well for you and I can't believe that Clive Thompson doesn't want to write for you any more.'

Tony Cavendish answered for her. 'Yes, but Clive's gone off to Hollywood to work on some big musical for Twentieth Century Fox, and it's high time that Sharon made her first LP. Honestly, she's always admired your work Nick and you and Tim know that Sharon has a super voice and will do your songs justice.'

'Oh, I've no doubts about that, and speaking for myself, I'd love to help out,' replied the writer, looking down at Sharon's upraised pretty face. 'The only problem is that Tim and I have a mountain of work for the next six months and I just don't think it would be fair to you or our present clients to take on any more commitments until we've ploughed through some of the stuff we're contracted to finish by the end of the year.'

'Let's think about all that later, let's have a dance first,' said Donna. She naughtily squeezed Tony's cock as she lifted herself up from the sofa and went across to a pile of records and selected the new Georgie Fame LP. She switched on the record player and clapped her hands. 'Come on you lot, where's all your energy? It's not even midnight yet!'

She cajoled them all onto the floor as the bluesy music echoed round the room but after a while even Donna tired and the two couples flopped down opposite each other with the two girls now sitting on their partners' laps.

'Phew, it's so warm in here,' said Donna, wiping her brow. 'I feel I should be lying on a sunbed on the beach back in Barbados.'

'What do you mean, back in Barbados,' teased Nick. 'You were born in Stoke Newington!' Donna chuckled and replied: 'Well, my Daddy came from Barbados and ever since I read a travel book about the island, I've dreamed of going there for a holiday.'

'Well, in the meantime, if you're too hot, you can always take off your clothes and pretend you're there, stretching yourself out on a bed of warm, white sand,' suggested her boss. Donna did not take offence at this brazen proposal. Instead, a sexy smile spread slowly over her face as she found a ska LP which she put on the turntable.

Then she walked to the centre of the room and gyrating her hips to the lazy beat of the music, Donna peeled off her silky mauve top and threw it across to Tony Cavendish who caught the garment and draped it over a chair.

Even Sharon watched in awe as the proud brown mounds of her breasts jiggled sensuously in the scanty scallop shells of her bra. Then she unzipped her black mini-skirt with a sensuous wriggle of her superb body, she let it fall down her bare legs onto the carpet.

Now her audience could see the rounded soft spheres of her beautiful bum cheeks between which the skimpy material of her white panties disappeared in a thinning strap to reappear at the base of her flat belly, moulding the swell of her prominent mound and almost mesmerising the three spectators who sat entranced as she stood before them, smoothing her hands over her high uptilted breasts.

Donna's eyes twinkled as she saw the effect she was having on Tony Cavendish, who was sitting upright as if transfixed by her sensuous strip-tease. She squatted down on her haunches with her back to him and in a husky whisper asked him to undo the clips of her bra. She turned her head and blew him a kiss as she covered her nipples with her forearms as he pulled off the straps from her shoulders. Then, cupping her bosoms in her hands, she swung herself round to Tony and with a dramatic movement, threw open her hands and exposed her bare breasts to his excited gaze. But when he reached out to touch them she skipped back with a cheeky giggle.

'Wait till you've finished, lover, I still have work for you to do,' she admonished him gently. She stood directly in front of Tony and ran her hands all over her gleaming supple body. Then Donna tweaked her nipples, rubbing them until they stood erect like two chocolate soldiers. When she was satisfied she stepped forward until his face was inches away from her heaving breasts. 'Take off my knickers, there's a good boy,' she purred.

Tony stood stock still and wiped away beads of perspiration before he reached forward with both hands and tugged down her white panties, exposing a full triangle of crinkly black hair through which peeked Donna's large cunny lips. She leaned back and slid her forefinger between them as she rocked gracefully from side to side to the soft rhythm of the music.

'Now it's your turn to show us what you have to offer,' she said as, with the other hand, she pulled Tony's unresisting head to her breasts. He took a rubbery nipple between his lips and wrapped his arm round her waist to draw her closer to him, but again she stepped back and this time extended an arm to pull him up from the sofa. Tony hauled himself up and stood in front of the naked girl, sliding his hands up and down her glistening brown body as she helped him to undress, first bending low to undo his shoe-laces and removing his shoes and socks before unbuttoning his shirt while he tore off his trousers.

Soon he was naked except for his Y-fronts and Sharon unconsciously slid her hand between her thighs as she saw the huge bulge in the front of Tony's pants. She began to tingle all over as Donna rolled down Tony's briefs and slicked her hand up and down his quivering stiff cock.

'Now that looks like a very tasty lollipop,' she breathed and dropped to her knees to lick along the sensitive underside of his shaft. Then she swirled her tongue all round his uncapped mushroomed knob, lapping the springy cap with the tip of her pointed pink tongue.

'A-a-h-r-e!' he groaned as Donna gobbled on his twitching tool. It swayed from side to side as she worked her mouth up and down the length of his pulsing prick.

'God, she knows how to give head, doesn't she?' muttered Nick as he moved his buttocks along the arm of the chair. Sharon squeezed his thigh and whispered: 'She's not the only girl who knows how to suck a cock, you know.'

Nick looked steadily into her eyes and replied softly: 'I can't tell you how delighted I am to hear you say so. Shall we go upstairs to my bedroom and you can prove it to me.'

He helped Sharon to her feet and as they left the room they took a last lingering look at the other couple who were fast reaching the point of no return, writhing wildly on the carpet, their lips joined together. Tony had slid a hand into Donna's crinkly dark bush and was frigging her soaking slit. Just before Nick closed the door behind them, Sharon glanced back to see Tony climbing on top of the dusky girl to begin fucking her in earnest.

Once upstairs in his bedroom they wasted no time and in a trice Nick's lips were over hers. Sharon kissed him back avidly, hooking her arms around his neck and then she squealed with surprise as he bodily lifted her up and, taking three firm strides forward, he tumbled her down on his bed. Then they were all over each other, squeezing and groping and giggling as they tore off each other's clothes until both were totally nude. Nick gasped at the beauty of the delectable young blonde while Sharon thrilled at the sight of Nick's powerful rock-hard cock which was long and thick, springing upwards from a forest of curly brown hair and a pair of large balls in his tightening, wrinkled scrotum.

The juices began to dribble out from Sharon's honeypot as she felt him caress her erect, pointy nipples. As he moved on top of her, the young girl spread her legs wide and raised her knees so that the swollen entrance to her love channel and the inviting red chink of her cunny were plainly visible to him. She grasped hold of his hot, throbbing shaft and, tensing the muscles in her backside and raising her hips from the bed to meet him, placed the tip of his knob between her pouting love lips.

For a moment he gazed deeply into Sharon's liquid blue eyes and then, with a hoarse, strangled sob, he thrust forward, sliding his pulsing prick inside her clinging cunt, his belly pressed against hers. He could feel her nipples rubbing sweetly against his chest as he started to fuck the ravishing teenager. Sharon's glowing curves vibrated as the muscles of her love channel contracted around Nick's delighted penis.

'Go on, Nick, I want you in deeper, as far as you can go! Fuck me with that great hard prick, you randy lad!' Soon they were locked into a pulsing rhythm as he fucked the quaking girl with long, sweeping strokes of his sinewy cock. He felt his shaft swell even further inside her juicy sheath as she drove her body upwards against the power of his punching hips, bouncing back from each encounter as Tony continued to ride his rigid rod in and out of her sopping crack until his huge truncheon triggered Sharon's cunt into the ultimate ecstasy.

Frantically he hammered his tool through her love channel and Sharon squealed with joy as a wonderful fully-fledged orgasm raced through her body in a series of exquisite electric shocks. Then it was Nick's turn to climax. With a low growl, his cock began to jerk and twitch as he lurched towards his peak, drenching her cunt with jets of sticky warm jism which spilled out of his palpitating prick.

For a while they lay exhausted on the bed, their drowsy satisfied bodies pressed together in a tight, contented embrace and Sharon murmured: 'If your next song's as good as that fuck, Nick, you'll have a world-wide smash hit!'

'Thanks for the compliment,' he replied with a little grunt. He felt Sharon's fingers sliding over his belly towards his shrunken shaft which was dangling over his balls. 'I wish I could give an encore . . .' Nick began unhappily but then his voice trailed off as Sharon moved up on her knees and, tossing her long blonde locks back over her shoulders, she pulled back his foreskin to expose his smooth helmet and then lowered her head to take his flaccid tadger into her deliciously wet mouth. She sucked lustily, slurping her way down to the base of Nick's burgeoning penis, covering every sensitive inch of his cock, with her tongue lapping on his swelling shaft like a sleek kitten with long sexy strokes.

She started to tease his plump purple knob, running her tongue all round its ridge and then her lips formed a wet suctioning ring which clamped itself around his cock while she gently manipulated his balls in their hairy pink bag of wrinkled skin.

Nick moaned as Sharon sent him into shivers of sheer ecstasy with a series of tiny, teasing nips with her teeth. She concentrated on his knob, washing it all over with saliva as she slid her fist up and down his pulsating prick, faster and faster until a gush of creamy spunk welled up from his balls and cascaded out of his cock into her mouth. She swallowed all of his copious ejaculation and licked a final blob before letting her hand fall from his rapidly deflating shaft.

'My turn now,' she said as she stretched herself back on the bed, parting her legs slightly so that the pink fleshy, folds of her pussy were revealed. She slowly undulated her hips, pressing her erect crimson nipples between her fingers in an attitude of wanton availability.

'Bring me off again, Nick,' she breathed, running her tongue lasciviously over her lips as if to signal to him how he could best perform this task.

He leaned over and their mouths locked together in a deep-throated kiss while Nick pressed his hand against her sopping wet pussy, letting his fingers delve through the fluffy moist patch of golden hair in a light stroking motion over her rubbery love lips. Sharon gasped as he opened her crack and applied his thumb to the sensitive bud of her clitty.

'Oh, that's absolutely marvellous,' she panted as Nick slid one hand under her bottom and moved his body downwards until his head was on the same level as her groin. With a little grunt of satisfaction, he rolled over between her legs and kissed her juicy pussy, sucking up the cunny juices which were already flowing out from her excited cunt. Then he breached a passage through her silky wheaten-coloured thatch with his fingertips and placed his lips over her clitty and sucked it into his mouth, feeling it expand as he lapped around the fleshy morsel. Sharon's legs began to shake and she drummed her heels on his lean buttocks.

'That's it, you've got it!' she squeaked as he found the tiny button under the fold at the base of her clitty and started to twirl his tongue around it. He could taste the tangy mix of his own salty spunk and

Sharon's pungent pussy cream as he sucked away even harder, lapping up the cocktail of their sex juices. Pushing his mouth up against her shuddering cunt, he moved his head back and forth along her juicy crack. With each stroke of his tongue Sharon arched her body in ecstasy, pressing her erect clitty up against Nick's flickering tongue.

'Y-e-s-s-s! Y-e-s-s-s!' she yelled out in a joyous scream of release. He felt Sharon's body shake as her clitty moved violently up and down inside his mouth. He gulped down as much of her feminine cum as he could, but the girl had climaxed so thoroughly that much of her cuntal juice washed over his face and dribbled down onto the bed. When her orgasm finally subsided, he gave her soaking pussy a final kiss before lifting his head up to see the sated expression of pleasure on Sharon's face.

Nick hauled himself up and enveloped the delicious young girl in his arms. 'You will stay the night, won't you?' he asked but before Sharon had a chance to reply, they were startled by the shrill ring of the telephone on the bedside table.

'Bloody hell, who can be phoning at this time of night?' muttered Nick as he stretched out his arm over Sharon and picked up the receiver. 'Hello, oh, it's you, Tim, what's up, mate?'

It must be Tim Lempert, thought Sharon as she propped herself up on her elbow and began to massage Nick's back as he listened carefully to what his writing partner had to say.

'So Adam Davies called from New York and said

what? Really? You're not having me on, are you? Stone me, Tim, that's fabulous news. Ha, I can't wait to tell my old Mum that Sinatra's going to record some of our songs! Yup, I understand, it's the big league all right but I wouldn't sign anything till Lewis Osborne has read through the contract with a magnifying glass. Okay, Tim, thanks for calling. I'll come over to your place at about ten and we'll see if we can get a good crack at finishing those last three numbers of Jilly Conway's new LP. Cheers, mate, see you in the morning.'

He replaced the receiver and turned back to Sharon with an excited look in his eyes. 'How about that then, did you get what Tim told me? Sinatra liked the material our American agent sent to him and he's going to sing a couple of our numbers at his next concert and record them early next year. If all goes well they'll want us to fly out to California next month and help his people with the arrangements.'

'Nick, that's marvellous!' exclaimed Sharon, giving him a big slurping kiss on his cheek. 'I'm really pleased for you, honest I am, although I suppose this means that it'll be absolutely impossible for you and Tim to write something for me.'

'That's where you're wrong,' he chuckled as he wrapped his arms around her. 'I want you to share in the celebrations so you're getting first refusal on the number we're working on right now. It's called *Ring, Telephone, Ring* and it's yours if you want it.'

'Oh thanks, darling! You are kind!' she squealed as Nick gave her a big bear-hug. 'Shall we tell

Donna and Tony the good news?'

Nick gave a wolfish grin and said: 'No, let's wait till the morning. I don't want to wake them and if they aren't asleep I don't think they would want to be interrupted!'

Although it was now almost half past one, the cabaret at *La Miraggio* was in full swing. Six scantily clad dancers were cavorting across the small stage of the fashionable nightclub just off Berkeley Square, only a stone's throw from the offices of Rose and Griffin.

Sitting alone at a small table at the side of the stage was a pensive-looking Adrian Klein. He had arrived at the club only half an hour before the cabaret started at one o'clock. Normally, Adrian would have enjoyed an evening's wining and dining at *La Miraggio*. He only had to sign the bill, for his visits were always connected with his work – entertaining clients, for instance, and occasionally bringing along producers to watch the acts of artistes on Rose and Griffin's books.

On this particular evening, he had come to the club on Teddy Dixon's instructions to see how Trevor Trenton was shaping up. He was a new comedian who the agency had signed up only a few weeks before. However, tonight, Adrian found it difficult to shake off a feeling of gloom, even after the dancers had finished their routine and Angelo Calabro had come lumbering on to the stage.

Adrian stared balefully at the owner of *La*

Miraggio. It was his own fault that he had fallen
out with his live-in lover, Gigi, a beautiful but
fiery half-Spanish girl. He had forgotten to tell
her about this late-night date. Indeed, he had
forgotten all about it himself until Gigi had slunk
into the living room wearing a transparent short
nightie and with a lascivious come-to-bed look in
her flashing dark eyes.

She had been anything but pleased when Adrian
announced that he had to see Trevor Trenton perform at *La Miraggio*. He had apologised about
letting this date slip his mind but added that Gigi
was welcome to come with him.

'I'm not getting all tarted up just to see some
rotten third-rate comedian for half an hour – and I
don't see why you should have to either, Adrian. I
think you should forget all about this Trevor what's-
his-name for now. You can always see him tomorrow night. Let's go to bed instead and fuck ourselves
silly. Doesn't that sound better to you?'

He sighed heavily and replied in all sincerity that
he would like nothing better than to ravish Gigi on
the spot, but he would be letting down Teddy Dixon
quite badly if he did not make his report on Trevor
Trenton tomorrow afternoon.

'Can't you say you had a migraine?' Gigi pouted
as she leaned against the back of his chair and let
her hand travel downwards across his body to his
groin. 'Come on, be truthful, when was the last time
you took any sick leave?'

'Not since January when I took two days off with

a stinking cold,' he reflected absently as Gigi's questing fingers brushed over his burgeoning penis, but then he drew himself upright and added: 'God, you don't honestly think I want to go, do you? I've one hell of a day tomorrow, a morning meeting with Dickie Segal and besides this report I've so much bloody paperwork to catch up on that I can't see myself leaving the office till seven o'clock at the earliest.'

However, the hot-tempered girl had not been impressed. She had flounced out of the room, saying she was fed-up with living with a workaholic and adding, just before she slammed the door, that if Adrian insisted on going out, he might as well put his prick in cold storage for the foreseeable future, as far as she was concerned.

This had caused Adrian to rise from his chair as he wavered between principle and expediency. He quickly decided that he could not allow himself to be blackmailed in this fashion and he picked up his jacket as he called out: 'I'm sorry, darling, but I must go. I'll make it up to you, I promise I will.'

So the hot-shot young agent was in sombre mood as he listened to Angelo Calabro give Trevor a nice build up: 'So put your hands together, ladies and gentlemen, for a new up-and-coming comedian who I know is on the way to the top. Will you please welcome TREVOR TRENTON!'

I must help our man, thought Adrian as he cleared his mind. He led a scattered round of applause as the fresh-faced young comic bounced up on to the stage.

He beamed all round at his audience and began his patter. 'Thank you, thank you so much, ladies and gentlemen, it's wonderful to work here at *La Miraggio*. Angelo looks after all the artistes so well. I've my own dressing-room and it's so new that it doesn't have a key, you need a penny to turn the lock. Yes, it'll be splendid once they put the roof on though when they do Angelo'll have to get a big case of air freshener from the cash 'n carry.

'No really, I don't care about things like that, I'm really glad to be here. I've already lost eighteen engagements this year through illness . . . they all got sick of me! Mind, I was on the telly last week . . . it's the only way I can get up to paper the ceiling . . . yes, times are tough. I was walking along Piccadilly last night and a girl came up to me and said are you looking for business, it'll only cost you a fiver. I went with her to her flat and gave her everything I had in my trousers . . . and I mean everything, and when it was over I pulled out two pound notes. That won't cover it, she said, so I told her to buy a doily . . .'

Despite the fact that his audience was more sophisticated than those in the northern working men's clubs he had been playing for the last two years, Adrian noted how Trevor Trenton's quickfire delivery had kept the punters' attention and had raised a few laughs.

'Any Americans here tonight?' asked the comedian. 'Yes? Well, a very good evening to you. I hope you're having a good time. I've got some relatives in the States, yes I have. My ancestors went out West a hundred years ago . . . the family name was Bi-carbonate because they were early settlers . . . my Uncle Bernie gave his life in the interest of electricity . . . the Governor wouldn't give him a pardon.'

Adrian observed how he crushed a drunken heckler by telling him: 'That's a clever remark, my friend, keep that up and it won't be long before you're able to use a potty. Why, with just a few more brains and a fair wind behind you, people might even take you for a half-wit.'

After a full half-hour of gags, Trevor finished his act to a storm of applause and ten minutes later he joined Adrian at his table.

'Well done, mate, that was a knock-out,' said Adrian, shaking hands with the comedian as Angelo Calabro himself brought over a glass of fresh orange juice for the star of his cabaret.

'Adrian, this boy's going places,' remarked Angelo generously. If we didn't have that French singer starting next month, I'd have asked if I could keep him on for another fortnight.'

Trevor smiled modestly as Adrian nodded and said: 'Yup, and as you took our word that he was good, we wouldn't have asked for more money either. However, I'm glad to say that Trevor's now booked up till mid-November. All being well, after that he'll be in one of Amalgamated's top pantos for Christmas.'

'That's terrific, I didn't know Dickie Segal had sent somebody over to give Trevor the once-over,' said Angelo reproachfully. 'Why didn't you tell me, I'd have been able to warn him.'

'I'm glad he didn't, Angelo,' grinned the comedian. 'I'd have been scared shitless if I'd known that there were any scouts from Amalgamated in the audience.'

'I doubt if Dickie's henchmen even know that Trevor exists – yet,' replied Adrian, pouring out a glass of champagne from the bottle which had appeared on the table seconds after he had sat down. 'To be frank, Angelo, Teddy Dixon wanted to know how he was getting on at *La Miraggio* before we told Dickie about him.'

At this point a waiter sidled up and said: 'Mr Klein, our telephonist took a call for you from a Miss Baroja.'

He handed over an envelope. After he had opened it and read the short message Adrian's face flushed. He crumpled the note in his hand and scowled as he placed it in the ash-tray. Gigi's terse missive had read: *I've gone to stay with Mademoiselle Melissa for a few days*.

Trevor Trenton could see that Adrian was upset and he asked anxiously: 'Everything okay, Mr Klein?'

'Could be better. I'm afraid my girl-friend's got the hump,' Adrian replied bitterly. He explained how a rift had developed that evening between him and Gigi.

87

'Oh Lord, I'd hate to think that I was the cause of an argument,' frowned the comic. 'Look, you've seen the act, there's no need for you to stay any longer, so why don't you go home and make it up?'

Adrian shook his head. 'There's no point – Gigi's gone to stay with one of her girlfriends. Anyhow, she's being totally unreasonable about the whole affair. I did apologise and I'm not going to go crawling back to her on my knees begging for forgiveness. If I did, she'd have me dancing round her every bloody time she snapped her fingers.'

'Women, women . . . what can you do? They drive us mad but we can't live without them,' sighed Angelo. He waved a beckoning finger to Luigi, the head waiter, to come over to him and he whispered some words in Italian in his ear. 'But you're quite correct, Adrian, you must not let this girl, how do you say, ride roughshod over you. That would be a terrible mistake – and to help you take your mind off this unhappy business, I have arranged for a lovely lady to come over here and cheer you up.'

'What a great idea!' said Trevor Trenton, as he downed his orange juice. 'Send along that gorgeous blonde who cheered me up when I was so worried before the first night, she did her job so well that I had to be carried onto the stage on a stretcher.'

'No, I'm afraid that Erica is already sitting down with one of our best customers, a Lebanese gentleman who seems to have money to burn, Thank God!' said Angelo with relish. 'But I don't think Adrian will be too disappointed when Tanya Gordon arrives. She's one of my own favourite girls.'

He let out a little chuckle and then added: 'Oh, by the way, Adrian, she lives in West Hampstead. That's not too far from you so, if you would give her a lift home, I'm sure she would be very grateful.'

'Tanya from the chorus?' whistled Trevor Trenton. 'Mr Klein, you'll need plenty of petrol in your tank to give Tanya a ride. I must be off, my wife's waiting up for me and, worse luck, we've been married ten years, that's a decade . . . And I've never seen such a decayed-looking woman.' Adrian interjected with a grin. 'Every time she walks past a beauty parlour they lower the blinds. And I'm not saying she's fat, mind but she rode a camel at Whipsnade Zoo last week and the hump finished underneath!' Sorry, Trevor, but I think Teddy Dixon used to use that script when he played the old music halls in the nineteen-forties!

'Ah well, I still say the old gags are best, guaranteed to raise a laugh from John O'Groats to Lands End,' he shrugged. 'Anyhow, here comes Tanya, and I just wish I could be your co-driver later on.'

A stunningly beautiful, auburn-haired girl sashayed her way across the dance floor to their table. She had not changed from the last outfit worn by the chorus girls in their final number except that she had taken off the gold-spangled headdress and shaken free her hair. She wore it in a fringe over her forehead, with long strands on the side of her face.

'Hello, are you Adrian Klein? I'm Tanya Gordon,' she said, holding out her hand to Adrian, whose mind immediately cleared of all his problems. He looked at the ravishingly voluptuous girl who was dressed only in a highly revealing cream bikini, out of which her luscious breasts almost spilled when she bent down to shake hands with him.

Against the stretchy shiny fabric, Tanya's skin was the colour of golden honey, except for the paler swell of her breasts which were clearly used to being covered by a bra or swimsuit top of more generous proportions. Another band of paler flesh ran around Tanya's tiny bikini pants which were a little more than a *cache-sexe*. A slender silver thong passed from her mound between the gleaming cheeks of her naked bottom.

'Hi, Tanya, nice to meet you,' said the agent as he stood up and looked around for a spare chair.

'Take my seat, love, I have to be going,' said Trevor Trenton and Angelo Calabro also stood up and asked to be excused, saying that he had to mingle with his guests.

Tanya accepted the offer of Trevor's chair. She blew the young comedian a farewell kiss as he waved goodbye and made his way through the throng of dancers back to the artistes' dressing rooms. Then she looked across at Adrian and remarked: 'Angelo tells me that you're Trevor's agent. I think he's a very bright, funny guy. So long as he keeps his cool, I'm sure he'll make it to the big time.

'The only trouble is that every one of the comedians I've ever known are such shocking depressives, always worrying themselves to death about whether they'll ever manage to make an audience laugh again.'

Adrian nodded his head in agreement. 'Yes, it's often the way. Comics tend to be such a terribly insecure bunch – like poor Tony Hancock, of course.'

'Oh, wasn't it just too awful, Adrian, his committing suicide like that in Australia last month. After all, everyone remembers *Hancock's Half Hour*. It was easily the funniest show on television. I could never understand why he wouldn't do any more.'

'Neither could I,' concurred Adrian as a waiter picked up the bottle of champagne from the ice-bucket on their table and poured out fresh drinks for them. 'They say in the business that Hancock was never really happy. He was always striving for new heights, even though he was at the top of the tree and the TV boys would give him anything he wanted.'

He gulped down a draught of champagne and went on: 'Of course that might have been part of the problem. Perhaps no-one could convince him that he needed good writers and a great foil like Sid James to make a great show.'

'Perhaps he began to believe his own publicity about being the funniest man in Britain,' speculated Tanya as they clinked their glasses together. 'And when his one-man shows flopped, he just couldn't believe it.'

'You're probably right,' agreed Adrian who was finding Tanya's superb semi-nude body too much of a distraction. 'What a tragedy, though, the man was a real genius. Still, I'm glad to hear you believe that Trevor has got what it takes.'

'Hey, I can't give you a written guarantee,' cautioned Tanya with a smile. 'I mean, he gets pretty worked up, I can tell you, though he's lucky that he's got Lizzie Farthing on hand to release his tension every night before the curtain goes up.'

Adrian pricked up his ears at this remark. 'Sounds as if he's on to a good thing there,' he commented hoarsely as, under the table, he felt Tanya's foot run up and down his leg.

'I'll say he is, the lucky so-and-so,' giggled Tanya. She began to slide her foot upwards over Adrian's knee until her toes were sliding along the inside of his thigh. 'Between ourselves, all the girls like Trevor. If Lizzie hadn't taken her opportunity, I can tell you that there would have been five other volunteers to take her place!'

'You'd better tell me the full story,' Adrian demanded with a smile. 'Trevor is under contract to Rose and Griffin so I should know exactly what he's been getting up to.'

Tanya continued to rub her foot suggestively near his groin as she said: 'It's his cock which has been doing all the getting up, and it all began at the dress rehearsal. We had done our opening number but there was an electrical fault somewhere as the lights kept going on and off. Angelo told us to take half an hour off while it was sorted out. The other girls decided to sit around and have some coffee but

I went backstage with Lizzie. It was a bit chilly out here without any heating and we were only wearing these little bikinis.

'Well, we heard some grunting and groaning when we passed by Trevor's dressing room and as the door was half-open we peeped inside – and there was Trevor, standing bollock naked, working out on a chest expander.

'Trevor's a cool customer all right because he didn't bat an eye-lid when he saw us but simply panted: "Come in, girls, I'll just have to finish this exercise and I'll make you both a nice cup of coffee while we wait for the lights to be fixed."

'Mind you, he's got a good body, wide chest, flat tummy and lots of muscles where it matters. Boy, was he well endowed! He didn't actually have a hard-on but his cock looked very thick and full. I could see Lizzie eyeing it appreciatively as she closed the door behind us while Trevor threw down the expander and wiped the beads of perspiration from his face with a towel.

' "Phew, I don't have that damned thing too strongly sprung but I believe in keeping myself fit," he informed us as he threw the towel back on a chair. "I'm just going to do twenty knee-bends to tone up the old muscles in my thighs and calves." We watched him squat down and then pull himself upright with his back ramrod-straight all the time.

'He took about a minute or so to finish the exercise and then Lizzie stepped forward and said, bold as brass: "What about exercising that thick muscle between your legs? That also needs to be used regularly to improve its stamina. Do you have to do that yourself, Trevor, or is there anyone here to help you out?"

'I think Trevor had been so caught up in his work-out that he only just realised that he had been talking to two half-naked girls. Only now did he look properly at us. Soon his thick cock began to jut out fully until it stood high against his tummy as he replied with a leer: "Oh, it can always do with being taken in hand, Lizzie, if you're interested."

'Lizzie's a randy slut and I could see she fancied taking Trevor in hand. She let her tongue slide over her top lip as she moved forward and slid her left hand round his throbbing shaft. Then with her right hand she started to rub his knob between her thumb and forefinger as, with the other, she worked on his shaft in long, slow, pulling strokes.

'Trevor closed his eyes and breathed heavily as he panted: "Ahh, that's super, Lizzie, keep going, I just love being wanked!"

' "Do you now," said the cheeky minx as, still holding his rigid chopper, she sank to her knees and carressed his balls while she licked up and down the length of his veiny stiffstander, taking her time to reach his uncapped helmet.

'Then, after teasing his knob with the tip of her tongue, she lashed her tongue round his thick pole and started sucking and slurping like a wild animal. Trevor grasped her head in his hands as he rocked backwards and forwards while Lizzie fucked his cock with her mouth. She gobbled in six inches or so of his shaft between her lips, sucked hard for a few seconds, withdrew and then plunged her head down again, building up and then quelling the pressure till Trevor could hold on no longer and with a bellow he spurted inside her willing mouth.'

Adrian cleared his throat and muttered hoarsely: 'Nice work if you can get it.' Tanya's toes continued their relentless journey over his swelling penis and she responded with a wicked little chuckle and murmured in a soft, sexy drawl: 'Well, you're all tensed up and if you want the same kind of relief, just unzip your flies and let me feel your nice thick tadger.'

Swept up in the heat of the moment, Adrian tore open his trousers. He gasped with pleasure as her toes gently caressed the sensitive underside of his circumcised cock. She arched her foot and gently prodded his pulsing prick, pressing it backwards against his abdomen with the ball of her heel. She rubbed his lurching organ so sensuously with both feet that Adrian's shoulders soon began to tremble. His chest rose and fell with the frantic need to fill his lungs with air as his climax rapidly approached boiling point.

Then, with deliberate carelessness, Tanya picked up a spoon and dropped it on the floor. With her impudent little toes still caressing Adrian's quivering cock, she bent down and, under the cover of the tablecloth, she grasped hold of his twitching tool. She pulled her hand up and down his smooth skinned shaft and Adrian stared down with unbelieving eyes as the girl's soft fingers gently coaxed his rigid tingling tool until he ejaculated and thick jets of jism shot out from his knob all over her dainty little hand. He slumped back dizzily in his chair.

'There now, don't you feel better after my special massage?' she enquired as she scrambled back into her seat and looked across the table with a merry twinkle in her eyes.

'I certainly do,' replied Adrian, zipping up his flies as he regained his composure. 'Believe me, if that was available on the Health Service, the country would save a fortune on tranquilisers!'

'Sorry, it's for private patients only,' cooed Tanya as she finished off her drink. 'Adrian, it's getting rather late, I'd quite like to leave now if it's all the same to you. Now Angelo tells me that you've been kind enough to offer me a lift home.'

'Yes, with pleasure – you live in West Hampstead, don't you? I'm only in St John's Wood so we're not far away from each other.' He waved at a passing waiter and called for his bill. If you'd like to change while I settle up, I'll meet you at the door.'

'Fine, I won't be too long, sweetheart. I've just got to change and take off my make-up. Give me about fifteen minutes and I'll meet you at the front door.'

'I'll be there,' promised Adrian as Tanya stood up and sauntered back to her dressing-room. Despite his orgasm just a few moments before, Adrian felt his shaft stir as he watched her splendid bare buttocks swing from side to side as she walked away, parted as they were by the narrow silver thong which raised and emphasised the curves of her nubile bum cheeks.

He called to a nearby waiter for his bill and Angelo Calabro himself came over shortly afterwards with his check. The club owner sat down at the table and said: 'So you're about to score with the lovely Tanya, eh? Good luck to you, my friend. But be told, she's a little tigress in bed.

'Tanya doesn't fuck with any old Tom, Dick or Harry. But when she does, oh boy! You can ask your chum from the Hippodrome, Charlie Nettleton, if you don't believe me. Charlie took her back to his place last week and had to call the office the next day and say he wasn't coming in till after lunch!'

'Is that so? Well, I've probably got more stamina than Charlie as I'm not screwing two or three girls from the Bluebirds troupe every afternoon. Anyhow, I can't afford the luxury of any time off tomorrow, I've a morning meeting with Dickie Segal. If I'm not fully awake, the crafty old sod'll run rings round me.' Adrian signed the bill and passed it back to Angelo, who flapped a hand in acknowledgment. A tall, tousled haired girl dressed in a baggy dark blue jumper, loose-fitting track suit trousers and scuffed tennis shoes passed by the table and called out: 'Good night, Angelo, see you tomorrow.'

'Good night, Julie,' he called back and then turned round to Adrian and said: 'I'll lay odds you didn't recognise that girl, did you?'

'No, I didn't,' confessed Adrian as he stared after the girl and Angelo let out a short laugh. 'Appearances can be deceptive,' he remarked with a knowing wink. 'Julie was the girl with long red hair in the middle of the chorus line tonight.'

'Was she? Well, you're right, I'd never have recognised her,' Adrian admitted in some surprise. 'The wig and the glamorous outfit certainly make all the difference.

Angelo let out a low chortle and said: 'Julie's only eighteen but she's one of those girls who disguises herself very well. She was wearing those old clothes when she came to audition for a job and although she'd brought with her a great letter of recommendation from Eric Williams, the choreographer at the Hunkiedorie over in Lancaster Gate, I thought it was hardly worth asking her to slip on one of the costumes. I was soon damned glad that I did!

'She needed no prompting to strip off and I got horny straight away when I saw that gorgeous body she'd been hiding under that scruffy outfit. True, Julie hasn't got the biggest bosoms I've ever seen, but they're lovely and firm with big dusky red nipples. She had the sweetest little thatch of hair nestling between her thighs.

'Then, blow me down, who should come into the office but Dawn, the blonde girl I'd been screwing since she joined the bar staff last March. She's a lovely kid and, instead of trying to stop anything happening between Julie and me, she stood there for a moment with her hands on her hips and said:

"Come on, Angelo, it's not very fair that Julie should be the only one here standing around with any clothes on!"

'She yanked her top off over her head and unhooked her bra, then unzipped her skirt and tugged down her panties. Then she came across and ripped off my shirt and trousers and then calmly invited Julie to pull down my pants!

' "Take them off, love, all the dancers do sooner or later," Dawn said to Julie, who grinned and tugged them down to my ankles. Then both girls sank to their knees in front of me. My prick was sticking out like a flagpole and Dawn slipped her hand round it and said to Julie: "Let's suck him off, that's what Angelo likes best."

' "That's okay with me, I love sucking cocks," said Julie and she leaned forward and started to lick my prick while Dawn opened her mouth and began sucking my balls. Jesus, what a sight! I tell you, Adrian, I nearly came there and then but somehow I managed to hold on while they took turns to suck my dick. Every so often they put their wet tongues on opposite sides of my stiffie and slowly licked up my shaft up over my knob and back again.

'But in the end I couldn't take any more so I gasped that I was going to come and Dawn was good enough to move aside and let Julie finish me off. She held my cock lightly in one hand and closed her lips over my helmet and then began washing my knob with her tongue while, with her other hand, she groped my balls.

' "That's the way," said Dawn encouragingly as she stood up and I diddled her tits with my hand. I felt myself on the verge of a huge cum.'

Angelo grunted and clicked his tongue against his teeth as he went on: 'Of course I came almost immediately and Julie jerked back slightly when the first spurt of sperm hit the back of her throat but she managed to suck up all my spunk and swallowed it down.

'Well, I'm not ashamed to say that I was so drained that I had to sit down and close my eyes for a few moments. But the girls' appetites were still up. The next thing I know is that Julie's lying on my carpet and Dawn's crouched between her thighs with her hands cupped under her bum and her face was buried in Julie's loveable little bush. I could hear Dawn's tongue slurping at a great pace up and down Julie's slit.

'It was so erotic to watch that it didn't take too long for my cock to swell up again. When Dawn came up for air and glanced at me, my shaft was almost back to full strength so she climbed off Julie and laughed: "Good boy, you've made a quick recovery. Now you can give Julie's cunt a taste of your cock, you randy old goat!"

' "Is that what you want, love?" I asked. Julie looked up all bright-eyed and panted: "Yes please, Dawn's made my cunny so tingly, I must have a cock to finish me off!"

'So I climbed on top of her and I could see that Julie wasn't joking! Her cunt juices had soaked the inside of her thighs and her pussy lips were all swollen and gleaming. I slid my cock inside her and after a couple of shafts she began to buck and twist like mad. I pulled my prick back and teased her by letting my knob just push to and fro between her pussy lips, but I could see she wanted more of my prick so I pushed in a little more, in and then out, then back in again. Each time I shoved my cock in a little deeper.

'Julie wriggled her bum as she squirmed from side to side and finally she cried out: "Ohhh! Ohhh! Fuck me properly, Angelo, you can come inside me!"

'That was all I needed to hear and I slewed my shaft in to the hilt and began ramming it in and out of her juicy cunt. Julie came first, soaking my tool with a great squirt of cunny juice and then I came as well and drenched the walls of her love channel with a fountain of sticky jism.'

Angelo paused and smacked his lips as he recalled the pleasant interlude. 'So the moral of this story is never judge a book by its cover,' he said jovially as he clapped Adrian on the shoulder. 'But I think it's safe to say that, as far as Tanya is concerned, what you see is what you get!'

'Thanks, Angelo, I'm sure you're right,' said Adrian. He shook hands with the plump club owner and made his way out to the entrance of *La Miraggio* where he had arranged to meet the sexy dancer. He went to the cloakroom and, after having a pee and washing his hands, he looked at his watch. It was almost three in the morning and he hoped that he wouldn't have to wait long for Tanya. He smiled when he saw her hurrying towards him. She planted a smacking wet kiss on his cheek and then they walked across Berkeley Square to Sampson Mews where Adrian had parked his red MGB-GT.

Whilst he fiddled with the key to unlock the car, Adrian could not prevent himself yawning. 'Here, how much have you had to drink, love?' said Tanya. 'Perhaps it would be best if I drove because I've only had that one glass of champagne but you must have polished off almost a full bottle. Don't worry, I'm a bloody good driver, I've even passed the Institute of Advanced Motorists test. I know the way home blindfold so chuck over the keys and you have a little nap while I take the wheel.'

Adrian hesitated for a moment but then he remembered how one of his close friends had been breathalysed by this new device which measured your alcohol level. He wasn't drunk but he was very tired and all he needed now was to be caught speeding or going over a red light. At this time of night, the patrols were probably cruising around looking for possible offenders. So he shrugged his shoulders and gave Tanya the keys, saying: 'Okay, my insurance'll cover you, but take it easy 'cos the cops are always on the look-out.'

When they were inside Tanya switched on the engine. Adrian noticed how confidently she revved the engine and swung the sports saloon out of the space between the two large cars which had parked at his front and back. As she zoomed through the top of Grosvenor Square he shut his eyes and quickly dozed off.

At first he thought it was just the car slowing down to a halt which had woken him up, but then he realised that they were only in Lisson Grove. 'Oh no,' he groaned as he noticed that a police car had pulled up in front of them and that two uniformed officers were getting out of their vehicle and walking back towards them. 'How fast were you going, Tanya?'

'Not more than forty-five,' she shrugged, hastily unbuttoning the top buttons of her blouse so the swell of her breasts would be clearly visible. Her friend Jacqui had recently informed her how she had managed to persuade a policeman not to report that she had crossed a red light by inviting him to her flat 'for a cup of tea and one off the wrist.'

Fucking hell, muttered Tanya as she hiked up her skirt. She looked at the two approaching officers in the driving mirror. If it proved necessary, decided Tanya, she would try to pull a similar trick for, despite her membership of the Institute of Advanced Motorists, her licence had been endorsed twice for speeding and a third endorsement would mean that she would lose it.

She wound down the window and smiled seductively at the constable who squatted down at the side of the MGB so that his face was level with hers. His colleague walked slowly around the car, making a note of the registration number and checking to

103

see if the vehicle tax certificate displayed on the windscreen had not passed its expiry date.

'Good morning, officer, is there anything the matter?' said Tanya, flashing a sweet smile at the young policeman.

'Good morning, Miss, yes, I'm afraid there is,' he replied sternly, although Adrian could see that his eyes had wandered down from Tanya's face to her heaving bosoms. 'Didn't you realise that you were travelling at almost fifty miles an hour in the middle of London. You must know there's a thirty miles an hour limit?'

Tanya affected an air of total astonishment. 'Oh, I wasn't, was I? I'm dreadfully sorry, officer. The fact is that I'm a dancer at a night club and this gentleman is my agent. As we were leaving the club, he said he was feeling unwell so I offered to drive him home.

'It's true I was trying to get Adrian back to his flat as quickly as possible, but I wouldn't go fast at this time of night because that's when people go a bit barmy. They think because there isn't much traffic about they can go through red lights and God knows what else.'

The second policeman now came round to the window and peered in while Tanya pulled the keys out of the ignition. As she opened the door and slid her legs out of the car, the keys slid out of her hand and fell onto the road.

'Oops, I've gone and dropped my keys,' she wailed. The first officer automatically bent down and picked them up for her. Adrian smiled inwardly as he noticed how she opened her legs so that the young constable was given a bird's eye view of her thighs and bikini-covered pussy. His hand shook slightly as he handed the keys back to Tanya who smiled sensuously at him.

'Thank you so much, you are a kind boy,' cooed Tanya, stroking the young man's fingers as she took the keys from him. 'I'm so sorry to have bothered you, it must be awful working the early morning shift. Gosh, I bet you're both ready for bed. When can you two call it a day?'

'Actually, we've just finished our stint and were just about to clock off,' he replied and Tanya pouted prettily: 'You're not attached to West Hampstead nick, are you? Yes? Oh, now look, I live round the corner in Messina Avenue so when you've signed off, why don't you lads come round to my flat for a nice hot cup of tea?

'Or something a little stronger, if you fancy it,' she went on, slowly passing her tongue between her lips. 'My girl friend Lesley, who's a cloakroom girl at the Hunkiedorie, will have just come home and we'll make you very welcome.'

They exchanged glances and then the constable who had first spoken to Tanya cleared his throat and said: 'Well, that's very considerate of you, Miss. I wouldn't say no. Would you, Phil?'

His partner hesitated for a second and then stuffed his notebook back inside the breast pocket of his tunic. 'Sounds like a great idea to me,' he nodded. Tanya clambered out of the car and standing only inches away from them, stood up and ran her hands sensuously down her body.

'Then let's introduce ourselves properly. I'm Tanya,' she said as she shook hands with him. She jerked her head backwards and added: 'And that's Adrian in the car.'

Adrian wisely decided to stay silent and merely waved a hand in greeting as the constable said: 'Pleased to meet you, Tanya, my name's Mark Briggs and this is my mate, Phil Lintern.'

'Okay then, fellas, let's go,' she replied briskly as she slid back inside the car. 'My pad's number three, Goldhill Mansions. It's on the ground floor, the first door on the left as you come in the hall.'

She switched on the engine and just before she wound up the window, Phil leaned down and said: 'See you later, Tanya, we'll be round in about twenty minutes. Drive carefully or you might be nabbed by some of our friends. They'll all be coming home after finishing their shifts, so watch out!'

Tanya waited till they had walked back to their car and then followed the police car at a sedate pace. After a while Adrian looked across at her and said in a resigned tone: 'I suppose I should congratulate you on wriggling out of trouble because you got out of that mess all right, but fancy making up an address for them! What'll you do if they ever see you again?'

'There's nothing they could do, if you stop and think about it,' she replied complacently. 'For starters, they're going to find it bloody difficult to explain why they didn't give me a ticket. Anyhow, who says that isn't my real address.'

He looked at her with a horrified expression on his face. 'Dear God, you mean that really *is* where you live? Well, what are you going to do when those two young coppers come back?'

'I'll put on the kettle and make them tea,' said Tanya with a shrug of her slim shoulders. 'And I wasn't making it up about Lesley. She'll be awake and I'm sure she won't mind helping to entertain the boys in blue. Anyway, if I know Lesley, she'll be pleased to take them both in hand. Of course, I'll help her out if need be, but I doubt if I'll be wanted because she loves threesomes.

'Don't look so glum, darling. You said yourself that you needed some sleep. If the worst comes to the worst, you shouldn't mind sharing me with those nice young men. Remember, what they say about the London coppers, they're the best money can buy!'

Adrian chuckled softly and switched on the radio, fiddling with the dial until he found Radio Luxembourg, the only station which stayed on the air in the early hours.

'Here, have you heard Bernie Harwin's new single, *Power of the Night*, Tanya?' he said as he turned up the volume. 'He's with our agency, you know. A young guy called Mark Matthews in our accounts department wrote it for him.'

'Yeah, it's good, isn't it? From what I hear about

Bernie Harwin, it's a very appropriate song. He's with your agency, is he? Well, is there any truth in those stories in the papers about Bernie being such a stud? Or is his reputation just a publicity hype?'

Adrian made a so-so motion with his hand. 'Bernie likes the girls and he often shags himself silly when the groupies come backstage after a gig. All we can do is try to make sure the girls aren't under sixteen which can be very difficult these days – but at least it's a darn sight easier than managing a pop star who prefers to fool around with boys in the shower after the show.

'You'd be surprised how many shirtlifters there are in this business,' he said darkly as Tanya swung the car into West End Lane and then turned into Messina Avenue where, miraculously, there was enough space to park the car just a few yards from the entrance to her apartment block.

'Thanks for the ride,' said Adrian as Tanya gave him back the keys to his car. As they walked back to Goldhill Mansions and she squeezed his arm and said softly: 'Thank *you*, sweetie, it was great driving an MGB. You wait, I'll give you an even better kind of ride once we get inside.'

'But without being stopped by our two PC Plods, if you don't mind,' said Adrian pointedly. Tanya giggled while she rummaged in her bag for her front door key. 'You mustn't worry so much about those two guys,' she declared, brushing strands of silky auburn hair out of her eyes. 'I doubt if they'll have the bottle to come round here but, even if they do, as

I told you in the car, my flat-mate Lesley will look after the lucky lads. Now come on, let's go in and make sure that she's back home.'

To Adrian's relief, Lesley had returned about twenty minutes before from her job looking after the customers' coats at the Hunkiedorie Club. As they were introduced, his eyes swept over the pretty ash-blonde girl's luscious body, which was covered only by a low-cut semi-transparent slip. Through it he could see the curves of her large breasts and the dark shadow of her nipples pressing against the fine white silk of her garment.

'Adrian's in show business,' called out Tanya from the bedroom where she had gone to put away their coats. 'He's a theatrical agent for that black singer, Bernie Harwin.'

'Are you?' said Lesley with interest as she sat down next to Adrian on a deep two seater sofa. 'Tell me, is it true that he's such a superstud or—'

'Is it all made up by his publicity people?' Adrian interjected with a smile. 'Tanya asked me the same question. Bernie's with our agency but I don't actually look after his affairs. I do know that yes, he likes to play the field, though no more than most rock stars. As I said to Tanya, at least he doesn't grope boys which is more than can be said for some.'

'Yes, though I don't think it's right for your publicity people to put it about how well-endowed Bernie is. It makes people believe in that old myth about West Indians having bigger dicks than Europeans.'

Adrian gave a short laugh, for with his own eyes he had seen Bernie Harwin's enormous prick slewing its way between the rounded bottom cheeks of one of his teenybopper fans. He replied carefully: 'I'm no expert on that matter, though I will say that I know for a fact that Bernie wasn't short-changed when willies were being handed out!'

'Lucky old Bernie! But then I agree with the old saying, it isn't the size of the ship that counts, it's the motion of the ocean.' Adrian turned his head to see Tanya who had padded quietly back in the room.

He caught his breath as he turned his head and saw that Tanya was stark naked. His eyes followed her round until she came and stood directly in front of him. His cock started to swell as he watched her lift up her arms and sweep back her shiny auburn tresses which accentuated her proud young breasts, topped with delectable strawberry red nipples, which jutted out so seductively towards him.

Adrian gulped hard as, with a lascivious smile Tanya smoothed her palm across the smooth, tanned skin of her belly. She let her fintertips swivel inside the silky brown curls of her pussy hair. He blushed as she playfully parted the yielding cunny lips and gently began to frig herself, dipping her forefinger daintily inside the glowing red chink of her love channel.

'Ohhh!' he gasped as he felt Lesley's hands slide across his bulging crotch. She deftly unbuckled his belt and in one swift movement she had unzipped his flies and plunged her hands inside his trousers to

110

bare Adrian's erect, throbbing member, which she grasped in her hand.

Her lips parted and he tore his gaze from Tanya's voluptuous nude curves to Lesley's pretty young face as she slicked her hand up and down his quivering cock. She whispered: 'Isn't she gorgeous, Adrian? Aren't you just dying to thrust your cock into her sweet little cunt and fuck her?'

'Yes, yes, yes!' he panted. Lesley's fingers began a slow, subtle kneading movement up and down the rigid stalk of his tingling shaft. He savoured the feel of his smooth circumcised shaft in her hands while Tanya flaunted her delicious nakedness before them, turning her back and then parting her shapely legs before bending down to expose, between her taut, dimpled buttocks, the crinkled opening of her anus as well as the juicy full-lipped crack of her cunt.

Tanya straightened herself up and turned to face Adrian and Lesley again. Now she frigged her pussy with two fingers as she gazed at Adrian's thick prick jolting violently between her flat-mate's soft, warm fingers. Lesley held his cock tightly at its base with her left hand while she pumped her right fist up and down his trembling tadger.

Adrian's heart began to pound and his muscles tensed as the first spasms of a huge, impending crisis raced through his body. Then, with a low, wrenching cry he ejaculated a wild arc of sticky white seed over Lesley's hand. His cock continued to pump out a flood of warm spunk as it lurched and jumped in a final ecstatic paroxysm of pleasure.

'Oh dear, now look what I've done,' breathed Lesley, looking down at her wet fingers which were still gripping Adrian's fast-shrinking shaft. She wiped her hands on her slip and then pulled the silk garment over her head so that she too was now totally naked.

'Why don't you go into the bedroom and undress?' she said to Adrian, cupping her hand over the fluffy foliage around Tanya's cunny lips and then sliding her fingers into the moist folds of her friend's pussy and applying her thumb to the hard, rubbery flesh of her erect clitty. 'We'll come with you and we'll all go to bed together. You won't be able to do much for a bit but you can watch Tanya and me enjoy ourselves till your cock gets back its strength.'

'Good idea,' wheezed Adrian and he pushed his flaccid prick inside his trousers as he staggered into the bedroom. He tore off his clothes and sank down on the bed, his chest heaving as he slowly regained his composure.

As Lesley had promised, the two girls joined him. Tanya lay down next to Adrian while Lesley climbed between her spread glistening thighs and rubbed the palm of her hand against her fluffy brown thatch. Then she stroked her fingers along the length of Tanya's slit and opened the pink love lips. She bent down to kiss the dewy pouting crack, her hands sliding under Tanya's bottom to clasp the soft bum cheeks and pull her cunny closer against her yearning mouth.

'A-h-r-e, a-h-r-e!' Tanya purred as she thrust her hips upward to receive the ardent ministrations of Lesley's wicked tongue flickering inside her. She could feel a climax rapidly coming on as Lesley licked and slurped on her juicy cunt, delighting in the pungent feminine scent of her arousal while her probing fingers now gently teased Tanya's wrinkled little bum-hole, making her gasp with added excitement.

Despite the lateness of the hour, this display of lesbian loving was now causing Adrian's cock to stir. He placed himself behind Lesley and parted her jiggling buttocks with one hand as he rubbed his prick up to a full, rock-hard erection.

Lesley turned her head and looking up at him, she panted: 'Yes, go on, fuck my bum, but grease your cock first. There's a pot of cold cream on the bedside table to your left.'

He reached forward and grabbed hold of the little jar and then, still kneeling behind her delicious backside, he smeared a liberal amount of cold cream on his burgeoning shaft. He thrust his knob into the crevice of Lesley's bum. The grease eased his passage into the tiny winking orifice and he was able to sheath himself fully inside her back passage as her bum cheeks wiggled lasciviously against his belly. He withdrew his cock slightly and then pressed home again, his balls slapping against the back of her thighs and her beautiful bottom responded to every shove as his shaft shunted, thrust, emerged and then thrust forward again.

113

Adrian snaked his arm around Lesley's ribs and played with her rubbery red nipples while his cock slid in and out of her backside and she continued to lick and lap on Tanya's tingling pussy.

Then Tanya started to shudder as the first waves of her orgasm began to course through her groin. Lesley had to hold her thighs down with her hands to keep her mouth pressed against her cunt as Tanya bucked and twisted with the force of her orgasm while Lesley lapped up and swallowed her spouts of tangy cunny juice.

This erotic scenario speeded Adrian towards his own climax. As his shaft spouted a gush of frothy spunk which lubricated Lesley's rear, he moved his hand downwards into her wet bush of pussy hair to massage her erect little clitty. He continued to work his cock back and forth until his shaft began to shrink and he was able to uncork it from her bum.

'Sorry you weren't able to come with me,' he apologised to Lesley as they rearranged themselves. Adrian lay on his back, with an arm cuddling each of the girls beside him.

'Never mind, perhaps we can try again later,' she murmured, a remark which made Adrian blanch because his cock was lying forlornly down over his balls and he felt terribly tired. But he did not contradict her and instead he went on: 'Tanya told me that you liked taking part in three-in-a-bed sessions. I've not been lucky enough to know many girls who are keen to share, but obviously you enjoy trios.'

'Oh yes, I've been with two men together but I prefer to be with Tanya or another girl,' she replied. Tanya giggled: 'Tell Adrian about the threesome we had a few weeks ago with your nice Ghanaian boy-friend, Edgar, the medical student at the Royal Free Hospital. With a bit of luck it might even rouse his prick up to another stiffie!'

Adrian could not let this pass by and he shook his head and said: 'Don't bet any folding money as far as that's concerned, though I'll do my best,' he remarked gamely. 'But I'd still like to hear all about it.'

Lesley laughed and settled herself down inside the crook of his arm and began: 'Okay then, here goes . . . Now, despite what I said before about this daft business about black men's pricks being bigger, I have to say that Edgar's got one of the thickest tools I've ever seen. More important though, he's a lovely fella who we met at a party down the road. He's a very good looking chap and Tanya and I both fancied him so we asked him if he'd fuck us both together. We didn't have to ask him twice, I can tell you!

'Well, to cut a long story short, that night was one of the horniest I've ever had. I'll never forget when we were all naked together with Tanya lying on me, our tummies breasts pressed together with her legs stretched out between mine. Edgar moved between her legs and after he had pulled up her bottom, he parted her cheeks and started to fuck her doggy-style. As he fucked her with his big black cock, she caressed my breasts and sucked my titties. When his thrusting brought Tanya near to a cum, she pushed her knee up against my pussy.

'We were both wet with love juice when Tanya started to rub her knee along my slit as she continued to lick my nipples. Then Edgar moved forward and began to kiss me. While Tanya rubbed harder against me, Edgar slid his tongue between my lips and we exchanged a deep, passionate kiss. It's hard to explain, but it was as if I was being fucked by two cocks – one in my mouth and one sliding up and down my groin pushing up and over my sopping pussy.

'I could feel myself building up to an orgasm and Tanya slid down across my tummy and pressed her face into my sopping wet muff. Edgar now pulled himself up on his knees and rubbed up his enormous tree trunk of a cockshaft until it was as stiff as a poker and placed it against my cheek. I licked my lips and took hold of the throbbing monster, wrapping my tongue round the dark dome of his huge uncapped helmet. A crackle of electricity shot through my groin when I felt Tanya sliding her tongue into my cunt just as I began tonguing Edgar's knob.

'God, it was all so exciting that a gorgeous climax soon swept through me and we continued fucking till dawn in a variety of positions. I think this was the best threesome I've ever had and naturally Tanya also enjoyed it tremendously, didn't you, darling?'

'I should say so,' said Tanya. Just then the door-bell rang and she jumped out of bed and slipped on a dressing-gown. 'Ah ha, this must be our two young rozzers – I was wrong, wasn't I, Adrian, for I didn't believe they'd turn up.'

In fact, when she opened the door Tanya discovered that she had not been completely mistaken for only one of the two policemen who had stopped them had turned up. He had changed out of uniform and was wearing a sports jacket and trousers. As Tanya smiled at the tall, fresh-faced young man, the old saying that you know you're getting older when policemen begin to look younger ran through her mind.

'Hello Tanya, you do recognise me, don't you?' said the fair-haired lad.

'I'm Philip, I was driving the police car when we stopped you for speeding in Lisson Grove.'

She clicked her fingers and opened the door wide. 'Oh yes, of course, come on in, I didn't recognise you for a moment out of uniform and away from your mate, what's-his-name, Mark.'

'Thanks, I'm on my own, I'm afraid,' he explained – 'Mark got caught up with some trouble at the station. A friend of ours hauled in a drunk as we were leaving and although he wasn't giving us any aggravation, three of his mates came in and started a brawl with the duty sergeant. We rushed in to give a hand and old Mark got swiped over the head with a chair. Luckily he's not too badly hurt, but we had to call an ambulance to take him up to the Royal

Free to get some stitches put in.'

'Ah, the poor lamb,' said Tanya sympathetically as she led him inside the flat. 'Never mind though, Adrian's woken up since you last saw him so we won't miss Mark too much.

'Now Philip, I seem to remember I promised you a cup of tea, so I'll put on the kettle unless you would prefer something stronger.'

'No, it's okay, thanks very much, I had a hot drink in the station canteen,' he replied. Tanya took the raincoat he was carrying on his arm and threw it over a chair. She smiled at him and said: 'Fine, then come through and I'll introduce you to Lesley.'

She threw open the bedroom door and stood still, looking up at the young policeman's face with an amused glance. She saw his jaw drop in amazement as he took in the erotic spectacle before them. For from his innermost resources, Adrian had somehow found the strength to produce a further throbbing stiffstander which Lesley was holding in her hand. He was lying on his back and Lesley was bending over him, low at the waist so that Tanya and Philip had a perfect view of her curvy bare bum cheeks as she leaned forward to wash Adrian's knob with the tip of her tongue.

'Oh, I say, look at that,' gasped Philip as he saw Lesley's lips close over the pink helmet of Adrian's circumcised cock. He watched in wide-eyed fascination as he heard Adrian sigh delightedly when she started to gobble on his twitching tool, working her mouth up and down the length of his pulsing shaft.

Tanya broke the spell by pulling off Philip's jacket and then leading him to a chair where she pushed him down and then settled herself in his lap. She threw her hands round his neck and in a trice their lips were pressed together in an excited, passionate kiss, their tongues fluttering wildly in each other's mouths. The young policeman was thrilled to find that Tanya was naked underneath her dressing-gown as he ran his hands over her lithe soft body. She shucked off the robe and then pulled his head to the taut, elongated nipples of her jutting breasts. He tweaked the tempting morsels with his tongue while he slid his hand between Tanya's thighs and revelled in the warm, furry touch of her moist thatch.

'Let's join the others on the bed,' she whispered and, nothing loath, with his lips still switching from one juicy nipple to the other, he picked her up bodily and carried her on to the bed. He laid her gently down next to Adrian, whose eyes were closed in a state of euphoric bliss while Lesley continued to suck his glistening stiff shaft.

'Lick me out, please,' breathed Tanya as Philip parted her thighs and, settling himself between her legs, he moved his head downwards across her heaving flat belly until his tongue found its way through the damp curls of pussy hair to the pouting lips of her cunny.

She moaned with pleasure when he parted the protruding pink love lips and she clamped her legs around his neck. Tanya twisted frantically from side to side when he slid a knuckle into her cunt, arching her back upwards while he rubbed her clitty with his thumb, making it pop out like a miniature cock as he lapped up the aromatic juices which were now flowing freely from her hairy crack.

Philip soon proved that he was a skilled muff-diver, for now he raised the tempo, wiggling his tongue between Tanya's yielding cunny lips, slurping between the grooves of her juicy honeypot in long thrusting strokes as she ground her dripping cunt against his lips. She climaxed quickly, sending a spray of pungent female jism into his mouth which he eagerly gulped down, smacking his lips loudly as Tanya sank back and relaxed as the force of her cum slowly died away.

'Wowee, where did you learn to eat pussy like that, young man? They didn't teach that at Hendon Police College, I'll be bound.' She gasped in admiration at the way he had brought her off. 'Now then, officer, why don't you lie back and let me take a ride on your thick, fat truncheon.'

This idea appealed to Philip and his eyes gleamed as obediently he took her place next to Adrian on the bed as Tanya swiftly clambered on top of him, straddling his legs. She reached down to let her fingers curl around his hot, throbbing tadger.

Then she wriggled herself down on his thick stiff tool, hugging his cock inside her tight, wet cunt. She moved slowly at first and then her movements became fiercer. Each time Philip met her downward push with an upward thrust of his own, Tanya's body lifted in the air. Her breasts bounced as she leaned backwards so that his prick reamed out the deepest recesses of her tingling love channel.

'Oooh, that's lovely,' cried Tanya which gave Lesley, as she looked up at her chum with Adrian's cock still inside her mouth, a sudden brainwave. She released his twitching knob from between her lips and quietly whispered some words in Adrian's ear. The lusty pair swung themselves off the bed and padded around to the foot of the bed, with Lesley slicking her head up and down Adrian's upright pulsating prick as he jumped up behind Tanya. Moments later Lesley did the same, kneeling beside him as she placed her hands on Tanya's creamy bum cheeks as they jiggled with the force of her fucking.

Tanya turned her head and gave a little yelp of approval as Lesley spread her buttocks wide, offering Adrian the narrow cleft of her bum and the prize of the small puckered entrance of her back passage. He took hold of his cock from Lesley and inserted his knob into the inviting crevice of Tanya's bum, lubricating his helmet with the greasy juices which were flowing down so copiously from her pussy.

'Don't rush, Adrian, your cock's a bit big for my bum-hole!' wailed Tanya as she felt his knob press into the winking little orifice. She leaned forward, resting herself on her forearms as Philip jerked his cock up high inside her honeypot. She let out a cry of delight as his knob tickled her clitty while Adrian thrust his cock forward, slowly advancing his bell

121

end inch by inch deep into the passage of Tanya's luscious backside until his balls were dangling against the back of her thighs.

She threw back her head in sheer ecstasy as Adrian and Philip's stalwart cocks breached her fore and aft. They came together as Tanya threshed around like a wildcat, throwing herself body and soul into this splendid double fuck. Then she drew in a long, shuddering breath and screamed out her delight before she flopped forward, almost fainting away with almost unbearable joy as simultaneously both lovers spurted their sticky tributes inside her, and she achieved a tremendous orgasm which rocked through her with such force that she almost fainted with excitement.

In the meantime, Lesley had been kneeling at the foot of the bed, frantically frigging herself while she watched her friend being plugged both front and behind.

'Hey, don't go to sleep, you guys, I also want to be fucked! After all, it was my idea for you both to screw Tanya together,' she complained. But then Lesley smiled when she saw that Philip's young cock was still stiff. With a happy little cry, she fastened her fingers around his gleaming wet prick and fisted his smooth warm shaft, pulling the loose skin up and down with both hands. His cock was soon swollen back up to its previous majestic girth and the wide purple dome of his helmet was fully exposed to view.

She pulled Philip's cock until he was sitting

upright and then she commanded him to change places with her. When he had done so, she lay herself down and looked with eager anticipation at his throbbing veiny shaft as he knelt over her and directly guided his uncapped helmet inside her squishy honeypot.

'Ahhh! That's better, *much* better,' she said cheerfully as he started to stab his pulsing prick in and out of her juicy cunt. 'Fuck the arse off me, you randy rozzer!'

Philip gritted his teeth and drove down at a furiously fast rhythm. His embedded prick was slewing a path at such speed inside Lesley that he felt it belonged to her as much as it did to him. He rubbed his lips against her stalky nipples as she gyrated her hips underneath him and he slid his hands underneath her to grab her lush bum cheeks as he pistoned his prick in and out of her clinging quim.

And despite the fact that he had spunked inside Tanya's cunt only minutes before, Lesley so cleverly flexed her cunny muscles to nip his cock that, sooner than he would have thought possible, a fountain of frothy hot spunk burst out from his knob and drenched the walls of Lesley's love channel as she too exploded into a delicious climax.

Now that Lesley had obtained her satisfaction, Adrian set the alarm on his watch for eight o'clock and Tanya turned off the light and the four lusty lovers snuggled up to each other to sleep away the few remaining hours till Adrian at least had to wake up and make his way home before leaving for the office and his dreaded meeting with Dickie Segal.

Surprisingly, although he fell asleep immediately after the exertions of the night's revels, Adrian woke up as soon as the irritating buzz of the alarm informed him that it was time to go. He switched off the alarm and saw that his three companions were still deep in the arms of Morpheus. He slipped out of the bed and began to dress.

When he had finished he found a ballpoint pen and a piece of paper on Tanya's dressing table. He scribbled a note for her which read:

Many thanks for a wonderful evening – I'll try and call you before, but I'm running around like a blue-arsed fly for the next few days. However, all being well I'll see you next Tuesday night in *La Miraggio*, we've a new singer called Marion Osbourne starting at the club courtesy of Angelo and I'll be there to give her some moral support – Much Luv

He scrawled an illegible signature underneath the message.

Then he picked up the note and tip-toed back to the bed, where Tanya was sleeping on her front, her arms hugging the pillow on which Adrian's head had rested. He was about to slip the note next to her when her long eyelashes fluttered open and she murmured: 'Adrian, must you really go so soon?

Come on back to bed and fuck me, lover. That'll set us both up nicely for the day.'

'I'd love to but, honestly, it'll have to wait till next time,' said Adrian regretfully, prising her arms away from his neck as he planted a chaste kiss on her cheek. 'Give my best to Lesley and to young Philip. Presumably he doesn't have to be back on duty till this afternoon at the earliest, the lucky sod. I'll be thinking of him wielding his truncheon as I'm locked in combat with Dickie Segal this morning.'

She opened her eyes wide and whispered: 'Did you say Dickie Segal? Old Nipper, do you mean? I've met him, he's a randy old goat, is it true how he got his nickname?'

Adrian grinned and replied softly: 'Well, his friends say it comes from his habit of saying "We'd better nip this in the bud before it causes any trouble," but those in the know say he got the name a good few years ago. The story is that he was getting a blow job and he got so excited that the bloody sofa overturned which startled the girl so much that she bit his cock and left poor old Dickie with a bruised prick for more than a week!'

Tanya stifled a snort of laughter and, not wanting to wake up Lesley and Philip who were still fast asleep, she threw back the corner of the quilt. Adrian's shaft shifted inside his pants as he looked down upon her perfect dimpled buttocks.

'Sure you don't have time for a quickie?' she whispered as she raised her arm and playfully stroked his burgeoning erection through the material of his trousers.

'No, honestly, I really must be off,' said Adrian but he found it impossible to move as Tanya sat up. Drawing down his zip, she pulled out his prick and began rhythmically pumping his throbbing boner. She looked up at him as she slowly increased the speed of her hand and said: 'Oooh, your cock feels so big and hard this morning. This is almost as good as having it stuffed inside my cunt – now let's see how much spunk you've got left in your balls after last night!'

She leaned forward and teased the underside of Adrian's knob with the tip of her tongue. She sucked it inside her mouth while, with her hands, Tanya pulled out his wrinkled scrotum, raising the low dangling bag high by its own loose skin. She teased his balls with her fingertips as they slid about in their tightening pink sack.

This was all too much for Adrian to bear. Tanya felt his prick flexing inside the wet circlet of her lips and he spurted a thick jet of creamy cum down her throat. She eagerly gulped it down, draining every last drop of sticky jism from Adrian's cock as it slid out from between her lips.

Adrian slid his cock back inside his trousers and zipped up his flies as he commented: 'Well, I've heard of going to work on an egg though I'm damned sure that a blow job is even better.'

'Of course it is, you silly boy. Don't you know the difference between an egg and a blow job?' asked

Tanya and when he shook his head, she smiled and said: 'well, you can beat an egg!'

He snorted with laughter and ruffled Tanya's tousled hair with his hand as he bent down. Tasting the salty tang of his own seed on her lips, he kissed her and said again that he must leave. 'Remember, I'll see you next week at *La Miraggio*,' he added as he went out of the bedroom. Picking up his coat, he left the flat, carefully closing the front door behind him. He opened the front door of the apartment block and stopped outside for a few seconds to take in deep breaths of the fresh, summery morning air.

Then he looked at his watch and tutted aloud as he realised that he would have to get his skates on if he were not going to be late at the office. The rush-hour traffic had already started to build up and he had to go home and wash and change before going to work.

And what would he say to Gigi if his live-in lover had telephoned his flat from Mademoiselle Melissa's? Come to think of it, might Melissa have told Gigi that he had fucked her yesterday afternoon? Probably not, but there was no time to worry about that, whatever might be happening in his private life, he could not afford to be late for his meeting with Dickie Segal . . .

Nevertheless, a happy smile of contentment slowly spread over Adrian Klein's face as he swung the MG out into the road and roared up the steep hill towards West End Lane. Although the coming day would soon see him having to cope with various heavy pressures, the memory of his raunchy night with Tanya and Lesley helped to prevent Adrian from worrying too much about them.

CHAPTER THREE

On With The Motley

After a refreshing shower and a change of clothes, Adrian gulped down a glass of orange juice. Under the empty glass he left two pound notes and a message to his cleaning lady asking her to iron all the shirts he had left hanging up in the bathroom. Then he locked his front door and marched swiftly back to his car. The traffic around the West End was almost at a standstill due to a van hitting the side of a bus at Oxford Circus. He reluctantly decided not to chance getting stuck in a jam and spend valuable time fretting about parking meters, so instead he drove to St John's Wood station, parked the MG and caught the tube to Green Park. To his great satisfaction, he was at his desk just after nine-thirty, only fifteen minutes later than he had planned.

The door to his office opened and Barbara, his perky new secretary, came in with a pot of coffee and a plate of chocolate biscuits on a tray.

'Good morning, Mr Klein, sir. Would you like a brandy in your coffee before taking on the dreaded

Dickie Segal?' she asked brightly.

'No thanks, Babs, it's too early in the day for me. Anyhow, I'd best tackle Dickie with a clear head,' said Adrian. He smiled at the attractive, lissome girl as she passed him a sheaf of letters which had arrived in the morning post.

Barbara Kennedy was an efficient, highly capable secretary but Adrian would have had to confess he had chosen her from the short-list prepared by Rose and Griffin's office manager not only for her short-hand and typing speeds but also for her looks. She was a head-turningly pretty girl with large liquid brown eyes, a well shaped nose and full, generous lips which parted to reveal two rows of sparkling white teeth. She wore her soft auburn hair with a fashionable fringe and long, loose strands tumbled down the sides of her face.

'Anything urgent in the mail?' asked Adrian, finding it impossible not to let his eyes sweep over her figure-hugging red mini-dress which accentu-ated the swell of her breasts and the curvy contours of her delectable backside.

She shook her head. 'Nothing that can't wait till you come back from your meeting,' and then after a little pause she added: 'You've had a telephone call from Gigi, though. She wants you to ring her back as soon as you get in – she's left me the number for you to call.'

Adrian stroked his chin and said: 'Um, I really don't have time just now, I have to see Teddy Dixon for five minutes before I shoot off to Amalgamated –

Babs, please do me a great favour and call Gigi back for me and say I'll telephone the minute I get out of this meeting.'

'For you, anything,' said Barbara, placing her hand across her heart and Adrian sighed: 'Promises, promises,' as he dialled his boss on the internal telephone. 'Teddy, it's Adrian, you wanted to see me before I go round to Dickie Segal's office. What did you say? Yes, I did see Trevor Trenton last night and he was terrific, he had the audience eating out of the palm of his hand. No, Teddy, I won't let him go for under three hundred and fifty a week, more if that TV show comes off. That's all, is it? Oh, fine, no problem, I'll be on my way.'

He put down the phone and said: 'Well, that's that, Teddy says good luck and don't let Dickie sign up Trevor Trenton too cheaply.'

'I'm sure you won't but now, if you don't have to see Teddy, perhaps you would like to phone Gigi yourself?' enquired Barbara. But Adrian shook his head. 'No, I don't think so, I've still got a million and three things to do. Look, be a pal and call her for me and tell her I'll definitely speak to her this afternoon.'

He stuffed a folder into his briefcase and rose from his chair. 'Babs, I'm off now to beard the lion in his den. I know I can leave you to hold the fort while I'm gone – knock out those letters I dictated yesterday, tell anyone important who phones in that I'll ring back after lunch but if old Sid Cohen calls from

Birmingham, tell him that I'm not in till next Monday.'

'Okay, Adrian, best of luck,' she said, waving him goodbye as he strode out of the office. Then she sat on his desk and picked up the telephone. I'm not getting involved in his private affairs, she said to herself as she dialled the number Gigi had given her.

'Hi, is that you, Gigi? It's Barbara Kennedy again. Look, I gave Adrian your message and he's asked me to ring you and say he's had to rush out but he'll call you back without fail this afternoon.'

'Did he, the rotten toe-rag? He knows I'm furious with him. Hasn't he got the guts to come to the phone himself?' said Gigi vehemently. Barbara rolled her eyes upwards as she protested: 'Please, Gigi, don't shoot the messenger! This quarrel has nothing to do with me, but for what it's worth, honestly, Adrian really did have to fly out to a meeting this morning.'

There was silence for a moment on the other end of the line and then Gigi apologised for her outburst. 'I'm sorry, Barbara, of course you're quite right. My row is with that bugger Adrian, not with you! Please, let me make it up to you – I know, let's have a nice gossipy lunch together. Are you free today? I'm modelling maxi-skirts at a showroom near Oxford Circus this morning but I could be at Rose and Griffin at any time after half-past twelve. We could even pop into *La Miraggio*, that bloody night club Adrian insisted on going to last night. He took me there a couple of months ago for lunch and there's a very good buffet to choose from. Do say yes.'

'It's not necessary,' began Barbara, but Gigi cut her short. 'No, please, I'd love us to get together. We've only had the chance to chat briefly at that party in your office for the Deltas and it really is about time we dished the dirt together on you-know-who!'

Barbara giggled and replied: 'Well, if you put it like that, how can I refuse? But let's keep away from *La Miraggio*, there are always too many people from Rose and Griffin there. Come to the office at about one and we'll go to a quiet little restaurant I know just off Bond Street.'

After Gigi had agreed to this arrangement, Barbara returned to her own small office and began typing the correspondence that her boss had dictated to her the previous day. However, she had only finished the first letter when Samantha, Tony Cavendish's secretary, ambled into her room.

'Hiya Babs, is Adrian not in this morning? What's happening to this place? Tony hasn't come in either and I haven't heard a word from him yet,' Sam was a pretty twenty-year-old blonde over whom many of the men in the agency lusted in vain. She shared her bed solely with Freddie Amos, the famous wise-cracking host of *Some You Win*, the most popular game-show on television. She sported a superb square-diamond ring on her hand from Freddie, although the only engagement in which the entertainer was currently involved was with his estranged second wife in an intense and expensive legal battle over her alimony.

'Adrian was here first thing, but he had to go out again,' explained Barbara patiently. 'Sorry, but I've no idea where Tony has got to. Don't you keep his appointments diary?'

'Yes, of course I do, and he has Marty Pachnos, the manager of that new group the Deltas, coming in to see him at noon, so Tony had better put in an appearance soon. Sam put her hand up to her mouth to cover a wide yawn as she slumped into a chair and stretched herself out like a sleek golden cat.

'Beg your pardon, Babs, I didn't get much sleep last night,' she said with a smug smile. 'Freddie came home early and I'd been worrying about him. Those solicitors' letters about his wife were getting him down so much that lately he could hardly raise a hard-on. I thought I'd try to give his wedding tackle a boost with a bit of unexpected rumpy-pumpy. So when he opened the front door last night, I was in the living-room wearing only my panties, stockings and a suspender belt.

' "Scotch or vodka, darling?" I asked him and he just threw off his jacket with a growl and gave me the most enormous bear-hug. He pulled me straight into the bedroom and began squeezing my breasts and tweaking my titties with his fingers. I dragged down his trousers and out popped his thick prick, as stiff as a poker! I started to wank him off and then he told me to sit on his face, and so I squatted over him while I rubbed his dick. Using his tongue, Freddie flicked the crotch of my knickers aside and licked all around my fanny.

'My panties were soon soaking wet so I ripped them off and he slid his tongue into my cunt. Then I sat fully on his face and swivelled my hips around while I leaned forward, popped his rock hard cock into my mouth and gave him a really good gobble. I enjoyed it so much that I took his shaft out of my mouth and licked it all over before sucking him off and swallowing his creamy cum, while Freddie continued to frig me with his fingers as his tongue flicked around my clitty. I soon came all over his face and we didn't get out of bed till ten o'clock when I made some sandwiches and a pot of tea.

'Afterwards we started fucking again, standing up, doggy-style with me bending over the bed, and God knows what else. Freddie is always saying that variety is the spice of life. So that's why I'm so tired. Who knows, perhaps Tony finally made it with Sharon Saxon! I know he fancies her like mad and they were going on to a party after the *Top of the Pops* recording last night, so I wouldn't be at all surprised. He's a terrible ram is our Tony, I think he'd fuck anything in skirts except the Scots Guards!'

Barbara slowly exhaled a deep breath and said anxiously: 'Sam, don't put that story about, because if it's true the papers might get hold of it and bang would go Sharon's naughty-but-nice image – and if it isn't true, Tony would be furious if he found out that you'd started a rumour about them.'

'Oh, I wouldn't do that,' replied Sam virtuously as she hauled herself out of her chair and prepared to go back to her own office. 'I'm only saying that to you, Babs, because I know that you don't go in for all that tittle-tattle you hear around this place.'

'Thanks, Sam, I didn't mean to sound off at you, and I know that you wouldn't do anything to upset the apple cart. Mind, if Tony's going to play silly buggers and not turn up for his date with Marty Pachnos, then he's asking for trouble, although I must say that I thought he would have more sense. You did say there was no answer from Tony's flat when you telephoned? Then where the blue blazes can he be?'

As it happened, at the same instant that Barbara Kennedy was posing this question, Tony Cavendish had just slipped out of bed and pulled open the curtains. When he had woken up just a few moments before, he would not have been able to answer Barbara immediately, for it had taken him a good ten seconds to remember just exactly where he was!

However, when he felt Donna's weight pressing against his side, Tony's face creased into a smile. He realised that he had spent the night in the spare bedroom of Nick Clarke's Prince's Gate penthouse, and that he had used much of that time in fucking the delectable girl who was still fast asleep beside him.

As the sunlight streamed into the room, Tony walked back to the bed and sat down with his head in his hands. The foggy mists of his deep sleep gradually cleared from his brain. Then he turned and lifted the corner of the continental-style quilt to expose Donna's gorgeous coffee-with-cream coloured body curled up in a ball, with her perfect bum cheeks facing him. Although Tony knew that he had to make a swift exit if he were going to arrive on time at Rose and Griffin, when Donna parted her legs and exposed the puckered little rim of her anus and the pouting pink lips of her cunny to his excited gaze, all thoughts except making love to this delectable, sensuous creature one last time rapidly fled from his mind.

Donna now stirred and swung over onto her back as she reached up and fastened her long fingers around Tony's burgeoning penis. She lovingly fondled his cock, sliding her hand up and down the veiny shaft, working his foreskin back and forth in long, slow strokes. Tony spread his legs to allow her access to his dangling ballsack.

She wiped her tongue over her lips and then with a lascivious smile, Donna moved her head forward to nibble daintily on his scrotum. Tony gasped and with a low moan he bent down and took an elongated browny-red nipple inside his mouth, wrapping his arm around her head to draw her even closer to him.

'Come back to bed and bring me off,' she murmured salaciously. Nothing loath, Tony swivelled his body over her, facing the foot of the bed and on his knees with his balls dangling above Donna's mouth. Then he leaned forward and kissed her dark crinkly bush and ran his lips over the rubbery love lips of her dripping love channel.

Now they both began to tremble with the fever of lustful passion as their bodies slid into a delightful *soixante neuf*. Donna was licking Tony's balls and masturbating his throbbing tool while he kissed her sweet pussy and the tip of his tongue sought out the secrets of her sopping slit. He lapped around the edges of her crack and when her clitty popped out he playfully scraped his teeth along the erectile fleshy button as Donna's love juices flowed over his face.

'Don't stop! Don't stop!' beseeched Donna as Tony lifted his head and pulled his cock out of her grasp. He swivelled his body round so that he could see the superb naked body of the gorgeous girl. Taking his pulsating prick in his own hand, he muttered throatily: 'Relax, you sexy beauty, I'm not going to stop but instead of licking you out, I'm going to slide my cock into your juicy cunt and fuck the arse off you!'

'Oh yes, yes, go on then,' she panted as she parted her thighs. Her curvy body quivered all over as Tony carefully guided his cock between Donna's inviting pussy lips, directly into her clinging quim. He fucked her in a steady, pacy rhythm and, cupping the firm globes of her breasts in his hands, he rubbed her pointy nipples till they were thrusting up stiffly against his palms.

Whilst his prick pistoned in and out of her clingy cunny, Tony glanced down at their joined crotches. A thrill shivered through his frame at the sight of his glistening shaft slicking its way into Donna's adorable cunt. She too was enjoying this magnificent fuck and whimpering with pleasure. She threw her legs around his waist, locking her ankles together as she fitted herself into his rock-steady rhythm and her body quivered with every pounding stroke of Tony's thick tadger.

Her superb backside was now raised above the sheets and Tony slid his hands underneath to squeeze her succulent bum cheeks as he pistoned his big cock between Donna's frilled pussy lips deep inside her.

'More! More! I want you deeper inside me, as far as it will go! Oh *yes*, that's *fantastic*! Fill my cunt with spunk, you randy rascal!' Donna cried and again and again Tony slammed his hips forward, embedding his cock inside her slippery cunt, his belly squirming against hers. The springy curls of his chest hairs rubbed with an arousing, earthy friction against her hard, erect nipples.

'You got it, lady!' growled Tony as he gritted his teeth. Soon they were locked into a new pulsing rhythm as he fucked her even more powerfully with long, sweeping strokes of his rampant cock.

As they fucked themselves up to a frenzy, Donna clutched a handful of flesh from one of his lean buttocks and Tony yelped with surprise as she began to slap his bottom. This seemed to make his member swell even further inside her sopping sheath.

'I'm coming! I'm coming!' Tony panted as he felt the spunk coursing up from his balls, as he plunged his raging rod inside Donna's squelchy cunny for one last final fling. She sensed he was about to shoot his load and her lithe body writhed beneath him, arching her back as a creamy torrent of sticky jism spurted out of his cock. Donna shuddered violently as the force of her own impending climax quickly rocketed through her body as Tony emptied the contents of his tightened balls inside her.

Tony rolled off her shuddering body and collapsed like a rag doll by the side of the lovely brown-skinned girl. She leaned over and cradled his head in her arms as his chest heaved while he lay drained from his herculean efforts.

'That was simply wonderful, really one of the best fucks I've ever had,' said Donna softly as she ruffled her fingers through his perspiration soaked hair. 'You're a great cocksman, Tony Cavendish, and if you can keep up that standard, you'll make every girl you take to bed very happy.'

He turned his face to her with a puzzled expression of dismay on his face. 'What do you mean *every* girl, Donna? Does this mean you're giving me the brush-off?'

She bit her lip and replied: 'Oh God, this is so difficult! Tony, perhaps I should have been more up-front with you before we made love, but I must tell you that I've made it a golden rule never to get romantically involved with anyone in the business.'

He stared at her hardly believing he had heard her correctly. 'Never to get romantically involved?' he repeated with an angry mixture of rising distress and incredulity in his voice. 'So are you saying that I'm just one of your studs who you take to bed when you want to be fucked? Okay, I know I have a reputation as a one-night stand but I really fell for you, Donna. Sure, I couldn't wait to make love to you but I thought this was going to be the start and not the finish of our affair.'

'I'm sorry, Tony, I can understand how you feel,' she said apologetically. 'But can I tell you something in confidence? The truth of the matter is that I'm practically engaged to a guy named Roger Palmer, whose firm have sent him out to Australia for nine months. I've tried very hard not to be unfaithful so I bought myself a vibrator, but I'm a horny bitch and I had to have an occasional cock inside my pussy. Well, as I told Sharon last night, lately I've been trying to get my rocks off with other girls and that's been okay as far as it goes, but I've had to admit that there's nothing to beat having a lovely thick prick pumping in and out of my cunt.'

When Tony saw that the girl was genuinely unhappy about the situation, the tide of his initial resentment swiftly receded and he gently said to Donna: 'No, I'm sorry, love, you didn't owe me any explanation. I was well out of order, flying off the handle like that. But there's no need to feel too guilty about enjoying an occasional no-strings-attached fuck – after all, with all those bronzed Aussie girls around him, do you think your chap is going to be one hundred per cent faithful for nine months and spend his nights alone jacking off without some Sheila giving him a helping hand?'

Despite herself, Donna chuckled throatily and nodded her head in agreement. 'No, I don't suppose he will, Roger loves to screw and for some reason he's especially randy during the summer. I can't explain why but it's as if the sunshine brings out the animal in him.'

'Well, he'll have plenty of sun while we're shivering away next winter,' commented Tony, who was about to slide out of bed and shower before making his way to work. But he could not break himself away from the warm embrace of Donna, whose elbow was pushing sensuously against his flaccid cock while her fingers lazily traced a pattern across his chest.

'Yes, won't he just, the lucky sod?' she sighed dreamily. 'He'll be on the beach every weekend eyeing up the talent, there's no doubt about that. Why, I'll never forget one weekend last summer when we drove down to the coast with a couple of friends, Camilla and Charlie, and we found a secluded little stretch of beach about seven miles outside Winchelsea. We had booked rooms in a little hotel owned by an old chum of Martin's, so there was no need for any silly nonsense about signing in as Mr and Mrs Smith.

'Roger could hardly wait to get me upstairs because I'd promised him that I'd let him screw me that evening. We'd only been going out for a month and though I'd let him finger-fuck my pussy and I had wanked off his big cock, I hadn't yet been sure enough about him to go all the way. However, although I was eagerly looking forward to sharing a bed with Roger, when he started to kiss and cuddle me in our room, I told him to cool down. I wasn't going to waste this wonderful weather by staying indoors. He would just have to wait a little longer for his oats!

'The afternoon was perfect, the sun was beating down and there wasn't even a wisp of a cloud in the sky. We had changed after we had arrived at the hotel and I was wearing a bikini under my clothes and Roger had a bathing costume on under his shorts. The boys had brought along two deck-chairs and a big air-bed which Charlie began to pump up while Roger set up the chairs. I slipped off my dress and then bent down and rummaged in my bag for the bottle of sun-tan oil I'd brought with me – but did I get a shock when I straightened up and turned round to speak to Camilla!'

She paused and started to giggle as she let the image of the memory float across her mind. Tony looked enquiringly down at her and kissed the tip of her nose. 'No, don't tell me, let me guess. I know, Paul McCartney suddenly appeared from nowhere

145

and begged you to marry him!

'Huh! If he had, I wouldn't be here now telling this story to you!' she replied promptly, dipping her hand downwards to give his prick a friendly little tug. 'No, I turned round to see that Camilla had pulled off her tee-shirt and skirt and was standing there wearing only a pair of white cotton panties!

'Now Roger was sitting down in a deck-chair and I saw his eyes gleam, but Martin didn't seem to be bothered that Camilla was showing off her tits to us. He just looked up for a moment and frowned: "Bugger it, I've gone and left our towels in the car. I'll have to go back and get them. Don't use up all the sunshine, I'll be back in about ten minutes."

'As he walked away, I said to Camilla: "Did you also forget your cozzie? It doesn't matter, though, as I've a spare one in my bag if you'd like to wear it." But she shook her head and replied: "No thanks, love, Martin and I like to sunbathe in the alto-gether. But I wouldn't mind a drop of that sun-tan oil when you've finished with it."

'Her reply really staggered me, Tony, for believe it or not, it had never occurred to me to sunbathe in the nude. I suppose my surprise must have shown on my face, because Camilla laughed as I passed over the bottle and said: "Oh dear, have I shocked you? Why don't you try it, you'll find it so refreshing lying out naked in the sun."

' "True, we don't often get such glorious weather as this, but the Scandinavians especially rush down south in the summer for their all-over tans. There are a few private places on some small Greek islands in which you can go naked and there are special beaches for naturists around Cap d'Agde in South West France. Martin and I might go out and see what they're like next month."

'With that, she opened the bottle and smoothed the sun-tan oil over her breasts. Camilla has perky little breasts with tip-tilted pointy nipples and they stood up even more as she massaged the oil over them. Then she tut-tutted and said crossly: "Damn, my hands are all greasy and I forgot to take off my panties."

'Before I could reply, as quick as a flash, Roger had leaped out of his deck-chair and was standing by her side. "No problem, I'll take them off for you," he offered. She gave him a cheeky grin and said: "Many thanks, kind sir, for helping a damsel in distress."

' "Call me any time and I will be proud to be of service," said Roger. Squatting down on his haunches, he took hold of the top of her panties and rolled them down over her hips, with his face only inches away from the pretty little muff of light chestnut hair around her pussy. When he hauled himself up and stuffed the knickers into my basket, I could see that a bulge had already formed in his swimming trunks.

'Now, before I go on, I should say in fairness to everybody concerned that except for Charlie (who's a teetotaller) we had quite a boozy lunch – anyhow, that's going to be my excuse why I acted as I did.

You see, I knew that Roger fancied Camilla and I thought, well, let's see how he acts if he has a choice of fucking me or her. So I stripped off as well and flaunted myself sexily in front of Roger as I called to Camilla: "Well, you can use as much oil as you like, but you'll never get as brown as me!"

' "That's true enough," she agreed and then she beckoned me over to her and whispered with a little giggle: "Just look at that huge stiffie bulging out between Roger's legs, the naughty boy. I've got a good idea, come and lie down with me on the mattress and we'll give him such a show that he won't be able to stop himself coming in his costume!"

' "Yes, why not that would serve him right," I muttered back and so we draped a towel on the mattress. The two of us stretched ourselves down on it and Camilla rubbed some oil onto my body. I lay back and relaxed, enjoying the way in which she was smoothing her hand over my belly. There was certainly something to be said for sunbathing naked, I thought. I gasped as Camilla moved her fingers upwards and started to stroke my breasts, making my nipples tingle as she tweaked my titties till they stood up like two little brown buttons.

'I could see Roger looking at us open-mouthed as Camilla moved her hand down inside the slippery warmth between my thighs and inserted a finger inside my sticky cunt which made me shudder with delight, especially when I felt the featherlight touch of her fingertip on my clitty.

'Then Camilla kissed my titties as she raised

herself up and knelt down in front of me, while she parted my legs as wide as she could so that Roger would be able to see my pouting pussy lips. Then she dived down and began to lick me out. She wasted no time and sucked on my pussy open-mouthed, rolling my love lips inside her mouth before slipping her tongue deep inside my moistening, musky cunt.

'I lifted my thighs and rested them on Camilla's shoulders. She circled my hips with her arms and grasped my bum cheeks, pulling my pussy deeper into her face as she flicked her tongue over the hard nub of my clitty. She must have felt the shock wave of her caress ripple through my groin as a low groan of passion rose from my throat and I cried out: "Yes, yes, eat my pussy and finish me off, you lovely girl!"

'I writhed and twisted like crazy as Camilla brought me off. I closed my eyes and screwed up my face and I was engulfed in a great shattering climax. But when I opened my eyes and looked round to where Roger had been sitting, I pulled Camilla's head up from my pussy and pointed towards my boy friend. For there was Roger with his trunks at his feet, masturbating wildly, his hand sliding up and down his erect naked truncheon.

'Now I thought that would be the end of the affair but Camilla had other ideas and she called to him: "Roger, don't waste that thick prick by wanking by yourself, come over here and I'll suck you off!"

'Roger didn't have to be asked twice! He came and knelt down next to us. Camilla substituted her hand for her mouth between my legs, pressing her palm against my pussy as her free hand stole up and down Roger's cock and then she eased his straining uncapped knob between her lips.

'However, although I found this exciting to watch, I must admit I had decidedly mixed feelings about seeing Camilla's tousled head bob up and down on his veiny shaft. After all, Roger's cock belonged to me – it may not have been the biggest prick that I'd ever clapped eyes on, but it was beautifully proportioned with a huge purple dome and a hot, throbbing shaft which she now held onto with both hands as she licked and lapped on it as if it were a delicious lollipop.

'So I sat up and squatted down with my bottom on the back of my legs and nudged Camilla's mouth away from Roger's cock. I took hold of his tool and washed his knob all over with my tongue, the first time I had ever sucked his cock. To be fair, Camilla didn't attempt to push me off but simply transferred her lips to his hairy tight ballsack and began licking his balls, taking them into her mouth for a light suck.

'Roger was now breathing heavily and I guessed that he wouldn't be able to hold out for much longer against this double helping of licking and lapping. Sure enough, as I slurped away on his throbbing stiffie, his shaft began to twitch and I knew that the spunk would soon be rushing up from his balls.

'What would it taste like, I wondered. I found out almost at once as his cock bucked wildly between my lips and my mouth was suddenly filled with huge squirts of frothy jism. I tasted his creamy cum which had a nice, salty tang to it. I gulped it all down, licking round his knob to gather up any stray splashes. At last his spongy knob started to soften as I rolled my tongue around it for one final time.'

Donna stopped and looked up to Tony Cavendish with a saucy glint in her eyes as she felt his cock swell up and pulsate stiffly between her fingers.

'Oooh, I see that my little tale has turned you on,' she murmured. Tony nodded and replied hoarsely: 'Well, what did you expect, you little minx?

'But I want to hear the end of the story. Tell me, what happened when Charlie came back with the towels. He couldn't exactly have been over the moon to see his girl sucking off lucky old Roger!'

Donna shrugged her slender shoulders. 'Oh, Charlie wasn't that bothered because he knew that Camilla fancied us both and that we'd probably all finish up in a whoresome foursome that night. When he saw what was going on when he got back to the beach, he just tore off his clothes and ran over the sand to join us.

' "Come here and I'll oil your prick," ordered Camilla, and I moved to the side so as to let Charlie lie down on the mattress. Then she rubbed the sun-tan lotion on his cock as well as around her pussy. She knelt across him, arching her hips forward so he could see the red chink of her cunny. She spread her pussy lips wide and frigged herself and Charlie's circumcised cock shot up like lightning and I saw a tiny white bead of cum appear round the slit of his fat red helmet. Then, holding her oily love lips open, Camilla lowered herself over Charlie's prick and started to slide to and fro on his greasy pole.

The erotic aroma of her musky feminine odour mingled with the fragrant scent of the oil. Camilla thoroughly enjoyed the delicious sensations, rocking backwards and forwards on his slippery shaft and she groaned with delight as Charlie's pulsating prick reamed out the furthest, deepest nooks and crannies inside her tingling love channel.

' "God Almighty, I've never known a girl get so juicy!" Charlie groaned as he squeezed her proud, uptilted titties. She bounced away merrily on his thick truncheon, pumping her bum up and down and digging her nails into his muscular thighs.

' "And I'm going to make you even wetter," he grunted, arching his back upwards, jamming his glistening cock to the root inside her dripping cunt while Camilla rammed up and down, squeezing and releasing the muscles of her cunny and her backside as she prepared to milk him of his creamy jism. This exciting frigging of his twitching tool aroused Charlie so much that he let out a fierce growl. Camilla began writhing in orgasm herself as she ground down on him one last time, screwing her clinging cunny around his cock and gripping him like a vice until his hot spunk started to shoot into her cunt. She jerked her head backwards and abandoned herself to the thrashing throes of an incredibly powerful climax.'

Donna gave a throaty chuckle as she felt Tony's tadger thicken in her grasp. For a brief moment they gazed at each other's naked bodies. Then she released his quivering cock and pressed her warm breasts against his broad chest. Her slim hips undulated against his thighs as, with legs spread wide, she rubbed her excited little pussy against him.

'Fuck me, big boy,' she murmured with a vulpine gleam in her eyes. As any thoughts of returning to his office fled Tony's brain, he took hold of her shoulders and, pressing her body back onto the springy mattress, he quickly mounted her, his free hand delving down between her legs. His fingers opened up the pouting pussy lips while, with speedy dexterity, Donna seized hold of his swollen shaft and placed his knob with unerring accuracy at the entrance to her honeypot. Their pubic hairs matted together as Tony thrust forward, pushing his prick deep inside her. They threw themselves heart and soul into a frenetic bout of fucking.

With her thighs raised and wide open, Donna clawed at her lover in frantic passion. Her fingernails scored down his back and she writhed and twisted sensuously while her superb breasts were crushed under his weight. Tony felt her juicy cunt swallowing in his delighted length with every plunge as her legs kicked high in the air above him.

'Y-e-s-s!! Y-e-s-s!' Donna screamed out triumphantly as she threw her legs around Tony's waist. She exploded into a mind-wrenching orgasm and he now came too with a great groan. He drenched

Donna's sated cunny with a tremendous jet of jism as the gorgeous young brown-skinned girl trembled beneath him.

Tony collapsed on top of her and gently eased his now-limp prick out of her soaking love hole as he scrambled to his knees. After a few moments to recover his strength, he slid off the bed and, standing next to her, he bent down and gently kissed her cheek as he covered her up with the duvet.

She looked up lovingly to him and murmured: 'Thanks Tony, I feel really spoiled! I mean, to make love after a super party, enjoy a good night's sleep and then wake up to a wonderful good-morning fuck – what more could a girl ask for?'

He smiled and said: 'What more could a boy ask for either? I wish I could stay all day with you, but I have to go. I'm sure you've got work to do as well. But we must see each other again, Donna. How about coming out to dinner with me on Friday night? I won't take no for an answer! Now, I'm just going to take a shower, don't go away I'll be back in five minutes.'

'I'm not going anywhere, this bed is too comfortable and Nick never starts work till ten o'clock at the earliest,' she replied. Tony leaned down and kissed her again. 'And so dinner on Friday is a date?' he repeated as he gazed steadily into her beautiful brown eyes.

Donna hesitated briefly before she replied, for her story about not getting involved with other men while Roger Palmer was in Australia was perfectly true. On the other hand, although she had known Tony only a very short time and knew little of his interests and lifestyle, there had undoubtedly been a fiercely compelling physical attraction between them. It had quickly led to an intense sexual intimacy, but only time would tell whether this would merely fade or lead them to an even closer, fuller relationship.

So she nodded her head and whispered: 'Yes, if you really want to,' and Tony ruffled her silky, tousled hair with his hand as he chuckled: 'Is the Pope a Catholic?' as he padded out into the bathroom.

As Tony stood in the stall revelling in the sensation of a cascade of hot water spilling over his head, in the next bedroom Sharon Saxon and Nick Clarke had just woken up. The pretty blonde teenager was caressing the songsmith's thickening cock with her fingers. It came to life as if by magic, throbbing sturdily in her sweet touch.

Nick gasped as Sharon continued to fist his palpitating shaft, allowing its swollen girth to slide deliciously to and fro in her hot little hands. She began to plant a series of quick butterfly kisses on his chest, moving her head slowly downwards across his flat belly and down into his tangled curly mass of pubic hair.

'M'mmm, that's fabulous,' he groaned in sheer ecstasy as, having licked all around his pubic bush, Sharon now lapped around the ridges of his uncapped helmet, pressing her face against his delighted member before letting strands of her fine blonde hair fall over his purple knob. Giggling softly, she made a web around his cock, stroking him gently. Then she moved her lips across his bell-end and stretched open her mouth wide, gulping in his knob between her lips as she cupped his big ballsack in her palms.

'Yes, yes, yes!' Nick panted as Sharon closed her mouth around his rigid rod as tightly as she could. She began to bob her head up and down his pulsating pole, sucking lustily as Nick's hands pressed down upon her head as if he feared she might stop palating his prick. But Sharon needed no further encouragement to continue, for it was abundantly clear that she was enjoying herself hugely, slurping uninhibitedly on his wet fleshy penis while she toyed with his balls.

Soon Sharon felt his prick begin to signal that he was about to come, so she released his twitching tool out of the tight ring of her mouth and swiftly sat up. Then she pulled out one of the pillows behind Nick's head and slid it under her bottom as she lay back and arched her body upwards, her groin slightly raised. Nick's heart started to thud as he stared at the inviting red chink of her pouting crack set in the golden bush of pussy hair.

For a moment or two he was motionless as he gazed upon the open flower of her pretty cunt but then Sharon broke the spell as she whispered breathlessly: 'Come on, Nick, ram your thick cock inside me! Remember, you can come inside my cunt because I'm on the pill!'

She just had time to run her hand sensuously across her moist pussy before Nick enveloped the trembling teenager in his arms and rolled on top of her. She held him tightly as he raised himself high and then guided his massive erection towards her cunt. He jammed his cock between her yielding love lips and Sharon's beautiful body bucked with delight as his shaft sank thrillingly home. Their bodies were now joined from mouth to groin as Nick's chest crushed down against her perky nipples while he pistoned his rock-hard cock in and out of her squelchy honeypot. He thrust his meaty boner inside her to the hilt and momentarily stayed stock still, delighting in the feel of her cunny walls clinging against his own pulsating prick.

Their bodies glistened with perspiration as they pressed together in a sinuous sexual frenzy, their tongues entwining wetly in each other's mouths. Sharon squealed with pleasure as love juices began to pour from her pussy. Nick's quivering cock massaged its way with a growing urgency in and out of her satiated cunt.

Then Sharon cried out with joy and her glowing young body tensed and vibrated wildly as a soul-shuddering orgasm swept through her. Her cunny muscles contracted in such rapid, rhythmic waves around Nick's throbbing stiffie that he surrendered himself to the ecstasy of the moment. Out of his prick spurted a frothy gush of sticky jism deep inside the long funnel of Sharon's love channel.

Nick let out a joyous growl as the last dribbles of spunk poured out from his prick and he continued to slick his shaft backwards and forwards until he felt his shaft go limp and he collapsed down on top of her. Sharon threw her arms around his neck and Nick's lips closed over hers in a protracted, passionate kiss as her pink little tongue snaked wetly around his mouth.

For a while there was silence as they lay entwined in each other's arms and then Nick said tenderly: 'You're a lovely kid, Sharon, I'd love to stay here and make love to you all day.'

She kissed his ear and asked: 'Well, must you really work this morning, Nick? Why don't you stay here and I'll go downstairs and make us some breakfast which I'll bring up on a tray.'

Nick shook his head sadly as he broke the embrace and swung his legs out of bed. 'I wish we could, love, but don't you remember the telephone call I had late last night from my partner, Tim Lempert? I have to be at his place by ten to put the final touches to three songs we've written for Jilly Conway's latest LP. We have to wrap them up soon as she's booked into the recording studios next Wednesday afternoon.'

Sharon bit her lip in frustration but she realised that the longer she delayed Nick and Tim from finishing their work for Jilly Conway, the less chance she would have in extracting a new number from the hit tunesmiths for her next single. So she sighed heavily and said: 'Fair enough, Nick, I understand that you can't let her down. But when will I see you again?'

'Well, I'll be working till God-knows-when today, but give me your phone number and perhaps we can meet up again for supper tonight if you're free.'

'I'm free,' she said instantly and the happy couple dissolved into peals of laughter. Sharon pulled him back onto the bed for one final hug before getting up and getting on with the day.

Back in the offices of Rose and Griffin, Teddy Dixon was doing his best not to fall fast asleep while Sir Montague Brooks-Patterson, the elderly, internationally distinguished Shakespearean actor, gave him the benefit of his advice on how to grow tomatoes.

Sir Montague rarely appeared on stage any more (due to his fondness for Johnnie Walker Black Label rather than old age) but occasionally surfaced in a cameo role in a high-brow British film. In the late nineteen forties, he had been one of the first major signings for the fledgling theatrical agency. Although Rose and Griffin earned very little commission nowadays from his work, Teddy Dixon could not bring himself to bring to an end the monthly visits Sir Montague insisted on paying to Dover Street. He would sit in Teddy's office for three quarters of an hour and pontificate on the subject of his choice.

'Why queue at your greengrocer for tough-skinned

tomatoes that have had to be gathered green?' declaimed Sir Montague who, in the absence of any theatrical offers, for the last few years had busied himself with his large acre and a half Oxfordshire garden. 'They can't compare with tender better-flavoured fruits which have been gathered only an hour or so before reaching the table. You have a lovely garden at your place in Hampstead Garden Suburb.'

'Yes, but I'm afraid we don't have a green-house,' said Teddy, looking at his watch and thinking that this reply would surely close the matter and enable him to bring the discussion to a speedy end.

However, Sir Montague was not to be denied. 'Oh, that doesn't matter, my dear chap. These new types don't need disbudding and staking like the traditional ones. All you have to do is plant them a yard apart in the sunniest part of the garden about now and lay straw under the branches to keep them clean.

'As soon as the fruits start to form, feed them with a fertilizer and bob's your uncle. In autumn you can gather the unripe fruit and place them in a warm dark drawer to gain colour or your Doris can use the green ones for chutney.'

Teddy again looked pointedly at his watch. I must get rid of the old fart, he thought as, with a smile on his face, he stood up and said with as much sincerity as he could muster: 'Monty, I'll certainly take your wise words to heart. You must excuse me now though, I'm giving an interview to Louis Baum from

Variety this morning so I must love and leave you.'

'By all means, dear boy, by all means,' said Sir Montague genially as he rose, a trifle unsteadily, to his feet. 'I'm lunching with young Freddie Newman at the Garrick. He has a play set in pre-war London and would like my opinion on one or two matters. Who knows, I might even accept a small role, it's been two or three years since I last trod the boards.'

'Enjoy your lunch and give Freddie my best regards,' said Teddy as he shook hands with the old thespian. He propelled him towards the door just as his nubile mini-skirted secretary came into the office carrying a thick file of papers in her hand.

'By Gad! I don't know how you can concentrate on your work having such a lovely filly at your beck and call,' said an appreciative Sir Montague. He now lived quietly with his wife in the country but in his younger days had enjoyed a notorious reputation for hopping into bed with pretty young actresses.

'Ah, Marlene, Sir Montague is leaving. Perhaps you would accompany him to the lift,' said a relieved Teddy Dixon. He took the file from his secretary and then he squeezed his unwanted guest's shoulder as he added: 'Bye Monty, see you soon.'

Once the door had closed upon Sir Montague and Marlene, Teddy breathed a sigh of relief. He went back and slumped down in his leather upholstered executive chair. He riffled through the file containing the morning's post which Marlene had brought him but he raised his eyebrows when, among the sheaf of letters, he came across an unopened air mail envelope which bore a postmark of Auckland, New Zealand. It was addressed to him and was marked *Strictly Private and Confidential.*

At first Teddy was at a loss to think who could be writing to him from that faraway little country, but then he remembered that Adrian Klein had secured a lucrative if punishing seven-week Australasian concert tour for Laurie Wilkinson, a fiery and sensuous cabaret singer, beginning with shows in Adelaide and Perth before going on to play Melbourne and Sydney and then finishing up in Auckland before flying home after a short rest.

But Adrian was Laurie Wilkinson's personal agent, so why was she writing to Teddy? And what could she have to tell him that was for his eyes only? True, like a good many of the attractive female artistes on Rose and Griffin's books, Teddy had spent a hot half hour with Laurie on the casting couch but he had not spoken nor corresponded with her since the agency threw a leaving party at *La Miraggio* for her a couple of months ago.

Blimey, I hope she hasn't got herself into any trouble, muttered Teddy, as he slit open the envelope with a paper knife. While Laurie had a superb, powerful voice and was capable of belting out a song like Judy Garland or Shirley Bassey at their best, she was also a temperamental lady who needed firm but gentle guidance from her management.

So it was with more than a little trepidation that Teddy took our Laurie's letter, which consisted of three closely typed sheets. Laurie had, in fact, been discovered by Adrian Klein when she was in the typing pool of a large insurance company. He settled down in his comfortable chair to read what she had to say. But he soon realised that there was no immediate cause to panic as the letter began as follows:

Dear Teddy,

Greetings to all at the old firm from New Zealand! How are you, Teddy? Who of the girls I know have you been fucking recently, you randy old sod! I'll wager folding money that you've already had the knickers off Marlene, that gorgeous young new secretary. Teddy, I hope you're not tut-tutting while you're reading this for let's face it, you must have shagged seventy per cent of all the chorus girls currently on stage in London!

Mind, I will say that as far as I know, unlike some rotten bastards in this business, you never promised the earth to any girl who would suck your cock and when any lass said 'no' you might have tried to persuade her to change her mind, but if she stuck to her guns the agency still did everything possible to further her career. So as far as we girls were concerned, there were never any hard feelings once you'd had your wicked way with our pussies for we knew what a cunt-struck old goat you were!

Forgive me, I'm rambling but this will probably be my last letter to you and I thought I'd get that little piece off my chest. Now why will this be my last letter? Well, believe it or not, Teddy, I have decided to stay in New Zealand and I want you to release me from my contract with Rose and Griffin and let me sign up with Billy Macfarlane, the local agent here who you assigned to look after me when I arrived in this country.

The reason why I'm staying in New Zealand is that I've fallen for a super young guy named Seth Rodney and when he asked me to marry him, I accepted his proposal. I'm not planning to give up singing, though, which is why I need your blessing so that Billy Macfarlane can look after my career.

This request will probably cause some surprise and the least I can do is to give you an explanation. In fact, I'd like you to know the full story – I've written to my mother but I can't very well tell her everything like I can tell you! I'm leaving it to you to inform Adrian, I'll be writing to him later, but not in such detail which is why I'd appreciate it if you didn't show this letter around the office.

I suppose the feeling that it was time I found a man with whom I wanted to spend the rest of my life began one quiet afternoon in Sydney (it's winter here and though the weather isn't cold like in London, it can get pretty dull and drizzly). Well, I was feeling a bit low, there I was all alone thousands of miles away from home – not that I had been seeing anyone special since Mike Harper and I decided to call it a day back in January.

So there I was, sipping a glass of vodka and looking out of my first floor hotel room on the grey *outlines of the city, when I happened to see some movement behind a bush in a secluded corner of the hotel gardens. It looked as if a couple were having it away in the dense thicket and I rushed to my drawer to grab hold of the binoculars which the staff at Rose and Griffin gave me as a farewell present at the party you threw for me before I left for this trip.*

I peered through the lenses and I could see that indeed there was a couple writhing on the ground, oblivious to the fact that they might be seen by any hotel guests and then suddenly I realised that I recognised the pair taking part in this randy romp. The girl was none other than my chambermaid, Belinda, a well-built filly in her early twenties, and unless I were very much mistaken, I made out the boy to be Franz, one of the handsome young commis waiters in the dining room. At the beginning, both were fully dressed but they must have just begun their kissing and cuddling for it soon became quite clear that they were planning to pass the point of no return.

Within less than a minute, Belinda was lying on her back, naked from the waist up and her boy friend was kneeling between her legs, pushing down his jeans until his stiff cock popped out and she grabbed hold of his thick tool as she lifted her bottom off the grass to enable Franz to pull off her panties. She then scrambled up on her knees and opened her mouth as Franz thrust his big dick between her lips and she began to suck off the lucky lad as she cupped his balls in her hands.

This was so exciting to watch that I decided to go down and take a closer look at the proceedings and by the time I got down to where they were threshing about, I guessed from the heartfelt moans and groans I could hear coming from behind the bushes that the naughty youngsters were now enjoying a fully blown fuck. Unnoticed by them (and I don't think either would have even heard the massed bands of the Grenadier Guards marching through the hotel grounds!), I crept round and saw that Franz was now on his back while Belinda had pulled up her skirt and was sitting astride his waist, lowering her wet pussy onto his knob. I stood there with my hand inside my panties as with a squelchy sound, she sank down upon his straining shaft, taking his full length inside her juicy quim.

'Oh yes, I'm coming!' she panted as Franz jerked his hips upwards in time with her downward thrusts and he gave her two more climaxes before she lifted herself off his twitching tadger and told him to spunk over her ample bare breasts. Then she sat down with her hand clasping his cock which she rubbed up and down and brought him off, guiding his knob across her cleavage as he spurted his seed over her pointy red nipples and I began to jerk myself off with my fingers as Belinda rubbed the creamy jism into her boobs, and I bit on a knuckle of my free hand so that I wouldn't make any noise. After I came, I stood there with my eyes closed and breathing hard, my soaked panties clinging to every fold of my pussy.

Then my post rubbing-off reverie was interrupted by the sound of a little cough and I opened my eyes to see Belinda standing in front of me. 'Hello there, Miss Wilkinson,' she said as bold as brass. 'Did you enjoy our show as much as we enjoyed yours the evening?'

All I could do was to blush and mumble an incoherent reply as Belinda went on: 'Oh, it's okay, we don't mind an audience, but it would be far nicer all round if we could continue somewhere more comfortable like your bedroom.'

'Be my guest,' I said immediately and after they had thrown on their clothes we dashed back to my room. I wanted to offer Belinda and Franz a drink but I could hardly call room service so I opened a bottle of Seagers Egg Flip which the hotel had left with a bowl of fruit when I checked in. This is a very popular drink out here, by the way, and though it didn't look like anything I would ever have picked up at a party, this tipple of wine, eggs and sugar wasn't as sweet as I had imagined and certainly packed a bit of a bite.

Anyway, at Belinda's urgings all three of us stripped off and she grinned cheekily at me and said: 'Laurie, I suppose you fancy a taste of Franz's cock. Well, you're quite welcome but neither of us can get fucked until his shaft stiffens up again. We'll have to do something to help him along.'

The little minx then took hold of my hand and invited me to join her on the bed and I guessed straightaway that she was thinking of a little lesbian fooling around, and although that isn't really my scene, I was so far gone that in a trice I was on my knees between Belinda's thighs and she was grabbing my hair and pressing my face against her pussy lips which I started to lick and lap for all I was worth. I slipped my forefinger inside her cunt and then a second and third, moving them back and forth as Belinda clamped her cunny muscles around them, contracting the muscles as I finger-fucked her up to a nice little cum and I gulped down her tangy love juice.

Then we switched round and Belinda began kissing my titties while she worked her fingers over my clitty and soon my juices were covering her hand. I'd never fucked with a man let alone a girl in front of anyone else before but the sensation of Belinda's mouth and tongue all over my breasts with her hand on my pussy made me forget that Franz was only a few feet away, watching goggle-eyed as Belinda moved her head between my legs and sucked at my clitty. She was frigging herself at the same time, making little moaning noises as she quickly brought me off.

We both heard some strange grunting noises coming from nearby and I looked round to see that Franz was now on his knees next to us, rubbing his rock-hard boner inside his clenched fist and the sight of his meaty cock, with the foreskin rolled down and his knob all shiny with pre-cum, was too much for me and I wriggled away from Belinda and closed my lips over his helmet. I wanted him to come in my cunt rather than my mouth so I gave his knob one last lingering swirl of my tongue and then positioned myself on all fours in front of him, thrusting my bum into the air, waiting for him to begin fucking me doggy-style.

I glanced over my shoulder to watch him stroke his thick, veiny length as he parted my bum cheeks and slid his cock into the crevice between them until the tip of his knob was battering against my arse-hole. 'Don't go up the tradesmen's entrance, Franz, I don't like being bum-fucked very much,' I gasped out and I think he was a little disappointed, but knowing that the best fucking is with a partner who is enjoying it as much as yourself, he moved his prick downwards and opened the lips of my cunt with his fingers and slid in his fleshy joystick.

'Go on, big boy, fill my cunt with cock!' I cried out as I moved to and fro so that my cunny walls rubbed deliciously against his swollen shaft. He stayed still inside me at first and then Belinda began to encourage him, whispering loudly as she fondled his balls: 'Go on, Franz, fuck Laurie's juicy cunny! Ram your rod inside her clingy quim!'

'Okay, okay, give me a chance,' panted Franz as he moved his throbbing tool in and out of my soaking love box, very slowly at first and then faster and faster while I yelled out with joy, not caring a flying fuck who heard me when he reached down in front with his hand and rubbed my clitty with one finger and slid another into my cunt next to his

prick which was plunging in and out of my honeypot at great speed.

I came off almost immediately and a flood of love juice gushed out of my cunt but he still hadn't climaxed and I shamelessly screamed out: 'Shoot your load, Franz! Come into my cunt, you randy fucker!'

Somehow he managed to increase the tempo even more, gasping away until he started to shake all over and then with a hoarse growl he duly shot his load, filling my honeypot with a gorgeous warm gush of sticky spunk which sent me off again into another wild shuddering orgasm.

To cut a long story short, we spent the rest of the afternoon locked in my bedroom. Frankly, I felt sorry for poor Franz who when it was time to leave, could hardly crawl out into the corridor after we had finished with his sturdy cock! He was only nineteen and had all the stamina of a lusty young teenager and by heaven he needed it, because when he had recovered from fucking me, Belinda sucked him off, and then later she demanded he fuck us both together and we lay down with our legs apart while he slid his cock into one pussy and diddled the other with his fingers before changing over and giving the other girl the thrill of feeling his hot prick pistoning in and out her honeypot.

Well, Teddy, you must now be asking what has all this got to do with my decision to marry Seth Rodney – and the answer isn't just that Seth's Dad owns about a million pounds worth of property in

Auckland, Christchurch and Wellington as well as a sheep farm the size of Watford, though I won't deny that this might have made it easier to accept Seth's proposal!

No, it was after Belinda and Franz left my room and I started to wonder whether it wasn't time I thought seriously about settling down. Okay, I'm still only twenty-six and I have a nice few bob in the bank so there's no reason why I shouldn't enjoy being young, free and single for a little time yet – despite all the heavy handed hints about settling down from my Mum who especially since my Dad was killed in that terrible rail crash four years ago can't wait to start a new career as a grannie!

And the fact is that Seth and I hit it off as soon as we were introduced by Billy Macfarlane, the very nice guy who runs your associate agency here in Auckland, at the party he threw to welcome me to New Zealand. It's been a pretty whirlwind courtship but he proposed after only six days after we met and my 'yes' came out so naturally that I'm sure it was the right answer to give him – it had better be because I'm already wearing a square cut diamond engagement ring with a stone as wide as a sixpence!

I'm also sure I'll miss all the glamour of showbiz even though I'm not giving up singing completely – that would be too sharp a break and fortunately Seth understands this – but for the most part as far as my career is concerned, I've been there, seen it and done it and I'm absolutely positive that I've made the right decision. So as your old mate

Englebert Humperdinck sings: 'Please release me, let me go!'
  All my love,
  Laurie

Wordlessly, Teddy put down the letter. He noticed that Marlene was standing next to him with an anxious look on her face.

'A penny for your thoughts,' she said as he slid his hand out and pinched one of the curvy cheeks of her delectable bottom.

'They're not worth it, love. I was only contemplating how I'd spend my time if I gave up this job,' he grunted. Marlene frowned as she bent down and planted a light kiss on his forehead.

'Teddy, what on earth are you talking about? I've never heard such nonsense,' she said angrily. 'You simply can't be seriously thinking of retirement. For heaven's sake, who would take over? There isn't anyone else at the agency with your experience. Anyhow, you're far too young to start sitting at home all day twiddling your thumbs or chewing the cud with all the old codgers at the golf club.'

He glanced up and smiled at her. 'Thanks for the vote of confidence. I wasn't actually planning to leave but this letter from Laurie made me wonder whether there isn't more to life than all this constant pressure. Here, read through it for yourself.'

Marlene picked up Laurie's letter and curled herself up on the black leather chesterfield to read through it. 'Huh, so you fucked her, Teddy and she wonders whether you've taken down my knickers yet, the cheeky cow! Still, I wish her luck and hope it all works out for her. I presume you are going to cancel her contract, aren't you?'

'Of course I am. There's rarely any point in keeping anyone on the books who doesn't want you to look after their interests.' Teddy heaved himself up and wandered across to her. 'Tell you what, call Allan at Godfrey's of London and ask him to send a whacking great bouquet by Interflora and book me a person-to-person call to her. You'd better ask for it to be made from my home number at about eight o'clock tonight because of the time difference. They're about eleven hours ahead of us in New Zealand.'

'Ah, you old softie,' she remarked as she scribbled Laurie's telephone number on her notepad. 'So all those stories about your being a tight-fisted old bastard aren't true, after all.'

Teddy looked at her indignantly. 'Who the hell has been saying I'm a—' Then he stopped and joined in her laughter as he realised that Marlene was merely teasing him. He sat down next to her and gave her a big cuddle.

'So it's just as well that I don't like hard men,' she remarked. As she eyed the tenting bulge in his trousers, she quickly added: 'Well, that's not entirely true, it depends on which part of them is hard.'

She placed her hand on his lap and squeezed the top of his straining shaft as she said in mock anger.

173

'Goodness me, what's brought all this on? Was it Laurie's letter? I'm sorry, Teddy Dixon, but if you think I'm going to be fucked by Carola Watforde or any other dyke so that you can get your rocks off watching us, you had better think again.'

'No, no, I promise you that the thought never crossed my mind,' he assured her as he unbuttoned her blouse and slipped his hand inside to squeeze one of her firm young breasts. She sighed and half-heartedly tried to move his hand away as she complained: 'Teddy, suppose someone came in, the door isn't locked, you know.'

'Then they would have a grandstand view of the hottest show in town,' he replied. Nevertheless he hauled himself up and scuttled over to lock the door. On his way back to her he pressed down the key on his telephone so that all calls would go through to Adrian Klein's office.

'There, now we won't be disturbed,' he added thickly. Marlene unzipped her skirt and revealed that she was wearing a cute frilly pair of silk panties of such fine material that Teddy could see the shadow of her bush and the outlines of her prominent pussy lips. She tugged down the skirt and stepped out of it.

'Now then, Marlene, let me show you that I'm a long way off retirement!' growled Teddy.

He ripped off his jacket and knelt before her. She arched her body upwards, allowing Teddy to pull down her panties to her ankles. He nuzzled his lips against her pussy, running the tip of his tongue all along her moistening crack while his fingers splayed open her outer love lips. Marlene shivered as he found the hardened nub of her clitty and he rolled his thumb around it while nibbling the sensitive flesh with his teeth.

'Teddy, you are naughty,' she murmured dreamily as his hands gripped her hips. His tongue probed between her rubbery love lips and when he began lapping inside her dripping honeypot, she felt herself begin to come. With a little squeal, she started to twist and turn and he had to hold her quivering soft body still so that he could keep his mouth pressed firmly against her delicious cunt.

He licked her out in slow, persistent strokes, kissing and sucking her cunny which sent her into raptures of delight. Then, with a gasp, Marlene suddenly climaxed and drenched her employer's face with a spray of cuntal juice as waves of ecstatic pleasure coursed through her.

Marlene sprawled on the luxurious leather of Teddy's notorious casting couch, pulled off her bra and lay back. Teddy tore off the rest of his clothes and mounted the gorgeous girl. She grabbed hold of his rampant truncheon, giving a few rubs on the palpitating shaft with evident satisfaction as she held his cock tightly while he bore down upon her and guided his purple capped prick between her yielding pussy lips.

'Go on then, Teddy, fuck the arse off me!' panted Marlene. He pressed home, cramming his cock inside her love channel until their pubic hairs were entwined. He stayed still for a moment and then he slid his hands under her bottom and clasped her jiggling bum cheeks as he whispered through gritted teeth: 'Here we go, darling, we're off to fuckland!'

Teddy pulled back and then started to slew his throbbing stiffstander forward and backwards though he was careful always to keep his helmet inside her juicy quim. He breathed deeply as his cock plunged into the clinging grooves of her tight young cunt. He drove in and out so powerfully that his balls slapped against her thighs. Marlene yelped with delight as an electric little series of spasms raced through her body. Teddy's cock started to tremble inside her saturated depths and then he shuddered with rapture, creaming her cunt with gushes of hot, sticky jism which dripped down onto the couch from her sopping slit.

Marlene wriggled to one side as he flopped down beside her and then slid down to the floor. With some difficulty she hauled herself up and began to dress.

'Come on, boss, you'd better get your clothes on as well. We've both got work to do,' she said briskly. Teddy watched her pull up her skirt as he ran his hands through his hair and then nodded his agreement. 'Quite right, Marlene. God knows how I'd manage without you. Let's face it, you're not only a most marvellous fuck but the most reliable, efficient secretary I've ever employed. You know which telephone calls I really want to take, your short-hand

and typing are first class and you keep all the files up to date.'

'Why, thank you, Teddy, I couldn't put it better myself, she beamed happily as he continued: 'And you'll see how I appreciate your work in your salary cheque next month – which reminds me that this afternoon I must give Eddie Sinclair the details about all the summer staff bonuses. We haven't had a bad year so everyone will have a few bob more in their pay packets for the holiday season from young Garry in the postroom to yours truly.

'And I can tell you now that there'll also be something special for those members of staff on my personal order of merit – that's a far shorter list. Only you, Adrian Klein, Mark Matthews and Annabel, Carola Watforde's personal assistant are on it so far,' added Teddy Dixon, walking back to his desk as he buttoned up his shirt.

He sat down heavily and opened up the latest file of press clippings on Bernie Harwin, the raunchy-voiced West Indian singer whose bedroom exploits regularly filled the pages of the tabloid press. He let out a deep sigh and remarked with some asperity as he read the latest *Bernie Bedded Me* headline: 'I see that Bernie's made page three of the *Daily Sketch* again. What are we going to do about him, Marlene? He's not a bad chap but the problem with Bernie is that when he undoes his flies, his brains fall out.'

'Well isn't that true of most men?' enquired Marlene with an impudent smile. Teddy frowned but, as he admitted to Adrian Klein later that afternoon, he found it impossible to find the words to contradict her as his sensuous secretary pulled up a chair, crossed her shapely legs and flipped open her notebook, her pencil poised, ready to take his dictation.

'I think I'll have to speak to Adrian about Bernie and see if we can curtail some of his high jinks,' said Teddy eventually. 'Short of chopping off his dick, though, I don't suppose there's very much we can do.'

'Sounds a bit drastic and anyway, it might affect his voice, I don't see Bernie's fans being so keen on him as a soprano,' said Marlene drily and Teddy pursed his lips and said: 'Then we'll just have to think of something else. Meanwhile, I'll get Adrian Klein in here this afternoon and we'll hear what he has to say about it.

Coincidentally, as he spoke, Adrian Klein's name was also featured in a conversation between Mademoiselle Melissa and Gigi Baroja in the bedroom of the former's plush apartment in Brechin Place, South Kensington – although, had Adrian been there, he may not have liked much of what he would have heard.

After her angry outburst the previous evening, Gigi had telephoned Melissa and asked her if she could spend the night on her sofa. When Melissa agreed to this request, she packed an overnight bag and, after leaving a message for him at *La Miraggio*, she stormed out of Adrian's flat. Less than an hour later she was sitting on her friend's sofa in her nightdress, sipping a glass of chilled white wine with the pretty astrologer.

Gigi recounted the story of her argument with Adrian, in blissful ignorance of the fact that only a few hours before, her lover's gleaming circumcised cock had been sheathed inside Melissa's juicy cunt. Although she was tempted to reveal this to Gigi (as she had earlier confided to Adrian, she was still slightly miffed at the fact that the feisty half-Spanish girl had fucked a boy she had been going steady with last summer), Melissa decided to stay clear of this lovers' tiff.

'Bloody men are all the same, my love,' commented Melissa as she refilled their glasses. 'And you must never forget that Adrian is a Scorpio, which is a "water" sign. This means he will be naturally secretive, although he is also emotional and passionate. On the other hand, it's no surprise that you have an occasional clash with Adrian. Your zodiac sign is Aries and you possess all its characteristics of vigour, aggressiveness and strong sexuality for Aries is, of course, the sign of the Ram.

'However, this doesn't mean to say that you can't live happily together,' she added hastily as Gigi looked down gloomily into her lap. 'And even I must admit that astrology is not an exact science. Why, a medieval English astrologer named Edmund Bartholomew wrote that Ariens have crooked hairy bodies, while I know several girls who would kill for such a lovely figure as yours. Such large firm breasts and such a nice flat tummy! So don't be too bothered about Adrian. When all's said and done, there are plenty more fish in the sea.'

Gigi raised her head and glanced gratefully at her friend. 'Thanks, but I don't know why we girls care so much about men,' she remarked thoughtfully. 'I truly believe that they're often more bother than they're worth.'

'Now I don't know whether I can fully agree with you about that,' said Melissa, with a roguish twinkle in her eyes. 'I bet you and Adrian have a great deal of fun between the sheets.'

'Well, sure, and I'm not saying that he doesn't excite me in bed. I will say that he knows that just sticking his cock inside me isn't enough – *anyone* can do that. He knows I like him to hover over me and let his stiffie slide up and down over my breasts and belly before rubbing against my clit.'

'M'mm, that sounds like a nice turn-on,' said Melissa, moving across from her chair to sit next to Gigi on the sofa. 'Does he then slam his shaft straight into your cunt?'

'Oh no! Give him his due, Adrian is more sophisticated than that,' replied Gigi with the ghost of a smile. 'He knows I prefer him to insert his cock a little at a time, so first he opens my cunny lips with his fingers and slides his helmet in between them, and then he pulls it out as a kind of tease. The feeling of the ridge of his knob rubbing against the entrance to my pussy is really terrific. Then he puts his prick inside a little further and then goes out again and each time he goes in deeper. The tension quickly builds up and I'm well juiced up when he starts pumping his prick in and out of my quim.'

'You'll miss his thick tool tonight,' commented Melissa with a soft throaty chuckle, sliding her arm around Gigi's shoulders. To her delight, the other girl did not move away but indeed snuggled her head against her shoulder as she gave a little snort of annoyance and replied: 'Yes, maybe I will, but then I can always bring myself off if I start to feel randy. I always keep a dildo in my overnight bag. Anyway, the way I feel just now, frankly I'd rather do without any sex rather than think about Adrian's cock.'

'Hey, that sounds a little bit drastic, Gigi. It doesn't have to be like that, you know,' murmured Melissa as she dropped her hand to stroke Gigi's warm knee with her long fingers. 'The tongue can be just as powerful an instrument as the penis.'

The dark-haired girl pondered on this remark for a few moments as she decided whether or not to accept this implied, if unspoken, invitation to share Melissa's bed. Then she raised her head and replied softly: 'Maybe so, Melissa, but it depends on whose tongue is doing the licking.'

'Ah, that's a very fair point and, with respect, I doubt even Adrian could bring you off as well as another girl. So many men seem incapable of realising the subtle nuances of eating pussy, observed Melissa as she let her hand stray higher and higher towards the top of Gigi's thighs.

'Perhaps you're right, but I don't care whose lips

are kissing my pussy so long as it's someone I like, said Gigi, parting her thighs to let the tips of Melissa's fingers run down the length of her moistening slit. 'Shall I tell you how I like to be sucked off?'

'Oh yes, please do, I'd love to know,' said Melissa eagerly. Gigi gave a tiny yelp as she felt Melissa's knuckle rub along the length of her moistening crack and then went on: 'Well, whoever's going down on me should start with a light little nibble on my clitty and then should cover my whole cunt from my clitty to my bum with long, slurping kisses. I like to be lifted too – my bottom half, anyway – so my bottom can be cradled while I'm being eaten. What always sends me to heaven is if I'm finger-fucked while being licked out. That never seems to fail. In fact sometimes I get too wet and so it's nice to stop for a bit to let me dry out a little and then go back to finish me off.'

Melissa now rubbed her palms against Gigi's damp pussy lips and nibbled her ear as she breathed: 'Let me pleasure your pussy, Gigi. Take off your nightie and we'll make love right now.'

Although it had been several years – indeed, not since her friend Alice had climbed into her bed when they were both fifth formers at Greystokes Academy near Basingstoke – since Gigi had participated in any lesbian activity, the idea of being sucked off by her ravishingly pretty friend now appealed to her. As Melissa moved her hand away from Gigi's pussy, she stood up and pulled off her nightie to stand naked in front of her.

Gigi looked at the other girl's proud jutting breasts and the neatly trimmed thatch of curly brown hair between her thighs. She felt herself being so swiftly aroused that she panted with passion. She raised her arms and Melissa tugged her frilly short nightie over Gigi's tousled dark, silky mane.

With their arms clasped around each other's waists, the two friends walked purposefully into the bedroom. After Melissa had laid Gigi down tenderly upon the crisp white sheets, she then placed a pillow under the quivering girl's peachy bum cheeks. Gigi parted her legs so that Melissa could smooth her hands up and down the insides of her thighs.

Their lips locked together in a deep, passionate kiss. Gigi whimpered as Melissa's probing tongue played around her mouth while her hands cupped and squeezed her jutting breasts. They were topped with luscious strawberry red nipples which stood out at rakish angles to each other.

Gigi moaned again as Melissa's mouth moved downwards to suck her erect titties, moving her head from side to side as she playfully lashed her tongue around each nipple in turn. The flat of her hand rubbed insistently on the furry nest of pubic hair around Gigi's protruding pussy lips, which opened like petals to her gentle touch.

'Now I'm going to kiss your lovely cunt and suck your pussy till you come in my face,' announced Melissa in a low voice. She lowered her head and pressed her lips against Gigi's moistening bush while she ran a questing finger all along her slippery crack.

'Oooh! Oooh! OOOOH!' Gigi cried out as she felt her clitty pop out of its hood. Melissa opened her pussy lips with her thumbs and started lapping up the first flow of tangy love juice. 'Yes, I'm almost there! Finish me off with your tongue, you naughty girl!'

Melissa buried her mouth in the wet padding of Gigi's silky pussy hair. The hugely aroused girl wrapped her thighs around Melissa's head as her salacious tongue whipped back and forth, up and down, boring deeper and deeper inside her tender pussy. She feasted with lascivious fervour on Gigi's soaking cunt, gulping down the cuntal cream as she attacked her stiff little clitty which trembled and twitched as her teeth lightly nipped the twitching flesh.

Then Gigi began to shiver and shake as she clutched at Melissa's head and screamed with joy as she climaxed. Melissa's fingers plunged in and out of her tingling quim and her hips bucked and she flooded her friend's face with a flood of feminine cum.

Gigi lay back with her eyes closed and a beaming smile of satisfaction on her face but Melissa now clambered up beside her and murmured: 'Hey, don't go to sleep, what about my turn?'

'Sorry, darling,' apologised Gigi as she heaved herself upwards and wrapped her arms round

Melissa and gave her a huge hug. 'What would you like me to do for you?'

Melissa licked her lips and then swivelled her body round to open the drawer of her bedside table. Then she hauled herself back into Gigi's embrace holding a pink plastic tube shaped like an erect penis, complete with a mushroom helmet and raised veins running along its length.

'Have you seen one of these new kind of dildoes before?' Melissa enquired as she smoothed her hand over the flesh-textured tube before passing it over to Gigi. 'A girl-friend of mine sent me this little beauty called the Swashbuckler from New York. These vibrators are all the rage. It's not just an ordinary comforter but is electrically powered. It quivers inside your cunny when you switch it on.'

'How fascinating,' said Gigi as she closely examined the thick shaft. When she snapped on the switch at the base of the imitation cock, she looked with amused interest as the tube vibrated in her grasp.

'Don't switch it on till it's inside my cunt,' instructed Melissa as she pulled the pillow from underneath Gigi's bottom and stuffed it under her own rounded bum cheeks. She parted her thighs and, with her hand on the glossy curls around her pussy, she extended her forefinger and began to caress her clitty as she went on: 'Ahh, that's feels good, but it would be much nicer if you helped to bring me off.'

She lay back and Gigi laid the vibrator down on

the bed as she rolled herself on top of Melissa. The two girls pressed their soft, warm bodies together as their lips met and they tongued out each other's mouths. Gigi's hand pressed down on Melissa's moist mound, letting her fingers delve inside the thatch of lustrous bush of brown cunny hair. Melissa let out a low moan and then began a rhythmic panting as her lover stoked along the length of her crack. When Gigi slid a knuckle inside her cunt she pushed herself upwards, arching her back and wriggling her hips as if to signal the questing finger inside her quim to penetrate more deeply into her tingling slit. Then Gigi rubbed the protruding clitty with her thumb as she bent her head forwards, tossing back the hair from her face with her free hand as she kissed Melissa's pussy, inhaling the pungent aroma which wafted into her nostrils.

Gigi paused for a moment to draw breath and Melissa groaned: 'Ohhh! Ohhh! Don't stop! Lick me out with that gorgeous tongue, darling, and then fuck me with the dildo!'

Obediently, Gigi took hold of the plastic imitation penis and slid the pink shaft between the yielding lips of Melissa's love channel. Although this was the first time she had used such a gadget on another girl, she slid the instrument in and out of Melissa's cunt with great skill, rubbing the knob firmly against her clitty at every stroke.

'Now switch it on,' Melissa gasped. Immediately Gigi flicked the button, she began trembling like a leaf as the vibrator began to buzz. Melissa let out a tiny scream of happiness as the throbbing shaft pulsated inside her squelchy cunt, while Gigi clambered up on her knees to straddle her writhing body and leaned forward to tweak Melissa's elongated crimson nipples between her fingers.

Then Melissa pulled out the vibrator from her honeypot and threw down the buzzing dildo as she pushed the dark haired girl's head back towards her groin. Understanding her friend's needs, Gigi thrust her tongue into the hot wet crack of her cunt, licking and lapping like fury as she slid her hands to clutch at Melissa's delicious bum cheeks.

'Yes! Yes! Yes! Ream out my pussy!' cried Melissa. Gigi's tongue flashed unerringly around the grooves of her sopping cunny, which was now gushing out a deluge of love juice. With each tonguing, her pussy seemed to open wider as she lifted her buttocks high off the pillow. Gigi pressed herself even more tightly against the quivering girl as she buried her face between Melissa's thighs.

Their movements accelerated and Melissa's clitty now swelled up like a plum. The lovely girl bucked and twisted under Gigi's relentless sucking and then spasms of sheer ecstasy racked her beautiful young body as, with a tremendous shudder, she screamed out her delight. An exquisite orgasm careered through her in a prolonged series of pulsing thrills, running from the base of her belly to the very tips of her hard, rubbery nipples and her strong, shapely limbs.

Gigi crawled upwards and rested her head on Melissa's soft, heaving breasts and they lay silent for a while until Melissa picked up the vibrator and waggled it in front of Gigi's face as she exclaimed: 'My God, that was an amazing, absolutely incredible one, darling. Would you like me to fuck you now with the Swashbuckler?'

'Thanks, but I think I'll pass just for the moment,' replied Gigi faintly as Melissa ran the ribbed shaft slowly down her shoulder.

'Okay, lovee, it's up to you,' Melissa shrugged. 'But if you fancy having a real-life cock to play with, I can always ring up Andy Whyte, a good-looking young chap who lives across the road in Cranley Mews. Andy's only twenty-eight but he's already been written about in the *Financial Times* as an up-and-coming big man in the City.'

'Never mind about being big in the City, how about being big where it really matters?' asked Gigi with a giggle but Melissa took her question seriously and answered: 'About average, I'd say but, more importantly, Andy's a good fuck. He knows what to play on his instrument and that is what's important, isn't it?'

'M'mm, the idea does appeal, but I've never met the guy before,' said Gigi as she considered the matter. 'But sex with a stranger – how naughty!'

'Well, why not, duckie? So long as a girl is discriminating, what's wrong with it? Now I don't mean flashing your knickers if you're waiting at the bus-stop after work and some nerd with bad breath in a Ford Anglia asks if he can give you a lift. No, I'm talking about spontaneous rumpy-pumpy like, for instance, after a guy at a party takes your fancy.

'This happened to me at a reception at a posh West End hotel last week which was given by his gallery for the artist Tommy Colchester, who's an old chum of mine from way back when we were at primary school together. Pete was there with his current bimbo – huh, talk about having one night stands, Tommy's had more pussy than I've had hot dinners, but that's neither here nor there. True, there were quite a few fairies at the party but there was one man at the party, a reporter from the diary column of the *Guardian* who, when Tommy introduced us, locked eyes with me and in that very moment, I knew I wanted him to fuck me. His name was Jimmy Ward and he had also been affected by that magic reaction because after we had talked together avidly for about ten minutes, he excused himself and said he would phone in his copy to the paper and see me back at the party in about fifteen minutes.

'Well, I guessed that Jimmy wasn't just spending this time calling his newspaper but was also busy at the reception desk booking a room for the rest of the day. So I wasn't completely surprised when soon after he returned, he suggested that he and I left the party to go somewhere more private for a quiet drink.

'Jimmy guided me to the lift and pressed the button to the sixth floor. There were no other passengers and while we sped upwards, we exchanged a quick hug and kiss. Then as we got out, he took the room key from his pocket. I burst into a fit of giggles when I noticed that the desk clerk had given him room sixty-nine. When I explained what had made me laugh, Jimmy's eyes twinkled and he said: "Do you think he deliberately gave me that key?"

' "I don't know," I replied as he unlocked the door. "But if he was trying to suggest something to us, I'm game if you are."

'He growled his approval as he swept me into his arms. I grabbed his cock through his trousers and rubbed his shaft up and down. We kissed again and he forced his tongue between my lips but I needed to go to the loo and so I whispered as I pulled myself out of his arms: "Don't be impatient, I'll be back in a moment."

'I undressed in the bathroom and came back stark naked. Jimmy began to stutter something as I sank to my knees and tugged down his zipper. He was reduced to silence as I slid my hand through the slit in his boxer shorts and grabbed hold of his big thick cock. It felt so hard and smooth when I brought it out that I started to gobble on his knob straightaway.

'Jimmy gurgled as he clasped my head in his hands while I opened my mouth and drew as much of his cock inside my mouth as possible. Then I bobbed my head back and forth on his palpitating prick while I played with his balls as he began tearing off his clothes.

'When he was naked we moved over to the bed and, still with his twitching tool between my lips, I climbed over him and lowered my pussy to his mouth. He lapped beautifully on my dripping pussy lips and soon we both came inside each other's mouths. I swallowed down all his tasty spunk.

'Jimmy continued to frig me with his tongue while I held on to his still semi-erect cock. Surprisingly quickly, it began to swell up again until it was back up to its former proud stiffness. The feel of his purple knob bulging in my hand made me tremble all over with lust and my slippery little cunny was now wet through and through.

' "Come on, I'm dying for a good fucking and a rock-hard cock like yours will be just the job," I hissed in his ear. Thankfully, I didn't have too long to wait for this much-needed relief because as soon as I let go of Jimmy's throbbing tadger and rolled myself over onto my back, he climbed up on top of me. He parted my pussy lips as he guided his hot velvet helmet into the inviting red chunk.

'Jimmy thrust his thick prick way up my juicy cunt, pistoning in and out with lovely long strokes. He had all the skill of an older man with the stamina and eagerness of a teenage boy. We fucked away like crazy and I was in the seventh heaven as I turned my head to look in the big mirror on the wall and watch his glistening shaft squelch in and out of my juicy love channel. The sensations in my quim were driving me insane and I started to come again and again, coating his cock with love juice as he pumped backwards and forwards. I wound my thighs round his waist as his jerking cock sent ripples of pleasure all through me. I climaxed just as he began to shoot his load, sending a flood of hot, creamy jism into my cunt.

'We slumped down together and when Jimmy had recovered he fucked me once more, this time doggy-style and then we went out for dinner at *La Garonne*, this new French restaurant in the King's Road. Lovely food, but I felt a bit guilty as it was very expensive. Honestly, my darling, poor Jimmy got little change from a tenner though we did have an aperitif and a good bottle of wine with the meal.'

Melissa stopped and giggled as she remembered how much she enjoyed that heady encounter as Gigi gave a little smile and remarked: 'Did you say that Jimmy was a journalist? He didn't have to pay, you silly billy, he must have put it on his expenses.'

'Do you think so? Oh good, I like to be taken out but even though the food was wonderful, I would have enjoyed the dinner more if the restaurant hadn't been so pricey,' Melissa replied as she picked up the telephone.

'Now then, shall I call Andy Whyte or not?'

Gigi ran her fingers over her lips as she considered the matter. 'Well, I wouldn't say no if he's a decent sort of fella. Listen, Melissa, I loved our little session but I'd never give up having a nice big prick to play with. I dare say the Andy guy would be happy to hear that even if he doesn't have the biggest cock in the world.'

'Fine, I'll see if he's in, but there's no need to worry about the size of Andy's shaft,' said Melissa as she dialled his number. 'He knows how to use it and that's what's most important. After all, you don't have the longest tongue I've ever had up my crack, Gigi, but you did things to my clit that no-one's done for a long time.'

She waited impatiently for Andy to answer. She was about to put down the phone when Gigi heard a click on the line and Melissa said: 'Hello, is that you, Andy? It's Melissa here, did I get you out of bed? No, but out of the bath! I'm so sorry, m'dear, one of these days they'll invent a telephone which will play a recorded message to callers to ring back whenever's convenient or let them leave a message on tape. Anyhow, I don't think you'll have minded being pulled out of the shower when I tell you why I've called. You haven't met my friend Gigi, have you? She's a beautiful girl and she's staying the night with me. We're already in bed but we can't get to sleep and I wondered if you'd care to tuck us up.'

Melissa burst out giggling and then went on: 'Now, now, you naughty boy, I said *tuck* but come to think of it, what you said doesn't sound like a bad idea either. What was that? Oh, I'm sure Gigi won't mind at all. Hold on, I'll ask her.' She turned to Gigi and said: 'Andy says he'd love to come over but could we help him out by sampling a couple of bottles of wine? He has to order the booze for some important shindig his firm is giving next week

193

and he'd like us to help him choose which wine they should serve.'

'Great, tell Andy my palate it at his disposal,' Gigi called out. Melissa grinned as she said: 'Did you hear that, Andy? Yes, well play your cards right and who knows what Gigi might want to taste! Okay then, I'll get some glasses out and we'll see you in about twenty minutes.'

The girls slipped on their panties under the short, frilly nighties and then they went back into the living room to wait for Andy Whyte. He arrived only a quarter of an hour later laden with a large carrier bag under each arm. Melissa ushered him in and introduced the good-looking financier to Gigi, who was sitting in a low chair.

'How do you do,' he said, looking appreciatively through his clear blue eyes at the inviting swell of the pretty girl's breasts at the open top of her nightie.

'Fine, thank you,' she smiled back seductively at his craggily handsome suntanned face. 'I understand that Melissa and I are going to help you decide which wines you should buy for some important company function. We'll do our best but, speaking for myself, I like a glass of good wine but I'm no connoisseur.'

'But those are perfect qualifications,' exclaimed Andy as he returned her smile and placed a bottle of red wine on the table. 'Would you mind if we started with a red? I didn't have the two bottles of white in the fridge so Melissa's popped them into the freezer for a bit.'

Gigi shook her head and declared sweetly as she picked up the bottle: 'Not in the slightest, especially a red as light and fruity as a '63 *Vin de Pays des Pyrenees-Orientales.*'

'Hey, I thought you said you weren't a connoisseur,' said Melissa accusingly as she came in from the kitchen with a corkscrew in her hand.

'Honestly, I'm no expert.' Gigi protested. 'It's just that my Dad was a wine buff and he taught me early to appreciate the difference between the good stuff and plonk.' Andy opened the bottle and poured out glasses of the wine for himself and the two girls. He lifted his arm and clinked his tumbler against Gigi's as Melissa murmured: 'Cheers! Here's to us.' Perhaps their previous exertions had made them thirsty for both Melissa and Gigi gulped down the delicious wine in less than half a dozen swift swallows.

'M'mm, what a scrumptious tipple, I love the fresh, fruity taste,' said Gigi enthusiastically. 'I'll give this lovely gargle eight of ten.'

'It is good, isn't it,' Andy agreed. He looked across to Melissa, who was looking thoughtfully into her glass, and asked her: 'What's your verdict, ma'am? Eight out of ten or do you think that's too high a mark?'

'No, it's really superb, marvellously soft and plummy and very drinkable,' said Melissa, smacking her lips as she held out her glass for a refill.

But Andy delved into his bag and brought out a second bottle which he opened and poured out into their goblets. 'Now try this bottle – I won't say from where it comes, though I'll tell you now that it isn't French.'

The girls studied the deep, richly coloured wine and then, after a hesitant sip, they downed their glasses enthusiastically. Melissa looked at Andy in admiration and shook her head saying: 'No, you're trying to fool us, Andy, it was far too good to come from Italy or Spain. Come on, own up, this was a chateau-bottled vintage, wasn't it?'

'I'm not so sure,' said Gigi thoughtfully. 'I agree that its a wonderful wine, lots of super, luscious fruit with a good bite to it. But you mustn't be snobby about wines that don't come from France, darling. It's not unknown for some of the chateaux to mix Algerian plonk with their own wines to make them go further, and lots of the Italian and Spanish wineries produce some excellent bottles. I wouldn't be surprised if this one comes from Italy – is it a Valpolicella, by any chance?'

'Well done! Your dad must have had an attentive pupil when he gave you lessons about wine,' exclaimed Andy admiringly. He poured out a tumbler for himself and refilled the girls' glasses. 'To be exact, you're drinking a 1965 Vignotti Casterna Valpolicella. I have to admit that I raised my eyebrows when the wine merchant recommended it because it wasn't French and I thought that this was the sort of stuff you drank with a pizza in a beach cafe in Rimini. How wrong can you get?'

They finished the bottle and then Gigi suggested they try one of the bottles of white wine which were lying in the freezer. First there was the bottle of French red to finish and by the time Andy popped open the bottle of a delicious though expensive 1961 Cabernet Sauvignon, all three imbibers were, to say the least, very pleasantly relaxed.

And so when Andy went out to the toilet, Melissa leaned over to Gigi and muttered: 'Well, darling, what do you think about him? You have first refusal but, in all fairness, I should say here and now that I'm in the mood for a good fuck if you don't fancy having Andy's cock up your crack.'

'Oh, but I do,' Gigi replied somewhat thickly, her face a little flushed from the effects of her enthusiastic wine-tasting. 'There's no need to squabble about who goes first, though. He's a very nice boy, so why don't we give him the pleasure of fucking us both together?'

Melissa kissed her on the cheek. 'What a splendid idea,' she replied as she rose a trifle unsteadily from her chair. 'I want to rub a little cold cream round my nookie, so I suggest that you start getting Andy in the mood and when I come back I'll join in the fun and, all being well, we'll all finish up in bed together.'

She tottered out to the bedroom and when Andy returned he saw that Gigi was by herself. He asked where Melissa had gone. 'It was too hot in here for her so she's just making herself a little more comfortable,'

Gigi explained as she pulled her nightdress to and fro as if fanning her body and added: 'It *is* very warm tonight, don't you think? Would you mind very much if I took off my nightie?'

The burly young man shook his head and then looked at her with a twinkle in his eye. 'So long as I can do the same,' he commented. Gigi took a step forward until there were only inches between them and, crossing her hands, pulled off her nightie over her head, treating Andy to a close, unconcealed view of her stunning bare breasts which jiggled so temptingly in front of him.

Andy drew a sharp breath and for a moment stood stock still as he drank in the sight of the gorgeous girl, who was naked except for a tiny pair of frilly white panties which barely covered the bulging mound of her pussy. Then his face moved forward to meet hers and their lips locked together in a long, impassioned kiss. He stretched out his hands and cupped her beautifully rounded breasts, running his palms across the erect, jutting nipples as their bodies pressed closely together. He breathed heavily with undisguised lust. A low purr of pleasure escaped from Gigi's throat when she felt his fast-thickening erection throbbing through the material of his trousers against her belly.

The electrically charged sexual atmosphere now intensified further when the gleaming nude body of Melissa emerged from the bedroom. When she saw her friends clinging together as they rocked gently from side to side in their rapturous embrace, she went across and knelt down beside them.

At first they appeared not to be aware of her presence as, with her own glorious breasts heaving sensually, Melissa slid up her arms between the aroused couple. With deft expertise, the fingers of her left hand rolled down Gigi's tiny panties to her ankles and smoothed their way across the panting girl's moistening hairy mound to caress the pouting pussy lips. Then, with her right hand, she unzipped Andy's trousers and inserted her fingers, rubbing sinuously against the protruding swell of his throbbing tool which was severely straining the cotton of his Y-fronts.

Andy moaned as Gigi unbuttoned his shirt. Melissa now took her hand off Gigi's cunt to pull off Andy's shoes and socks and then unbuckle his belt and tug down his trousers. Now all three were stark naked and when Andy pulled his mouth away from Gigi's sweet kiss and opened his eyes to the sensuous sight of the two nude beauties, a pearl of pre-cum glistened in the tiny eye of his organ. He was forced to take a series of deep breaths to stop himself spurting his spunk into Melissa's soft warm hand which was delicately sliding up and down the veiny length of his rigid, pulsing shaft.

He closed his eyes again and nodded quickly when he heard Melissa murmur: 'Would you like to fuck us, Andy? Then Gigi and I will take you to bed, you lucky boy.'

Andy's tongue slithered into Gigi's wet mouth and his hands continued to caress the smooth white hillocks of her breasts. Melissa climbed to her feet and, with Andy's stiff cock still held tightly in her grasp, she pulled him forward and the three of them stumbled hastily into the bedroom.

They crashed down onto the bed and Andy lay upon his back, his hands roving over the shapely bottoms of both girls as they knelt on each side of him. Melissa turned her head and slotted her wet lips over the uncapped pink helmet of his cock while he felt Gigi's teeth nibble sensuously at his earlobe. In a low voice, husky with lust she whispered: 'I want you to eat my pussy as I diddle Melissa's cunt while she sucks you off. Won't that be nice?' With a flourish she straddled Andy's inert body, swinging her luscious bum cheeks over his face. She leaned down towards his groin and began lapping at his tightening ballsack while she lowered her sopping pussy to his lips.

Andy could hardly believe that this scenario was real and that he was not going to suddenly wake up in his own single bed with only an aching stiff penis for company. But then he moaned with pleasure as Melissa bobbed her head up and down his palpitating prick. When he ran his tongue along the length of Gigi's crack, from her puckered little rear-dimple to the pouting rose-pink lips of her cunt, he knew that he was not dreaming after all. He was indeed eating Gigi's pussy while both she and a second delectable girl busied themselves in palating his cock and balls.

'Aaah, that's divine, Andy,' yelped Gigi as,

transferring her attention from his scrotum, she raised herself up and moved Melissa's right leg over Andy's thigh so that the trembling girl was sitting in front of her.

'Now flick my clitty with your tongue, there's a good boy,' she went on. Gigi lifted her hips slightly to give Andy more room to dart his tongue inside her cunny lips. Then she carefully lowered herself downwards and, with her face pressed against Melissa's luscious backside, she separated the rounded buttocks with her nose and licked around the tiny wrinkled bum-hole while her right arm snaked around Melissa's hips to jam two fingers inside her juicy honeypot.

'Oooh! You wicked girl, what are you doing to me?' cried out Melissa, as she lasciviously wriggled her beautiful peachy bottom from side to side. Gigi frigged her cunt, sliding her fingers rhythmically in and out of Melissa's tingling wet love channel while at the same time inserting the tip of her tongue inside the pouting circlet of her anus.

The lewd trio writhed in a voluptuous paradise of erotic sensation and, perhaps not surprisingly, Andy was the first to reach a climax. 'I'm coming! I'm coming!' he breathlessly panted. 'Keep sucking, keep sucking, don't stop now . . . aaaah, aaaah, aaaah,' as, with a final jerk of his hips, he shot a stream of sticky spunk into her waiting mouth. Melissa kneaded his balls and milked his cock of his creamy jism as she gulped down his emission, eagerly licking up every last droplet as she swirled her wet tongue over the shivering smooth-skinned helmet of his twitching tool.

Then it was Melissa's turn to orgasm. She caught her breath and her body stiffened as she came over Gigi's fingers, coating them with cuntal cream which dripped down onto Gigi's waiting extended tongue as she too spent profusely. Andy was hard-pressed to swallow the deluge of love juice which gushed out of her saturated cunny as his cock began to shrink and his knob disappeared under the cover of his foreskin.

This was viewed with horror by both girls, whose appetites were still not fully satisfied. They vied with each other to tease Andy's cock up again, frigging his soft shaft and sucking on his wrinkled ballsack in a vain attempt to make his obstinate member stand to attention.

'We could try an old West Country remedy I heard about when I was at school in the wilds of South Devon,' said Gigi as she slicked her hand up and down Andy's recalcitrant shaft. 'It would involve sticking the handle of a small brush up his arse.'

'H'mm, I've got a solid wooden hand-brush but the handle might be a bit thick,' said Melissa pensively. But before Gigi could reply, Andy hurriedly eased himself off the bed and informed his bed-mates that he was going to open a new bottle of wine for them to try. He walked out briskly into the living-room.

'Great, but don't you have any more, Andy, or

you'll never be able to get it up again tonight,' warned Gigi. Andy shouted back: 'Don't worry, I'll just watch you two knock back this excellent '59 Blanc de Blancs.'

He came back with two full glasses on a tray and the girls reached out and clinked their glasses together. 'Here's to our favourite cock, may it quickly recover all its strength,' suggested Melissa with a giggle. Gigi winked back at her and said: 'With the operative word being *quickly* because my poor pussy is getting so hungry for cock, I'll have to ask you to lend me the Swashbuckler if we can't manage to bring Andy's prick up to scratch. Is that okay?

'Sure it is, you're very welcome to borrow my vibrator, but think of it as a last resort. After all, we've yet to try out your plan with the brush handle.' Melissa sipped the golden-coloured wine and said to Andy: 'Nothing wrong with this stuff, either. A mite dry for my taste but lots of people will love it.'

'Yes, it's very good, although if it's a '59 you'll have to pay quite a lot even if you buy a couple of cases,' remarked Gigi. She put down her half empty glass. 'Frankly, I doubt if you would get away with paying under a pound per bottle though as it's your company which is footing the bill, perhaps that doesn't matter.'

'Oh yes it does!' he replied instantly with a wry smile. 'If I can bring in the booze bill under budget it'll be a feather in my cap, and I could do with that at the moment because I did something very silly last Saturday.'

'Such as what, Andy? Did you fuck the managing director's wife?' asked Gigi as she swigged down the rest of her wine.

'Funny you should think of such a thing, love. I'll answer that question in a minute. No, I did something much worse, I beat him at golf. Mr Elliott isn't the best loser in the world, so I badly need to earn some plus points. He'll soon be calculating what wage rises he'll be offering us next year.'

Melissa raised her eyebrows and commented: 'Tsk, tsk, tsk, I'm very surprised at you, Andy! I would have thought you would have had more sense.' He held up his hands and accepted the rebuke with a heavy sigh, saying: 'Sure, but my problem is that I'm a better golfer than he is, but not good enough to lose deliberately without showing that I wasn't trying! I thought I might get away with it at the start because he hit a good flukey drive at the first hole, but his game soon went to pieces and he started to curse and be bloody rude to his caddy. Honestly, it's as well we weren't playing in a foursome or I'd have been even more embarrassed.

'I tried to make light of it and when his chip shot landed in a bunker I said to him: "Never mind, sir. You know the old adage, unlucky shots come in groups of three. Unfortunately the fourth unlucky shot marks the start of the next group of three!" '

'But he didn't see the joke,' observed Gigi and

Andy went on: 'Yes, you could say that. By the time we reached the twelfth hole, I'd tried as hard as I could but I was still six up. So at best I had to tie the hole so as not to win the game, though I would have still had to stop myself winning any of the remaining holes just to let him draw the sodding match. That wouldn't have been so bad. If he'd insisted on a tie-breaker, even if I weren't able to let him win it, at least he would have only lost narrowly. But what happens? I put the ball on the tee, and just glanced up and swung my number one iron and guess what, the ball landed up—'

'Straight into the hole,' Melissa speculated.

He shook his head sadly and went on: 'No, I wish it had have done because at least that would have given me some satisfaction if that had happened. I've never managed a hole in one except on the putting green even though I've been playing regularly since I was fifteen. But of course I'd hit the ball so sweetly that, although it's one of the longest holes on the course, and I'd never reached the green in one shot before, blow me down, there was my ball resting not more than three inches from the hole!'

Andy gave a rueful chuckle as he continued: 'Tony Jacklin couldn't have disguised a deliberate miss at that range so I didn't even bother to try. I knocked the ball in and we walked back to the clubhouse in silence. I wondered if I could put him in a better mood if I told him a good joke, so I asked him if he'd heard the one about the middle-aged lawyer who put an advert in the lonely hearts column of a magazine saying that he was a wealthy professional man who was looking for a girl to marry.

' "No, but I suppose you're going to tell it to me," he said grumpily and I thought, well, I've started so I'll finish. Do you know the story, by the way? I thought it was very funny.' When the girls shook their heads he grinned and carried on: 'Well, he had a reply from this lady and they got on like a house on fire, so much so that the girl was bewildered when the chap said they had better finish seeing each other.

' "Why is that?' she asked him. "I thought we got along together very well." He said: "We do, but I must be honest with you. I want to marry a virgin and last night you told me you've already been married three times."

' "But believe it or not, I'm still a virgin," she insisted and when he looked doubtful she said: "I was so looking forward to going to be with you. You see, my first husband was a gynaecologist and all he wanted to do was examine it; my second husband was a psychiatrist and all he wanted to do was talk about it; my third husband was a politician and you know what they're like, all talk and no action – but you being a lawyer, I knew damned well that I'd be shafted!" '

The girls laughed out loud and Gigi said: 'What a jolly good story – surely that helped break the ice with your Mr Elliott?' But Andy groaned and said: 'You're joking! He glared at me and said frostily: "My two sons are both solicitors and I dare say they would find your so-called joke as unfunny as I do – if I could be bothered to repeat the story to them." '

He slipped back to his place on the bed between the two girls. Melissa let out an explosion of anger as he concluded his story and chided him forcefully for not standing up to his boss: 'Andy, how the hell can you work for such a bone-headed old bastard? I came across guys like this when I left college and started work in an advertising agency. God, I do hate these rotten shits who get their rocks off by deliberately humiliating people who can't answer back because they're frightened of losing their jobs. But I'm surprised you didn't tell him to stick one of his clubs up his arse, especially when, with a track record like yours, there would be a queue of companies offering you goodness-knows-what to work for them.

'Anyhow, I'm not so sure that telling your boss some home truths would have led to being given the bullet, because I've always found that the best way to deal with bullies is to stand up to them. If you do that, they'll leave you alone.'

Andy accepted her rebuke with a shrug and replied: 'I know, I know. I should have left the firm last April but instead I let myself be flattered into signing a three-year contract which means that not only could the firm claim damages if I left without giving three months' notice, but my name would be mud in the City if I didn't stick it out. You see, Elliott, knows a hell of a lot of people and you'd be surprised how much business is still done on the old boy network.'

'That's the trouble with Britain,' said Gigi gloomily

as she finished off her drink. 'It's not what you know but who you know which matters, though I dare say it's the same in other countries. Still, let's not get maudlin, Andy. I do believe I saw your prick twitch just now. Does this mean that one of us girls is going to get lucky?'

She reached out and squeezed his burgeoning member which, to her delight, began to rear up and thicken in her grasp. Immediately she began fisting his shaft, it rose up to a full, majestic erection, throbbing and urgent between Andy's well-muscled thighs.

'Oh, just look at that lovely big cock,' said Gigi proudly as she continued to masturbate the pulsing fleshy pole, pulling down the foreskin to expose the rounded mushroom dome as she glanced up enquiringly at Melissa who understood and immediately answered the unasked question.

'Go ahead, Gigi, I'll enjoy watching Andy fuck you,' she remarked coolly as she cupped Andy's large hanging ballsack in her hands. 'And I'm sure we'll be able to coax up his cock afterwards for my benefit, won't we, Andy?'

'I'll do my best,' he croaked as Gigi released his palpitating prick. When she lay back with her legs open to display her neat patch of dark hair and pouting pussy lips, his cock swayed. With his forefinger he traced a sensual trail between the bouncy spheres of her breasts and across her taut, trembling tummy, stroking and teasing a passage through her pubic bush before sliding straight inside her juicy quim.

Their mouths met in a clinging kiss of desire and Gigi reached up with both arms to take him round the neck and pull him across her, while she closed her legs to trap his pulsating stiffstander between her thighs.

'Now fuck me, Andy,' she panted. She parted her legs and drew in a long, shuddering breath as he took hold of his cock in his hand and guided the tip of the shiny knob into the moist red chink of her cunt. He paused for a moment and then, with a choking cry, he penetrated her with a solid thrust, cramming in every last inch of his rigid rammer until it was fully embedded deep in her slippery love channel.

'Oooh! Oooh! Andy, what a big fat cock you've got,' cried out Gigi. 'It's so long and thick that you've filled me right up! I'm going to fuck you for as long as you can hold out!' Andy's prick started up a strong pumping rhythm in and out of her cunny. She met his pistoning thrusts with upward jolts of her own, her knees drawn up to open her cunt as widely as possible for him as he crashed down upon her smooth white belly.

Beads of perspiration began to appear on his forehead as Andy looked to his left where Melissa was lying next to them, furiously fingering herself while she watched his gleaming shaft slew in and out of Gigi's squelchy slit. She followed his gaze and when she offered him her hand, which was coated in her cunny juice, he licked her fingers clean. He continued to slide his shaft to and fro, feeling Gigi's clinging cunt joyfully accepting his tingling length with each of his lusty plunges.

'More, Andy, more!' she shrieked as her body writhed under him, gyrating in ecstasy with the force of her oncoming orgasm. Her fingernails clawed at his bum cheeks and he responded with all his remaining strength. With a final mighty heave he spurted a stream of creamy hot spunk inside the soaking depths of Gigi's honeypot.

Andy slumped down and saw Gigi help Melissa finish herself off by jabbing her fingers between her rubbery love lips. Melissa wiggled her hips and her body stiffened as she came and he watched the flow of love juice trickle slowly down her wet crack towards her puckered little bum-hole.

Despite her earlier optimism about being able to persuade his penis to thicken up for a third cockstand, even after an hour's rest it took a prodigious amount of rubbing and sucking by both girls to bring Andy Whyte's jaded prick up to the mark. As soon as his glistening shaft once again stood stiffly erect, Melissa began to rub her body against his. Her teeth sank lightly into his shoulder, nipping him as she rolled on top of him. Her elongated nipples traced tiny circles against his chest as she ground herself against his lithe masculine frame.

'I think I'd better do the hard work, Andy,' said Melissa cheerfully as she settled herself down over his thighs, sliding one hand up and down his quivering cock. 'Thank God you're not one of those silly chaps who feel that the man always has to be in the driving seat.'

'No, you go right ahead,' he panted excitedly while he watched Melissa rub her free hand between her legs. 'It makes a nice change to lay back and let the lady set the pace.'

Melissa smiled and let go of his throbbing tadger to lean forward and kiss him on the lips, sucking his tongue into her mouth. After they kissed, Andy ran his hands swiftly over her full dangling breasts, tweaking the horned-up strawberry titties. He licked each large erect nipple, rolling them in turn around his mouth while she reached down for his cock and gave it a loving squeeze.

Andy grunted in delight as she worked her juicy love lips over the uncapped helmet of his rigid boner. She gasped with joy as she bounced up and down with accomplished ease on his stiff staff. Unable to resist joining in the game, Gigi squir-reled her tousled mane down between his knees and with one hand underneath Melissa's bottom, she began to lick and lap on the hairy wrinkled skin of his scrotum.

'Aaaah! That's *fabulous*!' he gasped, holding Melissa's waist. She moaned with pleasure as she rocked backwards and forwards, and then she lay back, resting her weight on her knees and arms with her hands spread out on the bed. Andy slipped round a hand to play with her clitty, smoothing the rubbery button against his palm.

The panting girl drew great heaving breaths as she concentrated all her energies on the tingling buzz of her fast approaching climax, and clasped and unclasped her cunny muscles around Andy's sinewy cock.

'Y-e-s-s! Y-e-s-s!' she yelled out triumphantly as the first waves of her orgasm rippled through her body. Andy echoed her cry as he thrust upwards and shot his sticky emission into her saturated honeypot as Gigi cradled his pulsing, tightened ballsack in her hands.

All the tension drained out of the sated pair as though some huge tide had been undammed. Melissa crashed down upon Andy and they lay puffing and panting as they recovered from their strenuous sensual exertions.

They lay dozing peacefully, curled up together in a warm tangle of arms and legs. All too soon Andy sat up, kissed Melissa's cheeks and whispered softly: 'Wow, that was one sensational fuck, but I'm going to have to do a wham-bam-thank-you-ma'am routine and go home for a few hours' kip. I'm dreadfully sorry but I'm flying out on a three-day business trip to Frankfurt early tomorrow morning. I haven't even packed my case yet. Will you both please forgive me?

'There's no need for either of you to get up as I'll see myself out,' he added as he slid out of bed and began to search for his Y-fronts in the untidy heap of clothes on the floor.

'Of course we'll forgive you, won't we, Gigi?' murmured Melissa sleepily and Gigi gave a little purr of agreement while she snuggled herself against her friend's back and wrapped her arms under the other girl's shoulders so as to cup her large breasts in her hands. 'Many thanks for bringing over the wine—'

'And for giving us a taste of your nice stiff cock,' interrupted Gigi sweetly as she squeezed Melissa's high uptilted bosoms. 'Have a good journey to Frankfurt. It isn't much of a city for sightseeing but I suppose you'll be too busy for much looking around. Still, I dare say you'll have time to pop into one of those naughty clubs on the Munichstrasse.'

'I doubt it. My hosts are very prim and proper international bankers and don't go in for that kind of entertainment,' grinned Andy. He had been to Frankfurt several times before and on his second visit had spent a very enjoyable evening with a chorus girl from the Pink Pussy cabaret club.

'Mind you, perhaps I might be lucky and they'll take me to one of those wicked places,' he chuckled quietly. He finished dressing and, blowing a good-bye kiss to the girls, Andy left his bed-mates sleeping serenely and shut the front door of the apartment firmly behind him.

The girls were so exhausted from all their vigorous fucking that they were both still fast asleep when the alarm clock at the side of the bed began to buzz at eight o'clock. The radio automatically switched itself on and the sound of *Paint It Black* by the Rolling Stones flooded the room.

Gigi was the first to stir and she looked round her in bewilderment for a few seconds. Then her mind cleared and she remembered that she had flounced out of Adrian Klein's flat and spent the night with Melissa.

After she had showered and shared a light breakfast of tea and toast with Melissa, Gigi telephoned Rose and Griffin. She spoke to Adrian's secretary, Barbara Kennedy, and made the arrangement for them to have lunch together. *It's lucky that the weather is still nice and warm as I only brought a few clothes with me*, she thought to herself. She looked quickly at her watch before pulling on a green minidress over her bra and panties.

Then she scowled as she realised she would have to dash if she were not to be late for her midmorning job, modelling the new season's outfits at Harry Firestone's Margaret Street showroom. This was one more reason to make Gigi fume and say with some vehemence to Melissa: 'Bloody Adrian Klein, I'll give him what for when he calls!' But had Adrian been in Melissa's apartment at this time, instead of being deep in mind-numbing detailed negotiation with Dickie Segal, he would have had to tell her that he could not even begin to think about how he could make amends until he had concluded a deal with the ineffable Dickie.

And had he known about Teddy Dixon's decision to call him in that afternoon for a discussion about Bernie Harwin's randy romps, he would have been forced to tell Gigi that he wouldn't have been able to put his mind to making peace with her till he had worked out a campaign with Teddy on how to rein in Rose and Griffin's raunchy singing star.

CHAPTER FOUR

The Final Curtain

It was as well that Adrian Klein was in blissful ignorance of Gigi's anger as his negotiations with Dickie Segal dragged on. He needed to keep all his wits about him as he pressed his case for Trevor Trenton to star as Buttons in the production of *Cinderella* which the Amalagamated Entertainments Group was staging in Bristol at Christmas.

'Yes, I know he can sing and dance a big as well as tell a good story,' agreed Dickie Segal, inhaling a long puff from a huge Havana cigar which he had lit up after a secretary had brought a pot of coffee into the boardroom. 'And I'll admit that one of my people saw him do very well at *La Miraggio*, but you know how it is these days. If the chap hasn't had television exposure, the punters don't want to know.'

'Oh come on, that's not altogether true. I've already told you that Trevor's lined up for a *Billy Cotton Band Show* in September and he'll open a *Sunday Night At The London Palladium* a couple of weeks later,' countered Adrian, suppressing a yawn with difficulty. He was suffering from the after-effects of his enthusiastic participation in Tanya Gordon's 'whoresome foursome' with the lovely Lesley and Philip, the prick-happy policeman.

He placed his elbows on the table and spread out his hands as he urged the impressario to reconsider his position. 'My word of honour, Dickie, this time next year you'll be begging me to let you have him for a London panto season at double the money.'

'From your mouth to God's ears, I don't disagree that Trevor has talent and I wish the lad well,' said Dickie Segal piously. 'But right now we're talking about this Christmas and not some time in the future. The only reason I'm even considering him for the show is because you've booked the boy into that big Bristol working men's club for a fortnight in November.'

Adrian digested this statement thoroughly and then heaved a heavy sigh as with a gesture of weary resignation, he said: 'All right, Dickie, point taken. I'll tell you what I'll do, though Teddy Dixon will bite my balls off when he finds out. I'll offer you Trevor's services at twenty per cent off the figure I quoted but on the understanding that he gets an overall ten per cent salary bonus when weekly ticket sales reach ninety per cent. Could anything be fairer than that?'

To his relief, this offer broke the deadlock. Dickie Segal stroked his chin and replied: 'I'm taking a big chance here, Adrian. If it weren't for the fact that I respect your judgement, I wouldn't take him on at fifty pounds a week. Still, you've such faith in this young man that I'll go along with you – but the bonus figures are too high for my liking. Make it seven and a half per cent on ninety five per cent sales and you've got a deal.'

'Leave it out, Nipper, don't screw me into the ground here. As it is, you're getting a rising young star for peanuts,' said Adrian crossly, throwing in Segal's nickname to hammer home the close relationship between the two organisations. 'Amalgamated's been doing good business with Rose and Griffin for years and we've always come up trumps for you.'

'Okay, okay, let's split the difference, call it seven and a half per cent on ninety per cent and you can draw up the papers this afternoon,' offered the hard-headed theatrical magnate.

'Sometimes I think I'd rather have a tooth pulled than a bargain with you,' commented Adrian as he exchanged a handshake over the table. 'As it is, God knows what Teddy Dixon will say when he discovers what I've done.'

'He should kiss you on both cheeks for getting your boy onto my circuit,' Dickie Segal grunted as he took another puff on his cigar. 'So how is Teddy these days? I haven't seen him for some time and he didn't even turn up at the Variety Club meeting last week. Too busy screwing the girls at that flat in St John's Wood, I suppose.

'Not that you're much different, Adrian,' he went on with a short laugh. 'It was a surprise to see you here so promptly this morning as I understand you left *La Miraggio* early this morning with one of Angelo Calabro's young ladies on your arm.'

This remark caught Adrian on the hop. His mouth dropped open in astonishment as Dickie Segal leaned back in his chair and let out a hoarse chuckle. 'Don't worry, there aren't any private detectives following you. It's just that I sent Liz Thompson to *La Miraggio* last night to give Trevor another once-over. Obviously you didn't see her.'

'No, and I jolly well hope that no-one else saw me either,' said Adrian with genuine feeling. He explained how he had forgotten to inform Gigi about his late-night appointment and how he was now in the dog-house with his live-in girl friend. 'So I'm in a right pickle, Dickie. I'm phoning Gigi this afternoon but I'm damned if I know what to say to bring her round.'

'I wouldn't lose any sleep about it,' advised the managing director of Amalgamated Entertainments. Like Teddy Dixon, he had somehow managed to keep his own redoubtable track record as a cocksman secret from his wife for more than thirty years. 'Lay it on the line with her, Adrian. You must say: "Darling, I've apologised for not telling you about having to go out so late, but this is an important part of my job. It might be inconvenient but it pays for the flat, the car, the colour TV, and what-have-you. Now don't be such a silly girl and I'll take you out somewhere special for dinner tonight." Now I don't want to sound horribly hard, but if that doesn't do the trick then you'll be well shot of her if she decides to pack her bags.

While Adrian listened to this paternal advice from Dickie Segal, Gigi and Frank Henderson, an American freelance photographer who worked for all the top fashion magazines, were busy surveying a new range of maxi-coats for the coming winter season. They were in the stockroom at the back of Harry Firestone's premises, which were situated in the heart of London's wholesale rag trade around the streets north of Oxford Circus.

'I really wonder whether these maxis will ever catch on in a big way,' said Gigi doubtfully, as she pulled off the rail an attractive check tweed coat with a leather belt slung just below the waist.

'Yeah, one or two manufacturers are trying to hedge their bets, although Paris and New York think that women need a change from minis and macros,' remarked the photographer. He helped Gigi on with the coat. 'You're five foot six and can take a low belt, but I know that some buyers are thinking that shorter girls will be worried that maxis will make them look as if they're wearing dressing gowns.'

He pulled out a black coat and went on: 'Yet I reckon even petite girls won't have any problems so long as they choose high-belted number like this one. Even on a woman of say five foot two, this style will make it seem as if their legs go on for ever!'

'Frank, I'm sorry, but I can't agree with you,' said

Harry Firestone. He had overheard them as he walked into the stockroom with Chloe Roberts, his vivacious young designer and an old friend of Gigi. 'In my opinion, a maxi with a low belt will give smaller girls a nice stretched-out look so long as they don't drop their chins and slouch.'

Gigi pirouetted before a full-length mirror and commented: 'M'mm, you could have a point there, Harry, but then I'm five foot six. I'm still not too sure, though, whether shorter girls will be able to carry off these coats.'

Chloe now entered the discussion. 'Won't it all depend on the particular style they wear, Gigi?' she suggested brightly as she helped Gigi adjust the coat over her dress. 'For example, I would tell girls under your height to avoid bright colours with frogging unless they want to look as though they're on their way to or from bed. They'd also be well advised to wear chunky high-heeled shoes or perhaps a pair of small boots to give them a bit of a lift.'

'Well, let's hope you're right, my love,' said Frank as he checked the light meter and began to spool the film to the first exposure. 'Everyone I come across is hoping that the maxis will give trade a bit of a lift too, isn't that right, Harry?'

'Too true, nobody I know has had a good season so far this year,' agreed her boss. 'So we're all relying on some good publicity to help the fashion take off. Frank, you make Gigi look like a million dollars and if my coats start to sell in the stores, I'll see you right, don't worry about that.'

'Put that in writing please,' demanded the photographer as he tested his electronic flash. 'But for what it's worth, I think all will be well so long as no-one begins hiking up prices too much. This fashion isn't going to be as big as the mini. It'll only work if you can keep shop prices under the fifteen pounds mark.'

'That kind of price doesn't give anyone much of a margin,' Harry grumbled but Chloe cut in and said: 'Frank's right, we have to give good value. Alexon got a spread in the *Evening News* for a wool maxi at fourteen guineas. So we'll just have to match them.'

Nevertheless, the session went well, with frank Henderson taking shots of Gigi indoors and then getting her to parade up and down Great Titchfield Street in the warm morning sunshine. When they returned, Gigi pulled off her coat, flopped into a chair and blew out her cheeks. 'Did you have to make me work outside in this kind of weather?' she complained as the photographer stowed away his equipment. 'Who would ever wear any kind of coat in mid-summer?'

'Only overpaid models,' Frank grinned as he snapped shut the lock on his case. As Chloe came into the stockroom carrying two teaming mugs of tea he called out: 'Thanks, but I haven't time to breathe today. Martin Elstree and I have been booked to take some spreads for *Girls Illustrated* down in Richmond Park this afternoon and I don't want to be even five minutes late for that session!'

Chloe rolled her green eyes upwards and groaned:

'God, what men will do for the sight of a pair of tits!

'Waste not, want not. I'll just have to take a short break and drink his tea for him.' She sat down opposite Gigi who was sprawled out on a small sofa. 'So what's news, Gigi? I haven't seen you for simply ages. How's Adrian Klein been treating you?'

'Don't mention that man's name to me,' said Gigi darkly. She proceeded to recount Adrian's lapse from grace in full detail, but when she told Chloe about how it was all because of him that she had spent the night with Melissa and Andy Whyte, her friend put up her hand and commented: 'I think you're going over the top now, Gigi. I honestly don't see how you can say that it was Adrian's fault that you got fucked by this fellow as well as getting involved in a lezzie scene with Melissa.

'Not that I'm condemning you in the slightest, love, perhaps I'm not so sympathetic because I'm more than a mite jealous,' she went on hastily. 'You see, for the last couple of months I've been going out with a nice guy called Paul Adler. Adrian might have come across him as he's a top A and R man for Carlyle Records and plays centre forward for the Showbiz football team. My problem is that Paul's gone on a keep-fit kick since his brother gave him an exercise bicycle. He gets so bloody knackered after using the damn thing that he's too tired to do anything worthwhile between the sheets.

'Now I need to be fucked regularly and frankly, if I don't get enough sex, my whole body becomes one massive erogenous zone. It would take more than Manchester United's forward line to satisfy me!'

Gigi listened to her with interest. 'Oh you poor thing,' she said. Being a naturally kind person, she forgot about her own troubles and focused her mind on Chloe's difficulties.

'Perhaps you need one of these new electric vibrators from America,' she suggested thoughtfully. 'Melissa and I played around with one last night and I'm sure she would let you try it out.'

But Chloe shook her head and said: 'Thanks, but I can't think that anything made of plastic or rubber can beat the real thing. I know anything I tell you in confidence won't go any further and – between you and me – I've found a good way to relieve my frustrations.'

She lowered her voice and went on: 'Paul usually stays the night on Thursdays but last week he called me to say that after work he would pop back to his flat for a light supper and then go on to his tennis club for a game with three of his friends, and so he wouldn't be round at my place till about ten o'clock.

'This really upset me as I knew he wouldn't arrive till well after ten. After the game Paul likes to have a beer or two in the bar with his mates. Also, his car's in dock at the moment and he would have to cadge a lift or take a mini-cab which would make him even later. All in all, it was odds-on that Paul would be so whacked by the time we went to bed that I would be lucky if the silly so-and-so could even manage a single cockstand before he fell asleep.'

'Men! Sometimes they can be so selfish,' said Gigi bitterly and Chloe nodded and continued: 'And how! But then I had a good idea – my Dad bought me a Mini when I passed my driving test a few months ago and Paul's tennis club was only a couple of miles away, so I decided I would drive up there and drag him home as soon as he had finished his game.

'I was at the tennis club by half past eight and strolled around the courts but to my surprise Paul and his friends were nowhere to be seen. This was odd and I must admit that I was getting suspicious about what he might have been up to as I walked through to the clubhouse. Had he really been playing tennis this evening or was he actually elsewhere, two-timing me with another girl? However, when I enquired about Paul's whereabouts, I was told that he was in the dressing rooms and I felt quite ashamed of myself for thinking that Paul would be such a rotter.

'I was so caught up in mulling over how I would make this up to him by giving his prick a specially long sucking that it didn't occur to me that Paul might not be alone in the dressing rooms. I blithely opened the door to see not only Paul coming out of the showers but also the other three lads who had been playing in a doubles match with him. All of them were stark naked, wearing only their towels round their necks like football supporters' scarves.

'Neither Paul nor any of the others seemed put

out by flaunting their cocks in front of me. I found out later that they had only managed to book a court for an hour and had spent the rest of the time in the bar. This might well have been the reason why they were all so uninhibited about displaying their wedding tackle to me.

' "Hi, Chloe! You've met Allan, Colin and Laurence, haven't you?" said Paul with a slight slur in his voice which I guessed had come from having one Scotch too many. "Now what brings you here? I hope you've come in your car to give me a lift back to your pad after I've got dressed.'

' "I would be grateful for a lift down to Finchley Road if you have any room," said Colin, who at twenty-two was the youngest of the four. As I looked across at him, I couldn't help noticing that the lucky boy had been blessed with one of the most enormous thick cocks I had ever seen. I could hardly take my eyes off his huge shaft as it flapped from side to side between his thighs.

'Mike must have seen me gazing in admiration at his friend's tremendous tadger because he nudged Paul in the ribs with his elbow and said: "I'd get Chloe out of here fast, mate. She's seen Colin's tool and you know what the effect of his big dick has on lots of girls."

'Now to be kind to him, Gigi, I'll add here that Paul hadn't drunk any more than his friends. Let's just say that he was more tired and emotional than the others because earlier on he had been drinking at a business lunch.

'Anyhow, with a great flourish Paul plonked himself down on a bench and declared: "I'm all in favour of this new women's liberation movement. Why shouldn't Chloe look at Colin's cock if she wants to? I bet he would love to have a look at her tits!"

' "Bloody hell, we all would," said Allan who was sitting down with his towel across his thighs, although it was easy to see from the bulge in his lap that he was sporting a hard-on.

' "Is that so? Well, I don't see any reason why you shouldn't," I said. Perhaps it was the sight of Colin's monster member which made me feel so randy but, whatever the reason, I pulled off my top. I giggled as I heard a collective gasp when I flaunted my bare breasts at the four men.

' "Oh I say," murmured Laurence when I strode across to Allan, unbuttoned my shorts and boldly asked him to tug them down over my hips. His hands trembled as he wrenched them down to my feet. Then I stepped out of them and stood directly in front of Colin while I ran my hands over my breasts, tweaking my nipples between my fingers. I looked down and saw his enormous chopper rising up in salute.

'Perhaps if Paul had said something at this stage I might have stopped at just showing off my tits. I didn't think this was any big deal because in six weeks' time I'll be stretched out on the topless beach at St Tropez. It could be that he was too shocked at may behaviour but he didn't say a single word. I decided to carry on and enjoy myself with young Colin.

'I hooked my fingers into the waistband of my panties and slowly peeled them down my thighs to my knees. Then I placed my hands on Colin's shoulders to steady myself and invited him to kneel and yank off my panties completely. He sank down and in a trice my panties were on the floor and I said softly to Colin: "Well done, that deserves a little reward. Stand up and I'll think of something suitable to give you."

'I think the randy rascal knew what I had in mind as he scrambled to his feet. Now it was my turn to get down on my knees with my face only inches away from his huge cock and heavy dangling balls. As if in a trance, I took hold of his massive prick which swelled up even more in my hands as I slid them up and down the warm, velvety shaft. Then to my surprise I heard a familiar voice behind me whisper: "Go on, Chloe, we'd all like to see you suck his big dick!" '

Chloe paused for breath and Gigi leaned forward and gripped her arm. 'Don't tell me it was your boy friend who was egging you on,' she gasped with an excited gleam in her eyes.

'Oh yes, he most certainly did – not that I needed much encouragement! I pulled on Colin's colossal cock to make him step forward a pace. He let out a little moan as I flicked my tongue over his big bulbous knob and he tried to push my head forward to take his cock inside my mouth. I looked up at him and told him to be patient because his cock was so big I had to take my time or I would choke on it. Slowly I eased his helmet between my lips, straining my jaw open as wide as possible while I moved one hand down to cup his big hairy scrotum. I sucked on his meaty shaft and felt his prick throb hard against my cheeks as Colin's stupendous boner moved smoothly down my throat. The erotic sensation was fabulous with his thick tool sliding to and fro in and out of my yawning lips while I slurped on this wonderful monster cock.

'Then I sensed the unmistakable feel of two more erections pressing against my cheeks. I glanced up and saw that they belonged to Allan and Laurence who were standing by me, holding their pulsing pricks against my face. I released Colin's cock and, grabbing hold of these two truncheons in my hands, began to toss them off, fisting them up and down till they were both panting with pleasure.'

'Didn't Paul want to join in?' enquired Gigi and Chloe nodded: 'Of course he did! Seconds later he was behind me and his arms were wrapped round my ribs and his hands were caressing my breasts and rubbing my stiff nipples. Then he took his hands away and parted my bum cheeks so that he could slide his cock up my quim from behind. Gosh, how fantastic it felt, having Paul's prick pushing in and out of my juicy cunny while Colin's swollen shaft fucked my mouth and I jerked my hands up and down Allan and Laurence's throbbing tools.

'Colin was the first to climax and I could feel his

helmet throb hard on my tongue as the spunk rushed up from his balls. His shaft tensed before he spilled delicious thick jets of hot sticky jism down my throat. I gobbled furiously on his twitching shaft until I had milked his great cock dry and then the two boys I was frigging with my fingers also ejaculated, squirting their spunk on my cheeks. Then finally Paul and I came together and a shattering orgasm swept through me. I contracted the muscles of my love channel so that they squeezed his prick as he thrust his tool inside my cunt and shot his load.

'I let Colin's cock slip out of my mouth even though it was almost as big and hard as before! Now I was reeling even more randy and in a mood to be fucked by any prick in grabbing distance. I knew that Paul always needed at least half an hour to recover after he spunked and the other two boys' dicks were already limp in my hands. I could hardly say that I was upset that it was Colin who would have the honour of fucking me! I slicked a hand up and down his wet shaft until it had regained all its former stiffness and I led him by his cock to a small folding chair which had already been set up in a corner of the room. He sat down on the chair and I climbed astride him, leaning forward so that he could fondle my breasts and lick my titties.

'Then, as delicately as I could, I lowered myself upon Colin until I could feel the tip of his helmet nudge against my pussy lips. He arched his back and my flaps unlocked as he pushed his knob inside me. The other boys gathered round to watch Colin's knob disappear inside my cunt. His shaft nudged against my clitty and the flood gates burst as an electric little series of mini-orgasms shot through my pussy!

' "Ahhh! It's incredible, I've never been so full of cock! What a fabulous fuck!" I shouted out, past caring that Paul was standing next to us. My sopping honeypot opened up for him and my love juices poured down over his prick which was soon embedded to the hilt inside me. I flexed all my cunny muscles to squeeze his gorgeous cock and make that first entry tight for him. Colin now grabbed hold of my bum cheeks and, still with his lips glued round one of my erect raspberry nipples, he began to bounce me up and down on his thick truncheon which had slotted so neatly into my juicy crack.

'As I threw my head from side to side in sheer delight I saw Paul whisper something to the other two boys and I hardly had time to wonder what he was saying when it became all very clear! Paul called out: "Okay, lads, one, two, three, GO!" and on his signal they dived down and grabbed the legs of the chair and lifted Colin and me both up high into the air with my bottom resting on his slim thighs. All this shaking made his great pole of a prick quiver wildly inside me, reaming out my cunt quite wonderfully.

' "Put us down, you bastards!" Colin cried out as I gasped: "Oh, I'm going off again, come with me,

Colin, shoot your spunk!" And thankfully, perhaps because our combined weight made their burden uncomfortably heavy, my urgent plea had the desired effect and the boys carefully lowered the chair back down onto the floor. The three of them stayed to look on and Allan even squatted on his haunches to watch transfixed at the sight of my splayed pink cunny lips slithering up and down Colin's mighty cock. He jammed his thumb into my bum-hole while he sucked on my rosy titties and jerked his hips upward in time with my pushes.

'We came near enough simultaneously – Colin climaxed first, his glistening shaft burying itself inside me as he shot a tremendous gush of spunk into my cunt. This triggered off my orgasm and although neither of us made too much of a din, I dare say we were lucky that no-one else came in to find out what all the hullaballoo coming from the dressing room was all about!'

Chloe sighed happily as she recalled the erotic incident and concluded pensively: 'And you now something, Gigi, when we finished this lovely fuck, it suddenly occurred to me that Paul's feeling for me might change after seeing me being screwed by one of his friends – but not a bit of it! In fact, afterwards, while I was driving him home, I happened to look down at his lap and saw that he was sporting a gigantic hard-on.

'I did my Mae West number and when we stopped at a red traffic light I tapped him on the shoulder and said to him: "Goodness me, Paul Adler, have you stuffed a tennis ball down your trousers or are you just thinking about what we're going to do as soon as we get home?" '

Gigi shrugged as she commented: 'Oh-ho, so watching you being fucked by Colin was a turn-on for Paul. It's strange but quite a few men like to see their wives or girlfriends enjoying themselves with other men. This always surprised me but as they say in Yorkshire, there's nowt so queer as folk.'

'God knows that's true enough. Between you and me Harry Firestone gets his rocks off with his secretary by muff-diving every lunchtime.'

'Well, she's a very pretty girl, what's so strange about that?'

Chloe gave a little chuckle as she answered: 'Nothing, except that before they begin, Harry smears her pussy all over with butter and drapes smoked salmon round her cunny lips so he has a nice snack while he's on the job.'

The girls burst into laughter and Chloe continued: 'Well, as I said, Paul was getting very excited and as soon as we got home he tore off my clothes and carried me up to the bedroom. But then instead of flinging me down on the mattress, he sat himself down on the edge of the bed. As he bent me over his knees he hissed: "Now it's my turn to take charge. How do you think I felt as you gave Allan and Laurence hand jobs while you sucked Colin's cock. Did you think that I wouldn't punish you for such wanton conduct?"

'Actually I guessed what he had in mind so I

entered the spirit of the game and looked up at him and whispered: "Oh dear, I have been a rather naughty girl, haven't I?"

' "Yes, you have," thundered Paul. Even though I more than half-expected it, I let out a yelp as I felt the flat of his hand smack the bare cheeks of my bum. Then he panted: "Girls like you who flaunt themselves in the nude in front of their boy friends' pals and play with other fellows' pricks with impunity must be shown that they can't get away with such shocking behaviour."

'He smacked my bum three or four more times, hard enough for me to feel but well short of actually hurting me. I felt a lovely warm glow spreading across my buttocks. Then Paul made my whole body jerk as his forefinger slid abruptly up my crack and he rasped: "Your pussy's soaking wet, Chloe. You wretched girl, I suppose you're still thinking about Colin's thick, spurting cock!"

'Honestly, my senses were beginning to swim as I squirmed helplessly on his knees while he alternated the slaps on my arse with a probing little finger-fuck. "Oooh, oooh, you're making me come," I moaned. I started to gasp for breath as I felt his stiff shaft prod against my bum cheek. Now he pulled me up and threw me down on the mattress. I opened my legs and he fell on top of me, driving his rock-hard boner inside my cunny, humping me with a fierce energy until I wailed out that I had come and he flooded my honeypot with his sticky cum.'

'So Paul wasn't really cross,' Gigi observed and

Chloe gave her a saucy smile as she giggled: 'No, of course he wasn't – in fact he asked me if I would like to invite Colin to fuck me again, saying that he didn't mind at all so long as he could watch and then "punish" me afterwards. Paul and I had such a passionate fuck after he'd smacked my botty that I'm very tempted to take up the offer. After all, I've always been in favour of people coming out into the open with their sexual preferences, though it's terribly important for both partners to agree beforehand on whether they fancy swapping around occasionally.'

Gigi nodded sagely as she mulled over Chloe's remark, thinking hard of her own participation in an orgy the previous night with Melissa and Andy and how Adrian might react if she ever told him about this randy escapade. 'I'm sure you're right,' she said slowly as she slipped on her coat. 'What was it that famous Edwardian actress, Mrs Patrick Campbell, used to say? Um, oh yes, it was that consenting adults should do what they like to each other in bed so long as they don't do it in the street and frighten the horses.'

'Must you go, Gigi, why don't you stay for a bite of lunch?' asked the pretty girl. 'There's a good sandwich bar across the road – or if you fancy something different, we could always ask Harry if we could watch him eat his secretary's salmon-flavoured pussy!'

'Sorry, darling, I already have a lunch date with Adrian's personal assistant at Rose and Griffin,' said Gigi as she scribbled down Adrian's telephone number on a piece of paper. 'I'll probably go back to Adrian tonight or tomorrow night so give me a ring in a few days time and we'll fix a time for you and Paul to come round for dinner.'

While Gigi was hailing a taxi to take her from Harry Firestone's showroom to the luxurious offices in Dover Street which housed the personnel of Rose and Griffin, the agency's managing director Teddy Dixon was now slightly concerned that Tony Cavendish had still not made an appearance that morning. There was no answer either from his flat or that of Sharon Saxon.

'I hope Tony's not bonking young Sharon somewhere,' he commented somewhat incongruously to Marlene, who was on her knees between his legs, flicking her tongue around her boss's purple knob. 'It's not professional to fuck the artistes! I'll have something to say on those lines to Tony when he does finally condescend to come in to work.'

'Why are you laying down the law all of a sudden?' said Marlene indignantly, as she slowly slurped her wet tongue along the underside of Teddy's throbbing tool. 'You've had more chorus girls than I've had hot dinners. You made a play for me only days after I started work here.'

'That's quite different,' he insisted, pushing her head down until his knob was fully installed between her generous red lips. 'You only have to work for me, while a pretty young singer like

Sharon has to persuade God knows how many other people – record producers, impressarios, songwriters, etcetra, etcetra – to help her claw her way to the top. Now I'm not saying that they will all demand to be laid, but it doesn't help if it's known that the girl's already involved with her agent.'

Marlene opened her mouth and Teddy's glistening stiff cock was exposed as she said: 'How bloody unfair! I'm sure that if Sharon were a man, she wouldn't have such hassle!'

'Hey, I don't make the ruddy rules,' protested Teddy while he sought desperately to slide his cock back inside Marlene's mouth. 'And there are plenty of confirmed bachelors in the business who have absolutely no interest in girls, if you get my drift.

'Anyhow, I've never refused any girl a favour just because she didn't put out,' he added virtuously. This answer seemed to satisfy Marlene who took hold of his straining prick with both hands, bending the stem to her mouth and running her tongue up to the rim and over the twitching scarlet helmet. No-one could teach his secretary anything about cock-sucking, thought Teddy as he closed his eyes and revelled in sheer ecstasy. She gobbled on his knob while one hand slicked up and down his pulsating pole and the other gently squeezed his tightening balls.

Teddy Dixon would have preferred to fuck Marlene before his lunch appointment but he had already enjoyed the delicious sensation of ramming his rod inside her creamy cunt earlier that morning.

He also planned to make love to Marlene all evening at his secret St John's Wood flat, so he made no attempt to hold back the tide of jism from shooting up from his scrotum. Seconds later, great gouts of spunk arced out from his leaping cock. Marlene chewed on it happily, sucking hard on its thick, twitching length as rivulets of frothy white jism dribbled down her throat.

He buttoned himself up and she scrambled to her feet as his telephone rang. 'Teddy Dixon here,' he said crisply as he picked up the phone. His face visibly relaxed as the familiar tones of Barry Gore-Wharton, his solicitor and close friend, crackled through the line.

'Barry, how are you, to ~ hat do I owe the pleasure of this call? What's that about Bernie Harwin? Oh sod it, she isn't, is she? Look, we'll have to do something drastic about Bernie, he's beginning to believe our own publicity about his being the greatest stud since Casanova. Huh, you're quite right, I was saying only this morning, we'll have to tie a knot in it or Bernie will find himself up the creak. Yes, fine, let's talk about it over lunch at *La Miraggio*. I'll ask Marlene to book a table for one o'clock.'

Teddy replaced the receiver and shook his head sadly as he looked up at Marlene and explained: 'That was Barry on the line. It seems that two of Bernie's little trollops are going to sell their story to the *Sunday Pictorial*.'

'Well, so what's news? All the rags have run

239

stories about Bernie's bonking. Surely one more won't do any harm?'

'I'm afraid that this one will,' said Teddy with a gloomy sigh. 'It seems that the silly fool has been playing around with a pair of seventeen-year-old twins.'

Marlene looked puzzled and said: 'But that's hardly new. Don't you remember that piece in *The People* last year about Bernie with two young groupies?'

'Yes, but this is far more serious,' explained Teddy and he struck off points on his fingers. 'First, these twins shared Bernie's bed together; second, they allege he made them smoke marijuana cigarettes; and thirdly, they happen to be the daughters of a prominent Tory MP!'

'Ouch! Still, it's only the druggie business that matters, isn't it? I mean, there's no law against bonking seventeen-year-olds even if Ted Heath happened to be their Dad!'

'Huh, I suppose that's some comfort,' said Teddy as he pursed his lips with annoyance. 'But look what happened last year to Mick Jagger – he was given three months until he got off on appeal just for possession. Can you imagine what a magistrate will do to Bernie? He's got a reputation like Jagger's but worse, he's a Jamaican. Marlene, if this ever gets to court he'll be crucified. Funny thing is, although Bernie's one of the most pussy-struck men I know—'

Marlene could not resist interrupting him. 'Takes one to know one,' she said brightly, but Teddy

240

ignored this aside and went on: 'But not so long ago, Adrian told me that Bernie didn't smoke and never drank more than an occasional beer. You know, it could be that poor old Bernie's been set up. I'll find out all the details from Barry at lunchtime. If necessary I'll call Warren and see what he can find out about these girls.'

'Hold on,' he called out in reply to a knock at the door and got up to let a slightly dishevelled Tony Cavendish step into the office. 'Ah, our man missing in action returns. We were about to send out search parties for you and Sharon Saxon. Where the hell have you been, Tony? You look as if you haven't had any sleep.'

'Sharon's probably back home by now, Teddy. I'm sorry I'm so late in to work but we stayed over with Nick Clarke after the *Top of the Pops* party. The good news though is that Nick has agreed to write a song for Sharon's new single.'

'Has he now? Well, that's some good news and we can do with some of that just at this moment,' exclaimed Teddy as he turned to Marlene and added: 'I don't think I've anything else for you, love. But would you just ring Angelo and book a table for Barry and me for one o'clock?'

'Okay, boss,' she said. Tony also moved towards the door but Teddy put up a warning hand to him and added: 'No, hold on a moment, young man, I want a quick word with you before you rush back to work.'

After Marlene had shut the door behind her he

told Tony to pull up a chair and, trying hard not to sound pompous, Teddy scratched his ear and began: 'This isn't the first time I've had to make this little speech but for some reason I always feel a bit awkward about it. I suppose it's because we've a reputation in the business of being an easy-going kind of firm. I mean, we've a pretty mixed bag of people here, haven't we? Why, I even engaged a fanatical Arsenal supporter like Adrian Klein!'

Tony had an inkling of what might be on his managing director's mind but nevertheless he managed to smile faintly at Teddy's reference to Adrian Klein. Only recently Adrian had told him that Teddy Dixon's idea of Paradise would be to score the winning goal for Spurs against Arsenal in the FA Cup Final, followed by a night of debauchery in a suite at the Savoy with Jane Fonda and Goldie Hawn.

'Seriously though, Tony, at Rose and Griffin we don't pry into the staff's personal lives,' continued Teddy warmly. 'But you've been here long enough to know that I very much discourage any personal relationships between artistes and their agents. The reason is simple enough. You get involved with someone like young Sharon Saxon and, though you're both on the same side and you want to do the best for her, you might forget you also represent other artistes. Though they may not directly be in competition, they might find they aren't getting as much of your attention as they deserve.'

Fair enough, Mr Dixon, but one out of ten for

subtlety, thought Tony wearily. It was a bit rich for him to deliver this homily especially as the words were coming from a man who had fucked even more soubrettes and *ingenues* than the legendary Dickie Segal. However, it could not be denied that Teddy was right, even if he himself did not practice what he preached.

So Tony just quietly replied: 'You don't have any worries on that score, Teddy, there's nothing going on between Sharon and myself. On the other hand, I'm pretty sure she *is* getting involved with Nick Clarke.'

'Is she now? So just how sure are you?' Teddy Dixon demanded sharply, leaning forward over his desk.

'Um, dead certain, actually, because we both spent the night at Nick's place,' confessed the hapless Tony Cavendish. He felt it incumbent to explain his involvement with Donna, Nick's lovely secretary. This upset him, for he was very fond of Sharon and felt distinctly uneasy about giving any details of her sex life to his employer, even though it could be argued that he was duty-bound to do so. The young singer's relationship with one of the leading British songsmiths would have a genuine effect upon her career and was therefore of genuine concern to Rose and Griffin.

However, this information put Teddy back into a state of high good humour. 'Well, that's another matter entirely,' he beamed, all thoughts about giving Tony a piece of his mind now forgotten. 'So long as he doesn't fob her off with some old B-side material, I would say that Sharon should be guaranteed a number one spot for her next disc. What about production, though? Would we have to use Nick's people? Don't forget that we signed a deal with Louis Baum and Fred Newman to produce Sharon's next three records.'

'No problem, Teddy, they're old mates of Nick's from way black. All we need to do is to get Nick to write the song as soon as possible.'

'Good, good,' said Teddy, as he rose from his chair and walked across to his filing cabinet from which he pulled out a slim blue folder. 'It must have been quite a party! I'm sorry I couldn't have popped in and said hello. T'sk, t'sk, you young men don't seem to have much stamina these days. This girl has obviously knackered you out.

'If I were you I wouldn't go out to lunch today but get your girl to bring you in a sandwich and then have a snooze in my office,' he advised as he passed the blue folder to Tony. 'But when you're feeling a bit brighter, I'd like you to run your eyes over the note Bob Topping up in Manchester sent me yesterday about a coloured boy called Clyde Wells he heard sing in the Deansgate.'

Tony looked puzzled and the older man grinned as he explained: 'Ah, of course you're a born-and-bred London boy, aren't you? You think life ends north of Watford. Well, it doesn't and when she's a little more experienced and sophisticated, I hope we'll be able to book Sharon into the Deansgate. It's one of the most successful night-clubs in Manchester and it has made my old friend Bob an extremely wealthy man, especially since he got his gaming licence and opened up a casino.

'We used to be on the halls together just after the war,' he reminisced as he walked back to his seat. 'Bob was one of the best conjurers on the circuits. There was one trick he performed with a book and a box of matches which baffled me for years, even though I'd watched it dozens of times from the wings. Anyway, like many magicians, he married his assistant and then, would you believe it, seven months later the jammy bugger wins almost eleven thousand pounds on the football pools! With the money he made a few very shrewd property deals around Manchester and a few years back he took a controlling interest in the Deansgate.

'Bob and I have kept in touch on-and-off over the years and whenever he comes across an act he thinks has got that something special, he always lets me know. So give him a ring and arrange to go up to Manchester one day next week and hear this fellow Clyde Wells gargle. If he's any good, we'll want him on our books before any of the big boys sniff him out.'

'Okay, Teddy, but if we did sign him up, wouldn't that put Bernie Harwin's nose out of joint?' queried Tony. Being unaware of Teddy's current problems with the raunchy singer, he was taken aback at the lack of concern about the feelings of one of Rose and Griffin's most profitable artistes.

'Fuck Bernie, he needs a good kick up the arse!'
Teddy replied sharply. 'If he has any sense, he'll
realise that if this kid Clyde is any good, it's just as
well that Rose and Griffin are looking after him. It's
in our interest to keep all our artistes at the top,
while another agency will probably want to promote
someone like Clyde at Bernie's expense.'

Tony nodded and then heaved himself up and
walked to the door. 'I'll go up North next Tuesday
and call you as soon as I've seen Clyde Wells
perform,' he promised as he left the office. Teddy
waved a hand in acknowledgment and was about to
summon Marlene back to help him clear his in-tray
when his secretary came back to the office of her
own volition with a large buff envelope in her hand.

'Teddy, this envelope came round ten minutes ago
from Barry Gore-Wharton. He's just telephoned to
say that you must open it before you meet him for
lunch,' said Marlene excitedly as she placed it on the
desk. 'He sounded very dramatic, just like those
characters at the beginning of a James Bond film.
You know what I mean, the ones who are just about
to tell Bond who the villains are and where the
treasure's been hidden when they're bumped off by
the baddies.'

'Just as well, or there wouldn't be anybody left for
007 to blow away, would there?' said Teddy, reaching for his paper knife and slitting open the top of
the envelope while he chuckled. 'Anyhow, we'd
better take a look at what's put Barry's knickers in
a twist. Perhaps it's his bill – it can't be a writ or a

bounced cheque, he wouldn't make such a fuss.'

He slid his hand inside and brought out a clutch of colour prints held together by a large elastic band. 'Now what in heaven's name has he sent me here? A selection of the Gore-Blimey holiday snaps?'

Marlene craned her head over Teddy's shoulders to look at the photograph at the top of the pile. It showed an attractive teenage girl smiling seductively at the camera holding an empty crystal champagne glass in her hand. She was dressed in a denim jacket and blue jeans tucked into a pair of calf-high leather boots. She stood on the lawn of someone's back-garden which Teddy vaguely recognised, although at first he couldn't immediately place the location.

'Oh my,' he said softly as he pulled off the elastic band and peeled off the first print from the pile to reveal the next photograph, which showed the girl with her jacket off and in the act of unbuttoning her shirt. 'I have an awful feeling that I know what's coming next.'

'Well, what's so terrible about these pics?' demanded Marlene as she looked over Teddy's shoulder at the third shot, in which the girl's shirt was now off and she stood with arms akimbo, thrusting her bare white breasts towards the unknown photographer.

'You'll soon see,' said Teddy grimly, for he had now recalled exactly why the background of the well-kept garden shown in the photographs was so familiar to him. 'These snaps were taken at Bernie

Harwin's place up in Muswell Hill, and I'll bet a pound to a penny . . .'

His voice trailed off as they pored over the next picture which showed the girl taking off her jeans. Teddy breathed hard as he gazed at a shot of her lying stark naked on a white rug which had been placed on the lawn with her hand between her legs. Then came the shots which Teddy had guessed would now appear – the first showed the girl on her knees holding a thickly erect black penis which she was pressing against her cheek, in the second she was licking round the mushroom helmet and in the third, her hands were clamped around the dark shaft and her lips were stretched over the huge knob which was now inside her mouth.

'Presumably that's Bernie's dick,' said Marlene thoughtfully. 'Do you think that he was photographing himself being sucked off?'

'No, I don't think so, love,' said Teddy as he picked up the phone and dialled Barry Gore-Wharton's private number. 'There are two girls involved in this *Sunday Pictorial* story, the randy seventeen-year-old twins, remember? It's my guess that one twin had it away with Bernie while the other was busy with the camera and deciding how many noughts should be on the cheque Bernie would have to write to buy the negatives.'

'You think Bernie's being blackmailed? But the press couldn't print these photographs, they're far too rude. And anyhow, the girls didn't need them to sell their story to the *Sunday Pictorial*.'

'I'll explain in a moment,' said Teddy as he heard his solicitor's phone ringing. 'Barry, it's Teddy here, I've just seen the photographs. Were they sent directly to Bernie? Oh well, it's not the first time we've had this problem, is it? At least Bernie's not fooling around with fourteen-year-old boys like you-know-who! I'll keep these under lock and key and we'll have a chin wag about them at *La Miraggio*.'

He replaced the receiver and let out a heavy sigh. 'Don't breathe a word about this to anyone,' he said to Marlene. 'I don't think these girls are professional blackmailers. All this will cost Bernie is a few grand, but hopefully he'll learn his lesson and stop fucking every girl that throws her knickers at him.

'It's true that the papers don't need these photos to run stories about Bernie the Bonker. But you know what this business is like, it thrives on gossip. Remember that we want to launch Bernie in the USA next year. We don't want any hassles from immigration about his involvement with young girls and drugs, do we? So frankly, it's easier all round to pay off these two beauties, especially as it's Bernie who'll have to fork out, and not us!

'Anyhow, as I said to you earlier, I'll call Warren, our tame private 'tec, after lunch and see if we can find some skeletons in their closet. If these girls want to play dirty, we'll get our retaliation in first!'

As Teddy was explaining how he hoped to solve Bernie Harwin's problems, the subject of blackmail was also being discussed in Tony Cavendish's office. He had just finalised an agreement with a Midlands pop music promoter for Sharon Saxon to head up a Sunday-night concert in Leicester in the autumn. He put down the phone and punched the air in evident satisfaction as Adrian Klein's secretary, Barbara Kennedy, came into his office.

'Not bad, not bad at all, four hundred and seventy five pounds plus a five per cent cut of the box-office take. I don't think Teddy will grumble too much about that little deal,' he said to Barbara as she set down a letter for him to sign on his desk. 'Mike Randall was after Dusty Springfield or Sandie Shaw and, of course, he would have offered much more for them, but Sharon will still be enough of a draw to put bums on seats. I can't yet talk telephone numbers for Sharon but, with a bit of luck, she'll be right up at the top by Christmas.'

'It's certainly a feather in your cap arranging for Nick Clarke to write her next song,' commented Barbara who, in the absence of Adrian, had kindly offered to hold the fort for Tony's own secretary. The blonde bombshell Sam, had gone home complaining of a severe headache, but Barbara suspected she was planning to spend the rest of the day in bed with her boyfriend, the ineffable Freddie Amos, who had returned to London early that morning on the overnight train from Manchester. 'But did you *have* to fuck his secretary to pull that one off?'

'No, that had nothing to do with it,' Tony answered in an offended tone. But he soon broke into a chuckle when he looked up and realised from the impish grin from Barbara's face that she had only been teasing him. 'I wish I could claim the credit but, as I said to you before, it was Sharon who did the persuading.'

'On her back,' added Barbara and Tony held up his hands in surrender. 'Okay, Babs, I won't deny that the fact she is a sexy young kid didn't help. But to be fair to Nick, she was the one who came on strong. It isn't as if he tried to blackmail her on a no-fuck, no-song deal.'

'I'll take your word for it, but it wouldn't have surprised me if he had tried to trade music for pussy,' she said drily. 'Which reminds me, can I slip off in fifteen minutes? I'm meeting Gigi, Adrian Klein's girl-friend, for lunch and I think she's going to cry on my shoulder about how he's been treating her. Honestly, some of you men are enough to make a girl think twice about lesbianism. I'm seriously thinking of asking Carola Watforde to take me to the Red Parrot Club in Great Titchfield Street.'

Tony looked at her in astonishment when he heard Barbara mention this notorious lesbian hangout, for only a few weeks ago he had enjoyed a luscious if quick fuck with the curvy girl after an office party to celebrate a member of staff's twenty-first birthday.

'I would be a terrible waste if you did, Babs,' he said with genuine feeling. 'I simply can't believe there aren't scores of guys queuing up to ask you out.'

Barbara shook her head and said: 'Thanks for the morale-booster, Tony, but there's been nobody since

March, when I split up with the guy I had been going out with for nearly two years.'

'Well, you surprise me, although I know how difficult it is after breaking-up,' said Tony as he dived into his desk and brought out two glasses and a bottle of Remy Martin. 'I finished with a long-standing girl-friend around that time and I'm still all at sixes and sevens. So join me in a little toast to the future. I'm sure it's going to be brighter for us both.'

He poured out a generous measure and handed a glass to her. 'Hey, how will I be able to do any work for Adrian this afternoon?' she protested. As if on cue, the telephone rang and it was none other than her absent boss on the line.

'Hi Adrian, how's it going?' she asked. From the bright smile on her face as she listened to Adrian's reply, Tony gauged that his colleague's meeting with Dickie Segal had ended on a happy note. This was confirmed when Barbara put down the phone and said; 'Well, here's to Adrian, he's managed to get Amalgamated to sign up all our artistes for the Christmas season and to celebrate he's taking Dickie Segal out to lunch. He won't be back till about four.'

'Teddy Dixon will be well pleased,' remarked Tony as he raised his glass. 'And as he'll be thinking about our summer bonuses soon, this couldn't have come at a better time. So let's drink to good old Adrian! May his ball-point never run dry!'

They clinked their glasses together and drank

Adrian's health, but Barbara refused the offer of a refill, saying that she had to leave as Gigi would be waiting for her downstairs.

'Okay, but as Adrian won't be rolling in till four, at least promise you'll join me for coffee and brandy here when you come back,' said Tony, giving her a peck on the cheek as he escorted her towards the door. Despite her long-held resolution about never becoming involved with any man in the office, she returned the light kiss before scurrying back to her room to pick up her hand-bag.

In fact Gigi had been waiting for less than five minutes when Barbara walked into the reception area and the two girls shook hands warmly. 'Nice to see you, Gigi. I was thinking of taking you to Vittorio's, a little Italian restaurant off New Bond Street. It's nothing fancy but the food's good.'

'Lead on, Barbara, but let's be clear about one thing here and now. This lunch is on me,' said Gigi firmly as they made their way out into the warm mid-day sunshine.

'If you insist,' replied Barbara with a twinkle in her eye. 'The dreaded Adrian just called me five minutes ago to say that he's completed a big deal with Amalgamated Entertainments and that I should go and have a slap-up lunch on his account. I know you two aren't seeing eye-to-eye at the moment but it seems an awful pity not to take up this offer. Rose and Griffin can well afford it.'

'Well, if you're sure,' said Gigi, although she was somewhat relieved to hear this offer. As usual she was waiting for her model agency to come through with fees from weeks before and her bank account was already in the red.

'I'm positive,' Barbara confirmed as they turned the corner into Piccadilly. 'We'll have a super lunch on Adrian's expense account.'

And this they did, polishing off Signor Vitello's salmon trout baked in fennel and wine with a bottle of Soave. By the time the waiter had placed two small glasses of strega on the table, both girls were feeling mellow and relaxed.

'So what am I going to do about Adrian? asked Gigi with a note of plaintiveness in her voice. 'I've had a wild time without him, but I do miss him. On the other hand, I don't want to go crawling back with my tail between my legs.'

'Oh, come on, Adrian wouldn't see it that way,' said Barbara reassuringly. 'He'll be only too happy to have you back. Do you really want to know what I think? If I were you, I'd go back to Melissa's, collect all my things and go back to Adrian's flat. Then when he comes home this evening, open the door wearing a big smile and at most a pair of frilly knickers. Then let Nature take its course!'

'Perhaps you're right. After all, I did fly off the handle a bit at him,' said Gigi thoughtfully. 'Now that's enough about me. How's your love life, Babs? I know you finished with Ray a few months ago. Has there been anyone else since then?'

Barbara shook her head. 'No, I haven't had much luck recently,' she sighed. 'I thought I'd found a nice guy a couple of weeks ago but it's not worked out. You might know him, Gigi, he's a photographer called Stan Messina and he does a lot of fashion work for the big advertising agencies.'

'Yes, his name's familiar, though I haven't actually worked with him. I'm really sorry that things didn't work out.'

'Well, I think we went too far too fast,' replied Barbara with a resigned sigh. 'We were introduced at a party. This hasn't happened to me very often but the minute our eyes met, there was a kind of instant mutual attraction between us. We had a couple of drinks and then we danced and had a great time together.

'To be honest, I couldn't wait to leave the party with him and, of course when he dropped me home, I asked him inside for coffee. I knew that Stan was feeling the same way about me and before I'd even put on the kettle, he swept me into his arms and began kissing my neck.

' "Hey, take it easy," I said but when he made his way up to my mouth I returned his kiss. I stood there twisting and thrusting my hips up against the huge bulge pushing against my tummy. I stiffened for a moment when I felt his hand at the zipper of my dress but I didn't try to stop him. He quickly pulled the dress free of my shoulders and down to my waist before his fingers were tugging at the clasp of my bra.

We shouldn't be doing this, I thought with a twinge of alarm, but my whole body was now shaking with excitement as he began licking my breasts, making his way from one globe to another. I thought I would fall but with his arm around me, I let myself be half carried into the bedroom where I soon found myself lying naked on the eiderdown.

'In no time, Stan was out of his clothes and coming towards me. His cock seemed immense, much thicker than Ray's, but before I could take a good look, he was hovering over me with his prick in his hand. I moaned with delight as I felt his knob slip tightly between my pussy lips and he rammed his huge cock into my cunt up to the hairs.

' "Stan, Stan," I gasped, clinging frantically to him. My legs flew up in the air as he sank his shaft to depths where no-one had been before. I clung to him as he fucked me, my nails clawing at his back. His firm bum cheeks were rising and falling as he pistoned that big tool of his in and out of my juicy honeypot. He was fucking me so hard that I thought I would go crazy. I was gasping for air, lifting my hips, arching them up to meet his insistent thrusts.

'I was coming like mad but I nearly fainted when he drove in even deeper and his twitching cock began to spurt deep inside me. Gigi, this was one of the best fucks I've ever had! Stan stayed the night and we made love again three more times before breakfast. This was Sunday but he said he had to finish some work off in his studio that morning and asked if he could come back that night. Well, I told him that I had made an arrangement with a couple of friends to go and see a film, which was the truth and anyhow I wanted to slow things down a bit.

' "Okay," he said, "I'll ring you tomorrow night, is that okay?" '

Barbara exhaled deeply and swallowed down the rest of her strega before finishing her story. 'I waited all evening for that call, but it never came, and the truth is that I haven't heard a word from Stan since.'

'What a rotter! It's his loss though, not yours,' said Gigi warmly.

'It's kind of you to say so, and I wouldn't have minded so much if he hadn't promised that he would call,' sighed Barbara. 'I don't make a habit of bonking on a first date, but it did seem as though we had something going. Shows how wrong one can be.'

'Chalk it down to experience,' advised Gigi as she pulled out a card from her bag. 'Look, I know you have to go back to work this afternoon, but see if you can get away early and come round to a party at the Meridew Galleries in Gerson Street. There's a happening starring Jason Howard, that *avant-garde* artist who's always in the gossip column, and it could be a lot of fun. Most of the girls from our agency have been invited and if Jason if as way out as the papers say he is, it could all be a lot of fun.

'It's supposed to start at half past four, but I'm going to take your advice and go back to Melissa's place to pack my bag and then I'll go home and change,' declared Gigi while Barbara signed the bill. 'Let's all meet up at half past five – I'll call Adrian and make it up with him and ask him to come along.

Perhaps you'll bring that nice guy Tony Cavendish who you were telling me about.'

Barbara thought for a moment and then said: 'Okay Gigi, thanks for the invite. I hope that Tony can come – I'm just in the mood for a bit of craziness to give me a lift.'

When she returned to the office, Barbara immediately told Tony about the happening and asked if he would like to come and take part. She was pleased, though slightly surprised, when he readily accepted.

'Sure, I'd love to. Jason's a real weirdo but he can actually paint a bit and is one of the better Op-artists in town,' said Tony enthusiastically.

'An Op artist, did you say?' said Barbara and he nodded vigorously. 'Yup, it's the new style for the late sixties, an abstract style concerned with optical effects such as the illusion of movement. Jason's one of the best in the field, along with Ben Bucknall and Carys Thomas.

'Now I've just put on the kettle so you sit down and let me make you a coffee,' he said firmly. 'And then we'll finish that drink we were having before lunch. Don't give me any argument, I won't take no for an answer.'

She grinned as she answered: 'I don't need much persuading, though make the coffee strong and only give me a thimbleful of brandy or I'll soon be asleep. Gigi and I went through a bottle of Soave at lunch and Vittorio insisted on giving us a strega afterwards.'

'Not to sorry, sit down and take things easy while

I make the coffee. Teddy's out at lunch at *La Miraggio*, Adrian won't be back for a while and it's much too nice an afternoon to work,' said Tony cheerfully. Five minutes later Barbara was still sitting in his office when he reappeared with two mugs of black coffee.

Barbara would have found it difficult to explain exactly why she began to feel sexy, especially after reminding herself only half an hour before of her experience with Stan Messina, the photographer who had walked in and out of her life so abruptly. But she had always liked Tony Cavendish. When they had finished their coffee, she rose from her seat to put the empty mugs on a tray. She did not remove her arm when Tony wrapped his hand around her wrist and looked wordlessly up at her from his seat.

He stood up and kissed her eyes, her cheeks and her nose in quick succession. She trembled all over as she whispered: 'Oh Tony, is this a clever thing to do?'

'I really don't know, but it just seems right, doesn't it?' he responded gently. Barbara offered no resistance as he took her into his arms and his lips covered her own. Their faces pressed closer together and their tongues slid wetly around each other's mouths as they exchanged a passionate kiss. She sat on his lap as Tony unfastened the buttons on her blouse and unhooked her bra. Barbara moaned with pleasure when he cupped his hands around her firm, rounded breasts, alternately pinching the nipples and squeezing the soft, creamy globes.

Her hand strayed down to his lap and Tony helped her unzip his trousers. She plunged her hand inside and grasped his hard, pulsating prick which sprang out to display itself, naked and twitching with desire. He snaked his hand underneath her short skirt and rubbed her mound with the palm of his hand, which sent shivers of ecstasy running through her body. Barbara still possessed enough self-control to place a restraining hand on his arm as she whispered: 'Tony, I'm going to lock the door.'

She heaved herself up from his lap and turned the key in the lock before running back into his waiting arms. With trembling hands, he removed her blouse and bra and then he unzipped her skirt and slid down on his knees as he pulled it down over her hips.

'You're a very naughty boy,' she murmured as he tugged down her knickers. She spread her legs invitingly, affording Tony a bird's eye view of the nest of fluffy brown curls which covered her mound. 'Very naughty indeed,' she added as his hands massaged her thighs and his fingers moved higher to stroke her moist pussy lips which peeked through the fleecy brown bush. Barbara growled with delight as he continued to rub his fingers at the entrance to her yielding crack.

Barbara leaned forward and dragged him upwards, positioning his head firmly between her thighs. Tony pressed his face closely against her hairy cunt and slid his arms round to clutch at her soft, fleshy bum cheeks. His heartbeat quickened as his tongue raked along the length of Barbara's slit. Then he kissed her pouting pussy lips and she gasped as he slipped the tip of his tongue inside her cunny and explored her smooth, warm dampness. Almost of their own volition, her legs splayed even wider as she sought to open herself even further to him. She moaned and sighed, tensing towards her release while Tony lapped up the tangy love juices which were flowing freely from her tingling honey-pot. Her hands clawed at his shoulders as she arched her body backwards to press herself even more tightly against his face. Tony's own excitement built up as his tongue fluttered inside her juicy quim.

'Ahhh! Yes, you've got it!' she squealed when Tony found her clitty, licking and sucking the erect little button which twitched and vibrated at his electric touch. She seized his head in her hands and yelped with joy as he brought her off, flicking his tongue at speed in and out of her seething cunt as she orgasmed, her hips bucking as a flood of love juice cascaded out of her pussy and splashed over his face.

Barbara's body relaxed as the tension of her climax drained away, but the sight of Tony's stiff, veined shaft soon recharged her batteries and, as he clambered to his feet, she pulled his trousers and pants to his ankles and murmured hoarsely: 'And now let me repay the compliment!'

He leaned against the desk as Barbara dropped to her knees and kissed the bared bell-end of his quivering cock. Now it was his turn to moan in ecstasy as she slowly swirled her tongue around the domed helmet, licking up the sticky drops of precum which had already formed around the tiny 'eye'.

Then she opened her mouth and sucked in half his shaft, closing her lips around the warm, soft skin of his throbbing boner. She was rewarded by a delighted sigh from the back of Tony's throat as she bobbed her head to and fro, sucking vigorously on his pulsating prick while she worked her pink tongue all round his trembling truncheon, running her teeth up and down the fleshy shaft which seemed to swell even more in her mouth.

'My God, I'm coming!' he cried out and this made Barbara gobble his cock at an even faster pace while she gently squeezed his tightening scrotum. A throaty growl escaped Tony's lips as his body went rigid. He climaxed with a sudden upwards jerk of his hips, sending an arcing jet of gluey hot spunk down Barbara's throat. She gulped down his jism with relish, milking his trembling tool of every last drop of seed until his prick began to wilt and soften as she twirled her tongue around the ridges of his knob.

She rested her head against his thighs and then Tony pulled her gently to her feet and said quietly: 'Babs, much as I'd rather make love to you for the rest of the afternoon, we'd better get dressed. Someone is bound to come in soon.'

'Yes, of course,' she muttered. After they had

quickly thrown on their clothes, Barbara looked across at him as she unlocked the door and said: 'Tony, I hope you don't think—'

He placed his finger against her lips. 'I don't think anything except how two friends followed their natural inclinations and let it all hang out,' he said firmly. 'And furthermore, I'm not the sort of shit who tells tales about his love life to his friends. But then I would have hoped you knew that and weren't going to make me promise not to tell anyone about what happened just now.'

Barbara blushed as she walked across and kissed him on the lips. 'I owe you an apology for even thinking you might spill the beans at one of those after-work drinking sessions with Teddy and Adrian,' she confessed as she wrapped her arms around him.

'Not to worry, I'll think of a way you can make it up to me!' Tony replied, kissing the top of her head before sitting down in his chair. 'Now let's get down to some work so we can leave a bit early tonight for this Jason Howard event. He's a real nut-case, you know, Babs. God knows what sort of show he's going to put on.'

A similar thought was going through Gigi's mind as she pressed the bell of Melissa's apartment. She chuckled as she remembered reading about the wild young artist's last exhibition when on the opening day, he had thrown a large pot of red paint over a critic who had dared to criticise his work.

There was no answer so she pressed the bell a second time. Melissa couldn't be out for she had told her that she had a busy day ahead with three clients to see in the afternoon. She waited patiently and was about to ring for a third time when the door opened.

'Come on in, Gigi,' Melissa said hurriedly. 'I'm sorry to keep you waiting, but I'm in the middle of a reading.' Gigi noticed with surprise that the astrologist was wearing only a short silk kimono, and apologised for interrupting her work.

'No problem, my three o'clock appointment had to cancel,' said Melissa as she led the way into the lounge. 'But Andy Whyte took the afternoon off so I told him to come over and I'd work out a forecast about his love life if he'd take me to Jason Howard's op-art exhibition later this afternoon. I have to be there early because Jason has asked me to sit a table and offer astrological readings to guests. I won't get paid but there should be some good publicity mileage in it for me.'

'What a coincidence! I'll see you there a little later,' said Gigi excitedly and she explained to her friend how she planned to make things up with Adrian. 'Thanks for letting me stay with you, I had a great time but hopefully Adrian and I have both learned something from my walk-out. So I've come back to pack my bags and go home. But all being well I'll see you at the art gallery at about half-past five.'

'I'm sure you're right, a hard man is good to find,'

said Melissa, smiling at the remembrance of how much she enjoyed being fucked by Adrian Klein's thick circumcised shaft. 'Do come through into the bedroom and get your clothes – actually Andy was just about to fuck me, you're welcome to join in if you like.'

'Thanks, but if I'm going back to Adrian I'd better turn over a new leaf,' said Gigi as she followed Melissa into the bedroom. Andy was sitting naked on the bed, fondling his erect cock which stood up stoutly between his thighs. Melissa shucked off her kimono and stood naked at the side of the bed. As she surveyed Andy's throbbing erection, she remarked: 'I do like your nice, thick chopper, Andy!' She sat down and grasped his prick at the base, playfully waggling his shaft from side to side as she swung herself across and straddled him with her hairy mound just inches away from his face. 'Now what do you think of my pussy? Be truthful, is she as pretty as your prick?'

'She's lovely, Melissa, really beautiful. I'm going to make her all wet with my tongue before I fuck her,' he replied as Melissa ran her fingers through her forest of black pubic hair, combing out the thick curls to reveal the pink split of her pussy.

'Thank you, Andy. It always pleases a girl to hear a man praise her pussy,' said Melissa with satisfaction. 'You would be surprised how fellows do – in fact it always amazes me that there are some men who find their cocks things of beauty and a joy forever but have the nerve to say that they find cunnies ugly. The cheek of it!'

Andy kissed her pouting pussy lips and remarked: 'They're just immature, Melissa. I remember the first time I rolled my tongue over a girl's pussy. I shut my eyes because I was so worried about whether I was doing it right. But now I'm more than happy to look life square in the cunt.'

And as if to prove it, he ran his fingers along Melissa's exposed crack, teasing open the curled lips and gently inserting his forefinger inside her squelchy quim. He pulled out his finger and inhaled the tangy feminine odour before plunging his head forward into Melissa's hot, juicy love tunnel.

She tasted strong and clean and she gasped: 'Oh yes, now flick my clitty, there's a good boy, I want to come!'

Andy pulled his head back and panted: 'I'd much rather make you come by fucking you, Melissa. If you turn round and get on your knees we can do it doggie-fashion. I can play with your clitty while my cock's sliding in and out of your pussy.'

The idea obviously appealed to Melissa for she immediately did as he asked and bent forward in front of him, taking her weight on her elbows and knees. She thrust out her smooth broad bum cheeks and spread wide her pussy lips. Andy clambered up and ran his finger in the long furrow between her buttocks, giving the winking brown star of her arsehole an impudent tickle. This made the girl wriggle as she waited impatiently for his cock to slide inside her throbbing wet honeypot.

She miaowed with delight as Andy positioned himself behind her and slewed his sturdy stiff-stander between her bum cheeks, plunging his rigid rod all the way inside her until her backside was pressed tightly against his lean belly. At first he stayed relatively still, enjoying the erotic sight of Melissa's hips rotating in a sensual motion as she pressed her face down upon the eiderdown.

He reached round her waist and stabbed his finger inside her slit, nipping her erect clitty with his long fingers. This sent Melissa into a spasm of frenzied ecstasy and she yelled out: 'Ooooh! Ooooh! Brilliant! Marvellous! More, more, pump your thick prick inside my cunt, Andy!'

The bed rocked as Andy continued to diddle her clitty. Then he clutched at her breasts with his other hand, rubbing her big nipples until they stood up like two little red rubbery stalks. Gigi, who was standing transfixed at the foot of the bed, was tempted to lean forward and suck them, but she knew full well that if she became involved she wouldn't be able to stop until Andy's gleaming shaft had penetrated her own moistening pussy and reluctantly she turned away and began folding her clothes into her case.

Meanwhile, matters were swiftly approaching crisis point as Andy thrust home one final time and his quivering cock spewed out a luscious jet of creamy spunk inside Melissa's clinging love channel. He pulled her by the waist towards him as he pumped out a copious ejaculation into her cunt.

Gigi put the last of her clothes into her overnight case which she zipped up and turned round to face Melissa and Andy who were still panting with exhaustion from their frenetic coupling.

'I must be away,' she said and blew the lovers a kiss. 'Stay where you are, I can see myself out, no problem.'

'Okay, Gigi, we'll see you later,' said Melissa as she slicked her fist up and down Andy's semi-erect shaft. 'Oooh, look how quickly this thick prick is stiffening up again. Come on, Andy, we've time for one more fuck before we have to leave for the exhibition.'

'I'll leave you to it,' said Gigi hastily as she picked up her case and walked out of the bedroom. She looked behind her to see Melissa lying flat on her back with her fingers parting her pussy lips and Andy heaving himself over her, his erect shaft clasped in his hand, ready to be inserted into Melissa's moist, welcoming honeypot.

Twenty-five minutes later she was back in Adrian Klein's flat at St John's Wood and was waiting to speak to him on the phone. She was sitting naked on the sofa as, after she had cleared the air with Adrian, she was going to change into something more casual for this evening's festivities.

'Putting you through,' said the Rose and Griffin operator and Gigi cleared her throat and said softly: 'Adrian, it's me, Gigi. I thought I'd let you know that I've come back home, and, well, I owe you an apology. I'm really sorry I flew into such a rage last night. Please forgive me,' she said meekly.

Adrian had been half-expecting this call and had prepared a coolish reply, but his success in the negotiations with Dickie Segal had put him in such a mellow mood that his resolve to make Gigi suffer instantly dissolved and he simply replied: 'Oh well, let's forget it. I'll try and leave early and I'll take you out for a romantic candlelight supper.'

'That would be lovely, but there's something else I'd also like to do,' said Gigi, and she rapidly explained about how she would like to go to the Jason Howard exhibition. 'Are you very busy right now? I could come up to the office after work or meet you at the gallery.'

'I'm always busy these days,' Adrian grumbled as he looked at his watch. 'I thought I might be able to take it easy this afternoon but Teddy wants to see me in ten minutes. It seems that Bernie Harwin's in trouble again and we're going to have to perform another quick damage-limitation exercise.

'Still, I should be able to get away at a reasonable time – why don't we meet at the gallery at about six o'clock? I'll try and be a bit earlier if I can as I'd like to whizz you off for an early supper and then back to the flat. I'm so looking forward to seeing you again.'

Gigi blew him a kiss down the phone and she lowered her voice and said in a throaty whisper: 'Oh yes, I can't wait to see you again either, darling. I'm sitting here on the sofa naked and I'm thinking about you, lover, which is making my cunt all wet and tingly. My fingers are inside my pussy, squeezing my clit and I can't wait to have your thick, hard cock inside me.'

She was rewarded by the sound of heavy breathing on the other end of the line. Now genuinely aroused, she went on: 'Shall I tell you what made me feel so sexy? It was when I started to think about the first time we made it together. Do you remember where that was?'

'How could I ever forget!' he retorted with a chuckle. 'It was at Billy Macfarlane's gym, about a week after we'd first met at Les Cheetham's party. Tony Cavendish and I had gone for our weekly workout, but of course I had no idea that you were there.'

'No, you were blissfully ignorant of the fact that I could see you but you couldn't see me,' cooed Gigi as she slid back upon the sofa, running her fingers delicately across the bush of silky blonde hair between her legs. 'There I was standing in front of the mirrors doing my warm-ups and I could see you in your track-suit eyeing that pretty young singer on your books, what's her name, Sharon Saxon. It made me mad because I was wearing flesh-coloured tights and a pretty sexy leotard which barely covered my tits and bum which I thought would have already attracted your attention.

'So when I saw you drop to the floor for some push-ups, I moved across and stood directly in front of you. As I bent down and touched my toes, from between my legs I could see you were now looking at my bum stuck out right in front of your face, and when I straightened up and turned round, one look at the bulge between your legs told me that I was turning you on.'

She giggled as she heard Adrian growl deeply and then went on: 'You finished your press-ups and walked over to the exercise bike. My pussy began to moisten when you pulled off your track suit and I could see the outline of your tight little bum under your thin nylon shorts, especially when you stretched over the bike and started to pedal away like mad.'

'Yes, well that was because by now I had a gigantic hard-on,' explained Adrian and Gigi laughed delightedly as she went on: 'I thought I could see a bulge in your shorts and I could also feel the heat in my crotch too when at last you swung your leg over the bike and walked over to me. "Follow me," you whispered as you marched off towards the changing rooms and whisked me into a small cubicle. I watched wide-eyed as you dropped the lock into place and then, with one firm motion, you swept me into your arms and kissed me.

'As your mouth sucked at mine, your hands roamed all over my body, cupping my bum cheeks and squeezing my breasts. This made my pussy muscles clamp tightly together and I knew the only way to relax them would be to let your thick hard cock bring out the orgasm locked inside me.

'So I was more than ready when you peeled off my leotard and that's why I helped you roll down my tights. I gasped as your lips found my nipples and your hand rubbed against my clitty. Do you remember how I bit your shoulder as I felt the oncoming force of my pent-up climax shudder through me? I humped my pussy against your fingers and as I trembled all over, my love juices poured out of my pussy all over your hand.'

Gigi leaned back and began to diddle her fingers in and out of her sopping honeypot as she continued breathlessly 'Then I leaned back against the wall and you shoved that big meaty cock of yours up me. You were so strong that you slid me over your knob by holding me round the waist. I didn't have to do anything but let the feelings flow as you moved me up and down. I reached for your balls and gently lifted them, coaxing your spunk to the surface. It was so exciting as you moaned and buried your nose in my hair. I rolled your balls between my fingers and felt your prick pulsate inside my pussy as you got ready to burst. I could tell by the way you arched your back that you were ready to fill my cunny with a jet of your sticky white jism.

'A few quick pumps later and you pushed me hard against the wall as you shot your load. My pussy muscles tightened and held on to your cock as it see-sawed wildly in and out of my love channel.

'I ran my hand down your back which was all shiny with perspiration. I expected you to back away from me but instead you held me on your cock which was still stiff and lay me down on a rubber exercise mat. Then I wrapped my legs round your waist and you fucked me again with that gorgeous big prick . . . oooh, it felt so good.'

Gigi paused as she heard a series of fierce little gasps coming out of the receiver and she whispered: 'Adrian, are you frigging yourself? Go on, take your stiffie out of your trousers and play with it.

'Ooooh!' moaned Gigi as her finger sped in and out of her cunt at speed. 'Adrian, I'm coming, I'm coming, yes, yes, YES! Aaaah, I'm there, you should see all the cunny juice pouring out of my quim.'

She sighed as she heard a strangulated cry from Adrian and she muttered: 'Now it's your turn to finish yourself off! Squeeze that fat tool, rub your fingers all along the shaft, m'mm, I wish I were there to suck your helmet and make it happen even quicker for you! If I were there I'd cram your cock inside my mouth and draw out all that creamy seed and swallow it all down.'

There was silence on the line and Gigi shook the receiver as she called out: 'Hello, hello, Adrian, are you still there?'

'Yes, I'm here,' replied Adrian faintly. 'You naughty girl, it's as well I had a box of tissues on my desk or I would have had some pretty difficult explaining to do at the dry cleaners tomorrow!'

Gigi chuckled softly and said: 'Put your cock away now, darling, I want it to be in good shape when we come home tonight because we're not going to sleep until we've fucked and sucked ourselves silly. Then we'll wake up and begin all over again.'

'M'mm, why don't we skip this Jason Howard exhibition and I'll come straight home,' suggested

Adrian but Gigi shook her head and said: 'No, I've promised to go. Anyhow, there'll be a crowd of people we know there and with any luck we'll have a great time.

''Bye for now, darling. I'll meet you at the gallery. Oh, Tony and Barbara from your office have also been invited and it would be nice if you could all come together.'

'Sure, that's always a good thing to do,' he rejoined with a laugh. 'Gigi, I'll see you later.'

She put down the phone, purring happily as she heaved herself up and went into the bathroom to shower before she changed for the party. Adrian sat at his desk for a few moments, wondering why he was so much putty in Gigi's hands. It was sheer animal magnetism, he remarked to himself as he rose from his chair and walked out of his office on his way to Teddy Dixon's domain. *Let's face facts, Mr Klein*, he muttered aloud, *you still fancy the pretty girl like crazy*. It was certainly true that his cock was now conditioned to become erect as soon as he was anywhere in the vicinity of her ripe young body.

Well, that's hardly surprising, he thought. She was like a tigress in bed and he had never been with any girl who gave a better blow-job. But then a slow smile spread across his face as he thought about the previous night. He decided that Tanya, the hostess from *La Miraggio*, would give Gigi a good run for her money as far as cock-sucking was concerned.

It was weird how important sex was, Adrian

philosophised as he waited for the lift, although fucking was more meaningful with Gigi than with any of his previous girl-friends. With his previous girl-friends, the longing for a fuck was like wanting a drink or a quick snack. In his job he came across so many gorgeous girls who were easy lays that he seemed to be screwing day and night. But sometimes, as soon as he'd finished, he couldn't remember why he wanted it so much in the first place.

'Come in,' called out the managing director as Adrian knocked on Teddy's door. Adrian was surprised to see Barry Gore-Wharton, Rose and Griffin's solicitor, sitting opposite Teddy. Both men looked somewhat flushed as if they had been drinking more heavily than usual. As if to confirm his judgment, Teddy lifted a balloon brandy glass and said: 'Ah, here's the man himself! Let's hear what he has to say.'

'Adrian, help yourself to a liqueur and come and sit down. Barry and I want to talk to you about this problem we have with Bernie Harwin. There's not too much we can do about these teenage twins with whom he has been having it away. I've asked Warren to see if we can find out anything about them which might be useful, but I doubt if we can stop their story appearing in the papers.

'Hopefully we'll be able to ride out this business but we can't go on staggering from crisis to crisis. We have to look at the future if we're going to keep Bernie at the top.' Adrian poured himself a cognac from the beautiful lead crystal decanter on Teddy's desk. 'Now I don't care if Bernie wants to give himself a hernia, but somehow we have to stop him showing his cock to every groupie who throws her knickers at him. Now how are we going to go about it?'

'Why don't you introduce him to someone like Polly St George?' suggested Adrian with a grin. 'Believe me, if he became involved with Polly I don't think even Bernie would have enough strength left to screw anyone else.'

'Polly St George?' repeated the lawyer with some surprise. 'Do you mean that girl who's on the panel of *Press My Bell*? She's not one of your clients, is she?'

Teddy Dixon slowly drew his hand over his cheek before he replied: 'Not any more, Barry. We used to represent her but we parted company about five years ago. It was all very amicable though. I recommended her to Joe Bancroft and as far as I know she's still with him.'

'Not like you to lose a good client though – why did you let her go?'

'Well, between you me and the gatepost, Polly's a nice enough girl but she's hardly the most talented artiste in the world. I mean, she's well over forty by now and she's managed to make a career out of being one of those showbiz personalities who are famous for being famous. I mean to say, she can't act her way out of a paper bag but she tells a good story on a chat show so they're always inviting her back. Since she wangled herself onto the panel of

Press My Bell, she's made a nice few bob opening supermarkets and doing commercials.'

Barry Gore-Wharton looked puzzled at this explanation. 'So why does Adrian think she could help us out with Bernie Harwin?' he asked. Teddy let out a short laugh before he answered: 'Barry do you remember my telling you that Rex Harrison was supposed to have the biggest cock in Hollywood? Well, they say that Polly shagged him out so much last year when he came over to make *Doctor Dolittle* that she was banned from the set.'

'Good heavens, yet she looks as though butter wouldn't melt in her mouth,' exclaimed the lawyer. Teddy Dixon shrugged his shoulders. 'I don't know about butter but she's had more cocks between her lips than you've had hot dinners. He finished his cognac and refilled his glass from the decanter. 'And that includes yours, doesn't it, Mr Klein?' he added.

Adrian had the grace to blush as he nodded his agreement while Teddy continued: 'Yes, she seduced this innocent young lad less than a month after he started work here.'

'You lucky young devil!' said Barry Gore-Wharton with a note of genuine envy in his voice. 'Polly St George is a real woman and I've always fancied her. She might be past her prime but give me those luscious curves any day rather than those little waifs like Twiggy!

'So how did you get your leg over pretty Polly so quickly?'

'I just happened to be at the right place at the

right time,' said Adrian modestly. 'It was during the summer of '62 and Teddy had sent me down one afternoon to Polly's house with a contract for her to sign. In those days she was still married to that American actor Terry Farnham and they were living in this massive great house near Henley-on-Thames. Anyway, it was a very warm day, there had been an accident on the A4 so I'd been sitting in a traffic jam for the best part of an hour. By the time I got there I felt all hot and sticky.

'Polly answered the door herself and she was wearing only a striped beach jacket loosely belted at the waist. "Adrian, you poor boy, you look all-in," she said sympathetically. She led me through the house to the garden where she had been lying on a mattress at the edge of the swimming pool that had been built for them. I explained how I had been held up in the traffic. "Oh what a shame! Let me see if I can find one of Terry's swimming costumes for you to slip on. You can have a nice rest while I read this contract that Teddy Dixon seems so anxious I should sign."

'She disappeared into the house for a couple of minutes and then reappeared at the French windows of the lounge waving a pair of blue shorts. "Come in and change into these," she called out to me. As I went towards her I found it hard to keep my eyes away from her loose jacket which revealed the quivering curves of her bare breasts with every breath she took. I went into the house and changed into the shorts and when I came out Polly was lying face down on the mattress reading through her contract. She had taken off her jacket and was lying stark naked in front of me. I could hardly believe my eyes as I stared at her beautiful bum cheeks which wiggled so sexily every time she moved to turn over a page.

' "I hope it doesn't bother you if I sunbathe while I read this," she said. It was all I could do to blurt out: "Of course not" as I plonked myself down on a deckchair and gazed over her luscious nude body. To be honest, I'd never seen a totally naked woman before. Oh, I'd had a few quickies at parties or in the back seat of my Mini, but all the girls I'd fucked or petted with had always remained partially clothed, jeans down or skirt up. All I'd seen were glimpses of tits and pussies.

'So it wasn't surprising that I soon got a tremendous hard-on which began to throb like mad when Polly turned round and exposed her large bare breasts and curly bush of pussy hair. I thought I would take a swim which would hide my hard-on but when I stood up she looked pointedly at the bulge in my shorts and said: "Are you sure I'm not disturbing you, Adrian?"

' "Let's make you a little more comfortable," she added. I stood there trembling all over as she raised herself upwards and tugged down my shorts. She smiled up at me as she flicked the long red nail of her index finger over my knob and scooped up a drop of pre-cum. She brought her finger to her lips and licked it clean and then she put out her hand and slid her fingers around my throbbing tool.

' "Be a darling and rub some oil on me," she said, pointing at the bottle which was by my feet before lying back on the mattress with her warm hand still clasped round my shaft. I smoothed the oil over her skin, brushing lightly over her hard, erect nipples and then down over her tummy. I could hardly keep my hand from shaking when I reached her pussy and she parted her thighs, trapping my hand between them. My fingertips slipped over the moist lips of her cunt and when I touched her clitty her hand tightened around my cock.

' "Adrian, have you ever eaten pussy before?" she asked softly. Although I said I had I think Polly knew I was fibbing because she said: "Super, well you lie down beside me with your head towards my feet and we'll have a nice sexy *soixante neuf*. Remember to lick my crack slowly, slide your tongue all down my slit from top to bottom. A lot of boys are frightened to try it but once you start, you'll see how naturally it comes."

'And was she right! This was the first time I'd ever had a blow job let alone eat pussy. Once I got a taste of her creamy cunt my tongue seemed to have a life of its own, whipping back and forth, up and down, boring deep inside her juicy quim. Then I felt Polly's tongue flicking over my cock, down the shaft and over my balls until my prick was completely engulfed inside her mouth. Lying on our sides we came together and I gulped down her cuntal juice and then shot my load down her throat.

'She sucked my cock till it was hard again and then lay back with her knees up and legs wide apart. I leaned forward and pressed into her lovely wet snatch. She moaned with delight as she jerked her hips upwards to meet my thrusts. It didn't take long till I was spurting my spunk inside her cunt.

'What an afternoon! Before leaving I came again between her tits and she invited me back the next week. But Teddy had guessed what had happened and he sent me up to Manchester for a fortnight. By the time I got back, Terry Farnham had returned home and I never had to chance to make love to Polly again.'

Barry Gore-Wharton wagged a reproving finger at Rose and Griffin's managing director as he commented: 'That was a trifle mean of you, Teddy, it's not your usual style to take such a dog-in-the-manger attitude.'

'It was for his own good, I've always said to my staff that it's a bad policy to screw clients because it's bound to end in tears,' Teddy protested vehemently. 'Polly's a voracious lady who was known to have a penchant for younger men. I was doing Adrian a favour by keeping him out her clutches.'

'Although I certainly didn't think so at the time,' said Adrian ruefully.'

'Maybe not, but thanks to me it wasn't your name plastered over the papers when she and Terry got divorced, was it?' grunted Teddy Dixon. He turned to the solicitor and said: 'So now you understand what Adrian had in mind when he mentioned Polly's name.

Well done, lad, I should have thought of it myself. If we could get Polly and Bernie together, she would manage to keep him on the straight and narrow for at least a month.'

'And this would keep him out of the headlines till he goes to America,' remarked Barry Gore-Wharton. 'Well, it sounds like a good idea to me, but how do we know that Polly isn't currently involved with anyone?'

'Ah, but she is,' said Teddy knowingly. He fished out a gilt-edged invitation card from the pile of papers on his desk. 'Luckily, though, it's only a fling with that barmy young artist, Jason Howard. In fact, I've had an invitation to the press preview of an exhibition of his work at the Meridew Gallery this evening. I dare say Polly put up the finance.'

'Damn! From what you and Adrian have said, it's obvious that she would have been the perfect foil for Bernie,' grumbled the lawyer. Teddy waved his invitation in the air and continued: 'It's no problem, Barry, because from what I hear, Polly's begun to complain how Jason's been costing her a lot of money recently. This is probably just the right time for her to make Bernie's acquaintance. Adrian, why don't you bring Bernie along to the exhibition and make the introductions?'

'Bernie went down to Eastbourne today to start rehearsals for Sunday's concert,' replied Adrian hastily. 'Anyhow, it needs someone to set things up first and you're the man for that job, Teddy. You've known Polly much longer than me and I couldn't speak to her as frankly as you could.'

Teddy carefully considered this point and then remarked: 'Yes, I suppose it might be better for me to start the ball rolling. She might get the needle if I don't ask her myself – though I'd still like you to be on hand in case Polly needs some extra persuasion.'

'No problem, I've already been invited to come along tonight. As my girl-friend will be there too, I won't be able to offer any extra-curricular services,' warned Adrian but Barry Gore-Wharton immediately chipped in: 'Never mind, Teddy, if Adrian's suggesting what I think he is, I'd be happy to offer my services and I wouldn't even bill you! I've always wanted to meet Polly St George and who knows, she might even make one of my dreams come true!'

'Fine, but I'm not promising that you'll get the same welcome as Adrian did down at Henley-on-Thames!' said Teddy Dixon with a throaty chuckle. 'And you'd better not forget that we're trying to interest her in Bernie Harwin and not you! Still, as they say in the classics, nothing ventured, nothing gained. Barry, come back here at half-past five and we'll all go to the gallery together.'

Like actresses, models were often forced to spend long periods 'resting' and whenever Gigi Baroja found herself with time on her hands, she frequently spent a free morning looking around an exhibition at the Royal Academy or the National Gallery. As the commercial art galleries in Mayfair were always keen to have a gaggle of pretty girls swirling around at their parties, she was often invited to events such as Jason Howard's presentation.

So when she pulled open the door of the Meridew Gallery that evening, she was fully prepared to expect something wild and wacky from Jason Howard, for the galleries were not averse to mounting the most outrageous publicity stunts to attract press coverage. However, even such a regular party guest as Gigi was startled when at the entrance to the exhibition, she was offered a catalogue by a buxom blonde girl who was wearing a black highwayman's mask over her eyes. Moreover, her boxum figure was squeezed into a black lace-up corset with holes cut out in the cups in which her breasts rested to allow her nipples to peek through.

She smiled at Gigi and said in a lilting Welsh accent: 'Hi Gigi, don't you recognise me?' Though her voice was familiar, Gigi was forced to shake her head as she stared hard at the girl whose brazenly provocative outfit was completed by a tight white G-string through which her pussy lips could be seen pressing against the semi-transparent material. Her shapely legs were covered in black silk stockings held up by frilly white garters.

'No, but your voice rings a bell,' replied Gigi as she tried to remember where she had heard this girl speak before.

'Well that's not surprising, we've spoken quite a few times – in fact our last little chat was only a few hours ago while you were waiting for Barbara Kennedy to take you to lunch.' Seeing the puzzled look on Gigi's face she went on: 'Oh, I can see I'll have to put you out of your agony. It's me, Vicky Ashford, the receptionist at Rose and Griffin.'

Gigi snapped her fingers and smiled at her. 'Yes, of course! Sorry I didn't recognise you, Vicky, but you were dressed a little differently when we last met! What brings you here, Vicky?'

'Jason and I were at school together and when he called me this afternoon to say that one of his hostesses had let him down I said I'd help him out. Mind, I should have known what I was letting myself in for. It's just as well there's no-one coming here from the office or I wouldn't know where to put myself.'

Oh dear, I'd better warn her, thought Gigi. Before she could say anything, Jason Howard himself came up to her and with a low bow, kissed her hand. The artist was dressed in a silver cape underneath which he was naked except for a bulging white athletic support. 'Ah ha, you must be Melissa's friend, Gigi Baroja! She said you were one of the prettiest girls in London,' he exclaimed with a flourish. 'I'm so pleased you're here. I'm looking for girls to paint later in the evening when the press arrive. Would you do me the honour of modelling for me?'

'I'm sure that would be great fun, but my boyfriend is meeting me here in a few minutes and I'm afraid we might have to leave fairly early,' she replied, thankful that she had a good excuse to hand. It was not unknown for Jason to produce pictures of his female models in poses which left little to the imagination.

'Well, let's hope he's late so I can sketch you,' he said. 'Now you must excuse me, I'm under strict orders to circulate. Do enjoy yourself! Your friend Mademoiselle Melissa's down there on the right, if you'd like to say hello to her while you're waiting for your boyfriend.'

Gigi made her way through the throng of guests who were being served canapes and wine by six scantily dressed waitresses. She wondered why Jason Howard would want to distract attention from his paintings by having bare-breasted bimbos floating around the place.

After giving Melissa a hug she put this question to her friend, who was sitting in front of a large canvas painted all over in a dark blue with several background stars and a spaceship in the middle. It had obviously been modelled on the hit new television series, *Star Trek*, except that photographs of two naked girls had been plastered onto the gleaming silver side of the *USS Enterprise*.

'Ah, well Jason would probably say that the girls' outfits are actually works of art as he designed their costumes,' said Melissa drily. 'Remember that his style is all about the exploitation of optical effects. On the other hand, a more cynical explanation might be that the girls might make the critics better disposed towards all these crappy pictures! I'm sure that's why I'm here.'

She grabbed a glass of white wine from a passing

waitress and passed it to Gigi. 'Cheers! I should do some work for the twenty pounds Jason is paying me to sit here but I'm busting to go to the loo. Be a pal and hold the fort while I'm gone.'

'Here, I can't do that, I don't know anything about astrology,' Gigi protested but Melissa picked up a highwayman's mask similar to the one worn by Vicky Ashford and said: 'Don't worry, even I couldn't give a serious reading without all my books. So just busk it, give them some good news and you won't go far wrong.'

Melissa slipped the mask over Gigi's face and then, wrapping a long white scarf around her head, she went on: 'There, I wouldn't recognise you myself, especially in this muted lighting.

'Best of luck, darling, I won't be very long,' she said gaily as she slipped away into the crowd. After a couple of minutes Gigi breathed a sigh of relief. No one had asked her for an astral reading, but then she saw the familiar figure of Teddy Dixon walking purposefully towards her. At first she thought he had recognised her but then she realised that he was deep in conversation with a well-built man whom Gigi did not recognise.

In fact this was none other than Barry Gore-Wharton. When they were adjacent to her chair Teddy turned round to his companion and said in a jocular fashion: 'Go on, Barry, why don't you see what the stars have in store for you? Polly St George won't be here for half an hour so you might as well see if the stars foretell whether or not you're going to get your leg over! Now I'm going to get a drink and see if there's anyone else here from our office besides Adrian Klein. It's funny that Adrian didn't know that Barbara Kennedy was going to turn up on Tony Cavendish's arm. I wouldn't be surprised if there's a little rumpy-pumpy in the air between those two! I wouldn't blame Tony. Barbara's an attractive girl but didn't our receptionist, young Vicky, look ravishing in that costume? What a luscious pair of tits she has on her! She's been with us more than three months and I'm amazed I hadn't noticed them before. I really must be getting past it! Why, I can remember the time when I would have had those lovely boobs in my hands within days of the girl joining the firm!'

'Nonsense! That's only because they're not on display like that when she's working at Rose and Griffin,' said Barry Gore-Wharton. His slightly slurred voice was hardly surprising for, before the lawyer had returned to his own office, he had helped Teddy empty the decanter of cognac on his client's desk. 'I'm just off to point Percy at the porcelain but we both have the same star sign so I'll leave it to you to find out if stars predict that we're in with a chance tonight.'

Teddy turned unsteadily towards Gigi and grunted as he sat down heavily on a chair opposite her: 'Alright, Mademoiselle Melissa, do I cross your palm with silver or something?'

Gigi stifled a giggle and replied solemnly: 'Certainly not! Astrology is an ancient science and has nothing to do with crystal balls and all that hocus-pocus. Now, give me the date of your birth and I'll consult the charts and see what sexual prospects might be in store for you.'

He looked round and whispered something in her ear. 'Really? You don't look your age,' said Gigi diplomatically. 'But I'm not surprised that you're a Scorpio. With the Sun, Venus and Mars all in the right places in the sky, I would advise you to make sure you go on a proper diet. You're going to need a lot of stamina and your secretary wouldn't want you flaking out on the job!'

Teddy goggled at her as his jaw dropped open and he said shakily: 'How the hell did you know I'm screwing my secretary?'

'It's all in the stars,' Gigi informed him as she let her imagination run riot. 'Scorpios born soon after the end of World War One have a high sex drive and are usually irresistible to the opposite sex. They have no problems in charming their way into a girl's knickers. Now as you were born in 1919 and that tells me you're especially fond of having your cock sucked by your secretary whose name probably begins with M. Am I right so far?'

'Absolutely one hundred per cent accurate,' he gasped as Gigi continued: 'Furthermore it looks as if a chance meeting in an artistic surrounding may well lead to your taking part in an exotic orgy of kinky sex.'

There was now a gleam in Teddy's eyes as he rubbed his hands together and said: 'Wonderful!

How soon might that happen?'

'Oh, I can't be too exact, but it will be sooner rather than later,' replied Gigi hurriedly, as she saw Adrian push his way towards them. 'Why, it could even be tonight.'

She turned away as Adrian approached and called out to his employer: 'Teddy, you haven't bumped into my girl friend Gigi by any chance,. have you? Vicky told me that she arrived here about ten minutes ago but I can't find her anywhere.'

'Sorry, old boy, she hasn't passed this way. Don't worry though, she'll turn up soon. Now I'm going to get a drink and if I see Gigi I'll point her in this direction. Meanwhile, take my advice and have a chat with Mademoiselle Melissa while you're waiting. I tell you, Adrian, what she can see in the stars is nobody's business.'

Adrian's eyebrows shot up at the mention of Melissa's name. 'What the blazes is she doing here? Perhaps she knows what happened to Gigi,' he muttered as Teddy staggered off. Before he could speak to the masked girl with the shawl over her head, the lights dimmed even further and a spotlight picked out Jason Howard, who looked resplendent in his silver cape as he stood by a small table with a paintbrush in his hand.

'Ladies and gentlemen! As you know, I have always held that movement is essential to art. And so, with the help of the lovely Kathie, I am not going to demonstrate the technique of painting a moving canvas.'

There was a scattered round of applause as a thin wail of Indian music came through the loudspeakers. Then one of the waitresses, a lithe, slim girl with long auburn hair, came dancing gracefully into the spotlight. She was naked except for a tiny white *cache-sexe* and after pirouetting around Jason, she stood stock still in front of him, rhythmically moving her shoulders so that her high jutting breasts jiggled provocatively in time to the music. Then Jason discarded his cape so that he too was also nude, except for his bulging athletic support which covered his cock and balls.

The narrow belt round his waist had a thin strap which slid into the crevice between his dimpled buttocks.

He sank a paintbrush into a jar of blue paint and twisted it like a sword, bringing it out with a turn of the wrist to allow the excess to drip back into the container. At the same time, Kathie lifted her arms and ran her fingers through her silky hair and then let her hands wander down across her bare breasts. She lovingly caressed her nipples before she slowly dropped her hands to her waist and began to slowly pull down the minuscule *cache-sexe* down to her feet, treating the entranced spectators to their first view of her totally naked bottom. Then she turned round and, with her hand between her legs, faced the audience. To a cheer she flung her hand aside and exposed her fluffy fleece through which those nearest could see the pouting pink lips of her pussy.

Jason now tweaked her nipples with the tip of his

brush, teasing the hardening little bullets as he coated them with blue paint. 'Note how colour changes the entire perspective of the body,' he remarked as he changed brushes and stroked gold paint over Kathie's thrusting breasts.

'It's gilding the lily to colour such a lovely pair,' murmured Adrian to himself as he adjusted his trousers in a vain attempt to make more room for his burgeoning erection. Jason's brush encircled Kathie's belly-button, highlighting the dimpled flesh in a light green, finishing off the effect with a twisty line directly into her pubic bush.

'Hey, what's the idea?' he protested as a frisky hand slid across his waist and plunged downwards to rub itself against his stiffening shaft. He turned his head to see that the owner of the wandering hand was none other than Gigi, who was standing behind him.

'Hello love, I've been looking all over for you,' he whispered as they watched Jason splash wide strokes of pink paint across Kathie's bouncy bum cheeks. 'Where have you been hiding yourself?'

Gigi squeezed his pulsing erection and giggled in his ear. 'Actually, I've been here for the last five minutes informing Teddy Dixon what the stars foretell about his sex life!'

She rapidly explained about what she had said to Teddy and then tugging at Adrian's arm she murmured: 'Never mind Jason Howard's op-art, I can think of something far better to do.'

'Such as what?' demanded Adrian as he let himself

be pulled behind the canvas at the back of Melissa's stand where, out of sight of everyone, they hugged and kissed, their lips pressed together and sucking urgently, their tongues licking wetly against each other's, tasting the hot desire which was coursing through their bodies.

As if in a trance he helped Gigi throw off her clothes and she soon stood naked in front of him. She could sense his excitement as she unbuckled his belt and Adrian jerked down the zip of his trousers himself while Gigi sank down on her knees and pulled them down together with his pants. His throbbing erection sprang up to greet her.

'Oh, I hope you've missed me,' she cooed to his pulsating prick as she closed her hand around Adrian's straining shaft and slid her fist up and down the smooth love-truncheon.

Then Gigi leaned forward and, moistening her lips, opened her mouth wide to take his rock hard shaft between her lips, sucking lustily on his rounded knob, savouring the flavour of his cock and swirling her tongue over the domed helmet as she eased some three inches of his fleshy lollipop down her throat. One hand circled his quivering cock and the other cupped his srotum with her fingertips, concentrating on the exquisitely sensitive little area between his balls and arsehole. She bobbed her head up and down his glistening shaft in a sensuous regular rhythm.

Adrian's eyes were closed as he leaned back against the wall and groaned in ecstasy as he enjoyed these delicious sensations to the full. He did not see Melissa poke her head round the canvas and tip-toe to where Gigi was kneeling in front of him. But she immediately made her presence known for she squatted down beside her friend and started to tongue his hairy ballsack with long langorous licks. Adrian opened his eyes and shivered with delight as he saw Melissa's head of dark glossy hair jostling next to Gigi's tousled blonde mane. He almost swooned with excitement as he clutched their heads while the two pairs of soft wet lips brought him all too quickly to the point of no return.

'I'm coming, I'm coming!' he panted which gave Gigi enough time to begin swallowing in anticipation as the first spurts of sticky jism crashed out of its cock into her mouth. She gulped down his salty spunk and then Melissa took her place, squeezing his twitching tool and lapping up the final drains of his ejaculation from the wilting crown of his deflated cock.

Melissa lifted her head and smacked her lips. 'What a nice tasty prick, but it looks as if we've sucked him dry,' she commented as she flipped Adrian's limp shaft from one hand to another. 'So we'll just have to wait for his balls to recover.'

'Excuse me darling,' said Gigi acidly. 'You've been very kind to me and that's why I didn't mind letting you gobble Adrian's cock just now. But as far as I'm concerned, this was strictly on a one-off basis. I wouldn't let him stick his tadger in any other cunt but mine.'

'Don't fight, girls,' said Adrian hastily. 'I loved being plated by the pair of you but I'm sure Melissa doesn't have to be told that you have first refusal on my cock, Gigi.' He was very concerned that Melissa might blurt out that Gigi didn't have to make a fuss because he had already fucked her only the previous afternoon when he visited her for an astrological consultation.

He went on: 'Gigi, let's put on our clothes and take a peek at what's going on outside. Listen to that applause! I wouldn't be surprised if Jason's cabaret has got a little out of hand.'

Adrian was pleasantly surprised when the normally hot-tempered Gigi meekly agreed and bent down to pull on her panties. He was blissfully unaware of course that Gigi was also worried that Melissa might be indiscreet and mention the fact that she and Gigi had shared a bed last night, not only with each other and the Swashbuckler vibrator but also with the well-hung Andy Whyte.

'I'll go and see if there's anything worth watching,' said Melissa. She slipped out to join the other guests on the other side of the canvas while Adrian and Gigi quickly dressed themselves. She returned a couple of minutes later with an amused expression on her face. 'You were right, Adrian, she said. 'The entertainment's getting a bit wild out there and your boss is on stage right now.'

Adrian was shocked by this news. 'You mean Teddy Dixon? God, that brandy he was drinking this afternoon must have gone to his head.'

'Well, it's certainly done no harm to another part of his anatomy,' said Melissa with a wicked chuckle. 'Come and see for yourself.'

They followed her back and gazed down at the sight of a full-blown orgy taking place where Jason Howard had been painting the body of Kathie, the girl with long auburn hair. She was now covered all over with streaks of silver, blue and green paint and was bouncing on top of Jason Howard's hard oiled cock as he lay naked on a large mattress covered with a white sheet which was already liberally spattered with paint. Simultaneously she was having her nipples sucked by two naked men kneeling beside her and when Adrian moved round to get a closer look at them to his horror he saw that these acolytes were none other than Teddy Dixon and Barry Gore-Wharton.

Two nude girls, one white and one Eurasian, now entered the fray, each armed with a pot of paint and a paintbrush. The slight little Eurasian girl's small breasts wobbled as she bent down and dipped her brush into her jar of bright red paint. To a great cheer from the crowd she began to cover Teddy's back with Chinese characters.

'God knows what message she's written on him,' said Adrian hoarsely. The girl put down her brush and lay down next to Jason, whose hand snaked out towards her shaved mound and let his fingertips play inside the pink shell-like folds of her inner lips as he exposed the pink valve of her pretty cunt.

Teddy now removed his lips from Kathie's nipple

and, oblivious to anything but the gorgeous girl beneath him, took his cock in his hand. To a roar of applause, he plunged forward and buried his shaft between her love lips. Without further ado he began to fuck her, revelling in the delicious sensation of his cock rubbing against the slippery walls of her tight little cunt as he jabbed his excited tool in and out of her juicy honeypot.

Kathie continued to bob up and down on Jason Howard's sturdy boner while on his other side the second new girl was slapping blue paint all over Barry Gore-Wharton's chest as she used her other hand to masturbate him, flogging the rigid shaft of his twitching tool. When she had finished with the paint, she pulled his lips away from Kathie's nipple and led him by his cock round behind the girl who was still gaily sliding up and down Jason Howard's pulsing stiffstander.

'Is he ready yet, Michelle?' called out Kathie and when the girl shouted back in the affirmative, Kathie pushed out the peachy cheeks of her backside and reached round to pull apart her taut buttocks so that the crinkled opening of her bumhole was fully exposed to Barry's excited gaze.

Michelle slid her hand one final time down to the root of Barry's palpitating prick and then guided his quivering blue-veined cock into the puckered little opening of Kathie's anus. She wriggled sensuously as he slid the full girth of his shaft up into the clenching embrace of her tight, youthful bottom.

'Aaaagh!' Barry cried out as Michelle jammed her

finger into his own arsehole. He rocked backwards and forwards while Kathie leaned forward and stayed still for a few moments. Jason realised that he could no longer delay his orgasm and he jerked his hips upwards so that his cock was embedded inside her cunt.

'So two into one *does* go,' commented Gigi as Jason's cock spurted out a flood of frothy spunk. Barry grunted heavily as he reached the summit and lubricated Kathie's back passage with a fierce jet of jism.

This erotic sight spurred Teddy onwards as he sank forwards, the Eurasian girl's cunt enveloping his cock like a wet, warm glove. He slid deep inside the clinging walls of her love tunnel and she writhed in uncontrolled delight as Teddy's buttocks rose and fell. He drove his cock harder and harder into her honeypot and she shouted with joy as a series of orgasmic ripples shivered through her body. She wrapped her legs around his waist and pumped her pussy furiously against him so that Teddy felt that his shaft was somehow welded inside her agitated crack.

He paused to catch his breath and then ploughed on. Soon the hot, sticky seed burst out of Teddy's chopper, drenching the long funnel of her love channel as he spent himself to the limit, riding his twitching tool in and out of her juicy slit until he was milked dry. Then he withdrew his deflated cock, rolled off the girl's lithe, slim body and lay on his back with a glazed expression on his face, his heart pounding and chest heaving as he panted with exhaustion.

'I don't know how Teddy is going to live this down,' muttered Adrian. Gigi nodded and slipped a proprietorial arm around Adrian's waist as she sighed: 'Yes, it could be quite a problem. I doubt if any of this arty-farty lot know who Teddy is. Even if they did, they wouldn't care two hoots, but isn't that Denis Hammersmith of the *Evening News* gossip column over there?'

She pointed to a fresh-faced young man who was standing against the wall a few yards away, his pen in one hand and a small open notepad in the other. Adrian slapped his palm against his forehead and groaned: 'My God! If he writes anything about all this, Teddy's up shit creek without a paddle. His wife is away for a few days but when she finds out that Teddy's been playing around, she'll have his balls on toast.'

'And bang goes that CBE you said he was due to get in the next Honours List for his charity work,' added Gigi. She waved to Tony Cavendish and Barbara Kennedy who had sidled up to join them.

'Hiya folks, how did you enjoy the show?' said Barbara with a giggle but like Adrian, Tony was more than a little uneasy about the consequences of Teddy's behaviour. 'Babs, I've already told you this could badly affect everyone at Rose and Griffin. According to Vicky Ashford, the press weren't invited till later but one of the reporters has turned up early. God, if he writes up what he saw . . .'

His voice trailed off but Adrian finished off his sentence and said grimly: 'We could lose a hell of a lot of business. You all know how people can be so fucking hypocritical. If there was a front page story that Teddy had been caught fiddling his income tax, everyone would say "bad luck, old boy" but to be caught with your trousers down, that's another matter entirely. Nobody wants to know you.'

'Yes, in case they get tarred with the same brush,' said Tony. 'Look what happened to poor old Profumo!'

Gigi frowned and then said slowly: 'Hold on, there's only one reporter here and he's an old mate of Adrian. You've given Denis some bloody good stories, haven't you, darling? Can't you get him to forget about what he's seen? Bung him a hundred quid if you have to, it would be well worth it.'

'It wouldn't work,' said Adrian, shaking his head sadly. 'An exclusive like this will make his name and his paper will have to give him a bloody big bonus if they don't want to lose his services to some other rag.'

'There must be some way we can get to him,' Gigi persisted. 'He's quite a pretty boy, he's not gay by any chance? No? Good, in that case do you know if there's anything which particularly turns him on.'

Adrian thought for a moment and said: 'Well, funnily enough the last time I saw him he told me that he was going on to see a lesbian show at the Red Cabbage Club. I suppose like most guys he dreams about being the meat in the sandwich!'

'That's it, then! We'll make him an offer he can't refuse,' she said triumphantly. 'All is not yet lost. Adrian, give me fifty pounds!'

Her lover brought out his wallet and passed over five ten pound notes to her. 'That's all I've got, I'm afraid. What do you want it for anyway?' he asked but Gigi impatiently brushed aside his question.

'Look, there's no time to explain now. Just so as I say. I want you and Tony to borrow the camera from Vicky Ashford which I saw on the reception desk. Tony, you take charge of it! Adrian's hopeless at taking photos, either he forgets to wind on the film on or he sticks his thumb over the lens. Keep out of sight if possible and when you see Denis go upstairs, wait five minutes and then follow him.'

'Why should he go upstairs?' asked Tony curiously and Gigi answered: 'Because there's a nice little service flat which the gallery uses to put up important visitors. Jason and his crew are using it as a changing room but they'll be down here till the party's over so we won't be disturbed.'

She drew Barbara towards her and said: 'Babs, this is what I want you to do.' She cupped her fingers around her mouth as she whispered something into Barbara's ear which made the girl smile and say: 'Okay Gigi, you can leave it to me. If this works, I reckon we'll be entitled to an expenses-paid fortnight at a posh hotel in the South of France, courtesy of Mr Teddy Dixon!'

'I still don't understand,' complained Adrian but Gigi kissed his nose and said: 'Trust me, I know what I'm doing,' before sliding through the crowd towards Kathie, who had slipped on a tight white mini-dress and was talking to Jason Howard and a small group of listeners.

'Come on, we'd better do as she says,' said Tony and the two men followed her, leaving Barbara to make her way towards Denis Hammersmith.

Five minutes later the journalist was following Barbara out of the exhibition and up the stairs to the Meridew Gallery's small apartment. 'You are sure that the girls are already performing? I must phone in my copy soon,' he said anxiously.

'You'll see for yourself, Denis, there might even be a couple of titled ladies involved – think of the story that would make! Shush now, don't make a noise,' said Barbara as she quietly pushed open the unlocked front door.

Denis Hammersmith put his hand to his ear. 'Listen to that,' he breathed. He padded towards the half-open door, beyond which he could hear soft sighs and murmurings and a rhythmic squelchy sound which indicated that sexual activity was taking place. He peered round the door and his eyes widened as he gazed at a bed on which two beautiful naked girls were pleasuring each other's bodies.

Gigi was lying on her back while Kathie, who was sprawled out on her tummy between Gigi's legs, was sliding her fingers in and out of Gigi's juicy crack which lay open and exposed beneath the fluffy golden bush of pussy hair. Her love lips were pouting outwards to reveal the pink moist entrance to her moist, welcoming cunny.

Kathie's silky auburn hair was spread over Gigi's slim thighs as she continued to slip her fingers into her dripping slit, making the blonde girl tremble with desire. Then she lifted her pretty head and murmured throatily: 'What a naughty girl you are, to be sure! Look how my fingers slide in and out of your juicy cunt! Now I'm going to feast on your lovely pussy and bring you off!'

She was as good as her word. Gigi quivered with desire as she felt Kathie's hand stroke inside her churning love channel and found her erect, rubbery clitty.

'Ooooh, that's marvellous!' she whispered as Kathie finger-fucked her, faster and faster, using her thumb to massage the protruding tiny sex button. 'Oh yes, yes, I'm almost there!' she moaned as Kathie continued to stroke and caress her sopping pussy. Her hips jerked up and down, pushing wildly against Kathie's hand.

Gigi opened her legs wide and, in a trice, a mass of glossy auburn hair buried itself between her thighs. Denis Hammersmith watched with growing fascination as Kathie ran the pointed tip of her tongue up and down Gigi's musky pussy crack. His hand moved down to his crotch and he smoothed his palm over his thickening shaft as he saw Gigi lift her bottom from the bed, which enabled Kathie to gently titillate her wrinkled arse-hole with her forefinger.

Beads of perspiration now formed on the journalist's forehead as he stared at Kathie's rounded buttocks which were thrust high in the air. The puckered entrance to her back passage was winking up at him as he tore open his trousers and began to masturbate openly, furiously pumping his fist up and down his hard veiny shaft.

Then, to his astonishment, Kathie lifted her head and turning round with a smile on her face she cooed: 'Don't waste your time wanking, give us girls a taste of that nice meaty cock.'

No red-blooded man could have resisted such an erotic invitation, Denis Hammersmith was later to tell himself, but be this as it may, with a low cry he pulled off his clothes. Kathie dived back to resume eating Gigi's pussy and again deliberately thrust out her supple backside. He crawled onto the bed behind her and passed his arm around her ribs to caress her firm, uptilted breasts and rub his fingers against her stiff little raspberry nipples. Then he squeezed the smooth warm flesh of her delicious bottom and let his finger linger along the long furrow between her jiggling bum cheeks. They wiggled saucily from side to side as he passed his fingers below to feel the slippery wet lips of her pulsating quim.

Now Barbara stepped forward and grasped Denis's throbbing stiff chopper in her hand. She slicked her hand up and down his shaft before placing the tip of his uncapped helmet at the entrance to Kathie's arse-hole.

'It's what she wants,' Barbara assured him and the gorgeous girl reached round and squeezed his balls as in a muffled voice she cried out: 'Yes, go on, shove your thick prick up my bum.'

Denis pressed forward eagerly but Barbara pulled him back by his shoulder and said: 'Wait a moment, you don't want to hurt her. Let me just smear some cold cream on your tool.'

She rushed into the bathroom and came back with an open jar and liberally coated his cock with grease. Then she stepped back and Denis went to work with a will. As Denis was also later to say, he was so engrossed that he would not have heard the massed bands of the Coldstream Guards outside the bedroom window, let alone the tread of Adrian's footsteps or the click of Tony's camera. Like the cavalry arriving at a beseiged wagon-train at the end of a Western, the two Rose and Griffin agents had now arrived at the scene. However, they had no intention of interrupting this three-way fuck as, with a grunt of satisfaction, Denis pressed his knob into the tight dimple of Kathie's anus. She reared and bucked as he slewed his cock in and out of her tight back passage.

Kathie's bum cheeks slapped against Denis's belly as he bulled into her, but though she wriggled as his prick pounded in and out of her bum, she kept her lips pressed firmly against Gigi's cunt. Her tongue prodded in and out between Gigi's pouting love lips and the sight of Kathie sucking off the blonde girl while he fucked her backside sent Denis into a delirium of erotic ecstasy. He came quickly, sending a fierce torrent of sticky spunk deep into Kathie's glorious bottom.

As Denis pulled out his full semi-erect shaft from Kathie's bum, the girls changed positions with Kathie flat on her back and Gigi kissing and sucking her hard red nipples as she frigged Kathie's pussy. Her index finger was joined by first one and then two other fingers dipping into her dripping cunt. Gigi moved over her and kissed her fervently on the lips while the other hand snaked out and began to flog Denis's glistening shaft which soon swelled up and stood stiffly to attention.

'You'll find something interesting on the floor,' Gigi informed Denis as she slicked her hand up and down his tingling tool. He leaned over and grunted. 'Found it!' he called as he waved a dark plastic tube in the air. Kathie grabbed it from him.

At the doorway Barbara, Adrian and Tony gawped at the size of the thick penis-shaped dildo as they heard Kathie say: 'This model's called the Black Mambo. It's supposed to be moulded on a plaster cast of Cassius Clay's cock but that's probably only a rumour. Anyhow, I love to feel it sliding between my cunny lips.

'Denis, perhaps you'll do the honours,' she said as she gave the dildo back to him. Denis smacked his lips as Kathie opened her legs wider and displayed the flushed chink of her cunt to him. Then she squealed with joy as, on his knees, Denis plunged the dildo between her cunny lips. He slowly extracted the black tube from her quim, gleaming with Kathie's cuntal juice.

Gigi continued to slide her fist along Denis's swollen shaft while his balls bobbed and swung, dangling low beneath his bare buttocks. She abandoned caressing his knob and began to stroke the base of his shaft with one hand while the other gently caressed his balls.

Although his swollen cock was now bulging uncomfortably inside his boxer shorts, Adrian was hardly overjoyed at watching his girl friend masturbate Denis. It was not difficult to understand what she had in mind as the journalist's veiny shaft bounded and twitched in Gigi's grasp. Tony's camera clicked away as arcing spurts of spunk splashed out from the tip of Denis's prick. He was so overcome by the shuddering warm waves of pleasure running throughout his body that the Black Mambo stayed still in his hand and Kathie yelped out her need for somebody to finish her off.

'Leave it to me, dear,' said Gigi, and with her jism-coated hand she pistoned the dildo in and out of Kathie's honeypot, alternating a series of short sharp jabs with occasional longer, sweeping strokes which reamed out the furthest recesses of her shivering love tunnel. The lithe girl's hips jerked wildly as she came in a sudden release and Denis dived down to lap up her tangy love juice.

'Let's go, I've finished the film,' said Tony. Adrian muttered: 'Good, I know a discreet all-night chemist where we can get the pictures developed within the hour. Babs, we'll be off now but perhaps you would like to bring these proceedings to an end.'

Barbara guessed that Adrian was getting more and more upset at seeing Gigi's hand around Denis Hammersmith's cock. She said soothingly: 'Leave it to me, Adrian, I'll finish him off myself.'

She wet her lips and then strode to the bed where she sat down and unclasped Gigi's fingers from Denis's pulsing prick, Barbara let one of her own soft hands grip his trembling tool while with her free hand she kneaded and massaged his hanging balls. She licked slowly on the hairy wrinkled skin of his scrotum before taking each swollen sphere into her mouth, sucking on them with relish.

Then she slid his knob into her mouth and wrapped her tongue around it. Denis gasped with pleasure at the delicious sensation as she sucked him further in. With the tip of her tongue, she licked along the underside of his shaft, working her way along the full length of it.

The ecstatic young man groaned and clutched at Gigi's soft bum cheeks while Barbara probed round the smooth knob of his cock with her searching wet tongue. Soon she sensed he was on the brink of his climax. She pursed her lips and gulped in his entire tool until her lips were pressed into the wiry bush of his pubic hair. But she had no intention of swallowing his seed. A strangled cry erupted from Denis's throat as Barbara released his jolting prick and his jism surged out onto Gigi's backside with one thick spurt landing inside the cleft between her buttocks, trickling down the tight, private bud of her arse-hole.

'Right, the party's over,' said Barbara briskly. 'It's time to call it a day, folks. Let's all get dressed as quickly as possible.'

'Quite right, I've got a phone call to make,' said the sated journalist, but while Gigi wriggled herself into her knickers she said in a steely voice: 'Hold your horses, my thick-cocked friend! I wouldn't make that call if I were you.'

Denis Hammersmith frowned as he pulled on his trousers. 'Why ever not?' he queried and Kathie answered: 'Because if you did you'd ruin the reputation of two particular gentlemen we happen to care for.'

'You mean Teddy Dixon and Barry Gore-Wharton?' he replied as his lip curled with disdain. 'Well, they should know better than to fool around in public at their time of life.'

'Maybe so, but can't you give them a break?' pleaded Barbara as she stroked Denis's knee. 'When all's said and done, this is a private party and Teddy and Barry's sex lives hardly have any bearing on the way they carry out their work.'

'No, but its my duty as a reporter to expose them for what they are,' he added with a virtuous smirk.

'Oh, so does that mean you wouldn't be interested in negotiating a fee to keep quiet about the whole affair?' asked Gigi sweetly.

To her joy, the journalist took the proferred bait and grinned: 'Now I didn't say that, did I? What kind of nice round sum did you have in mind?'

'I didn't, but I'm delighted I discovered that you were prepared to be bribed, because it makes it far easier for me to tell you that if you call your paper with a report of the shinannigans you saw this evening, close-up photographs of your prick ploughing into Kathie's bum will be sent to a girl you have been chasing for the last months. The Honourable Hilary Norman, the textiles heiress, who inherits seven million pounds when she turns twenty-five, according to *Private Eye*. You've been romancing the lovely Hilary, but I doubt if she'll ever want to see you again if she finds out that you've been such a naughty boy.'

The colour drained from Denis's face as he gasped: 'But that's blackmail!'

'Yes, I suppose it is,' said Gigi cheerfully. 'And in case you don't believe us, my photographer will soon be back with some prints to show you. Sorry, Denis, you've been well and truly shafted.'

At half-past twelve the next day, Teddy Dixon was sitting in his office while Marlene proferred glasses of chilled champagne for his visitors. He rose from his chair and held up his glass to toast his guests. 'Lovees, what can I say? You all went beyond the bounds of duty to protect Barry and me from our own foolishness last night – especially you girls who had to let yourselves be mauled about by that rotten creep Denis Hammersmith.'

'That rotten well-endowed creep,' corrected Kathie with a smile.

'Whatever you say, but nevertheless, Kathie, I can't thank you and Gigi enough. After all, neither of you work for Rose and Griffin so please accept these small tokens of appreciation with my compliments.

He gave an envelope to each of the girls and then turning to the others he continued: 'As I know the rest of you acted simply for the good of the old firm, I wouldn't want to insult you others by giving you an extra summer bonus—'

'Oh, don't worry, we wouldn't be insulted,' said Tony quickly but Teddy Dixon shook his head. 'No, I wouldn't dream of it,' he insisted but then with a smile he added: 'However, that doesn't apply to Barry Gore-Wharton, of course, and he's asked me to invite you all as his guests for a fortnight at his villa in the South of France in August. He'll be buying the air tickets and taking care of all expenses, of course, even though he won't be able to join you himself.'

'How about you, Teddy?' asked Adrian. Teddy gave a wolfish smile, as he replied: 'I'd love to – only this time I'd better make sure that no-one sees me coming!'

A selection of Erotica
from Headline

SCANDAL IN PARADISE	Anonymous	£4.99 ☐
UNDER ORDERS	Nick Aymes	£4.99 ☐
RECKLESS LIAISONS	Anonymous	£4.99 ☐
GROUPIES II	Johnny Angelo	£4.99 ☐
TOTAL ABANDON	Anonymous	£4.99 ☐
AMOUR ENCORE	Marie-Claire Villefranche	£4.99 ☐
COMPULSION	Maria Caprio	£4.99 ☐
INDECENT	Felice Ash	£4.99 ☐
AMATEUR DAYS	Becky Bell	£4.99 ☐
EROS IN SPRINGTIME	Anonymous	£4.99 ☐
GOOD VIBRATIONS	Jeff Charles	£4.99 ☐
CITIZEN JULIETTE	Louise Aragon	£4.99 ☐

All Headline books are available at your local bookshop or newsagent, or can be ordered direct from the publisher. Just tick the titles you want and fill in the form below. Prices and availability subject to change without notice.

Headline Book Publishing, Cash Sales Department, Bookpoint, 39 Milton Park, Abingdon, OXON, OX14 4TD, UK. If you have a credit card you may order by telephone – 0235 400400.

Please enclose a cheque or postal order made payable to Bookpoint Ltd to the value of the cover price and allow the following for postage and packing:
UK & BFPO: £1.00 for the first book, 50p for the second book and 30p for each additional book ordered up to a maximum charge of £3.00.
OVERSEAS & EIRE: £2.00 for the first book, £1.00 for the second book and 50p for each additional book.

Name ....

Address ....

....

....

If you would prefer to pay by credit card, please complete:
Please debit my Visa/Access/Diner's Card/American Express (delete as applicable) card no:

Signature .... Expiry Date ....